SLEEPWALKER'S SANCTUARY

SLEEPWALKER'S SANCTUARY

REG RAWLINS, PSYCHIC INVESTIGATOR
BOOK NINETEEN

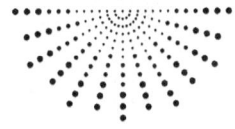

P.D. WORKMAN

 **PD WORKMAN**

ISBN: 9781774685648 (KDP Paperback)
ISBN: 9781774685655 (KDP Hardcover)
ISBN: 9781774685679 (Large Print)
ISBN: 9781774685686 (Lulu Paperback)
ISBN: 9781774685662 (ePub)
ISBN: 9781774685693 (Accessible Audio)

ALSO BY P.D. WORKMAN

FIND MORE BOOKS AT PDWORKMAN.COM

Reg Rawlins, Psychic Detective

Paranormal Mystery & Adventure

What the Cat Knew

A Psychic with Catitude

A Catastrophic Theft

Night of Nine Tails

The Immortal's Key

Yule's Sinister Spell

Fairy Blade Unmade

Web of Nightmares

A Whisker's Breadth

Skunk Man Swamp

Magic Ain't A Game

Without Foresight

Careful of Thy Wishes

Time to Your Elf

Undiscovered Tomb

Missing Powers

Thrice Spared

Cloaked Campaign

Sleepwalker's Sanctuary (Coming Soon)

Cat Tales in the Swamp (Short Story)

Tainted Truffle Treachery (Coming Soon)

A Fowl Play on Christmas Day (Christmas crossover story)

Lunar Lies (Coming Soon)

Zachary Goldman Mysteries
Private Investigator
She Wore Mourning
His Hands Were Quiet
She Was Dying Anyway
He Was Walking Alone
They Thought He was Safe
He Was Not There
Her Work Was Everything
She Told a Lie
He Never Forgot
She Was At Risk
He Drowned in Memory
Their Walls Were Empty
They Came for Him
They Sought Vengeance
She Was Their Target
His Fear Was Real

Stand Alone Suspense Novels
Looking Over Your Shoulder
Lion Within
Pursued by the Past
In the Tick of Time
Loose the Dogs

AND MORE AT PDWORKMAN.COM

To those who want to
transform themselves

* * *

CHAPTER ONE

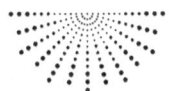

*R*eg listened to the voices. They started as whispers in her head. Like the other voices that were always there. There was always a background murmur; sometimes she could pick out the individual voices or feelings, and other times she could not. When she was doing a seance, the group consciousness and intention would help her to zero in on one voice, hopefully the voice that her client wanted to hear, but there was no guarantee of that.

She gathered her red box braids in both hands and swept them back over her shoulders so they all fell behind her. She smoothed her colorful gypsy skirt and tried to sort out the voices.

Some of the voices were harder to ignore or suppress than others. Her mother's voice was one that had always been foremost in her mind, the hardest to silence. Her mother, Norma Jean, had died when Reg was a child, but the voice had never left.

Then… things had happened and, even though Weston had changed the timeline so that Norma Jean had not died, Reg could still hear the living woman's voice in her head. And not only Norma Jean's but, lately, all of the other siren voices as well.

They were loud and discordant. It seemed like it was never just one of them speaking to her at a time; there had to be a whole Greek chorus wailing and calling to her.

One might think that sleep, at least, would be a blessed release from the voices. But one would be wrong. The voices were just as loud at night. Sometimes even louder and more intrusive than during the day. As Reg tried to relax and release all of the day's worries and put them aside for a peaceful night's sleep, the voices got louder and clearer. The shrieks, chants, and songs were overwhelming sometimes.

In her dream, it had started out as the shrieking, discordant voices that she had become accustomed to, irritating and difficult to block, but the same-old, same-old that she didn't feel like she *had* to listen to. If she could focus on other things, maybe play some YouTube videos on her phone to distract herself, they would become less intrusive.

But this time, it was different. The voices gathered and grew stronger and clearer. Rather than individuals trying to wail over each other, or the chorus chanting a warning together in different notes or melodies, the voices joined, the melodies synced up and harmonized instead of being discordant.

In the old Greek stories, the siren song was always alluring, enchanting, hauntingly beautiful. Reg had just assumed that those accounts were romanticized, since in her experience, the siren voices were loud, dissonant, and irritating. The reason that the sailors went crazy and jumped into the water was clearly not because they were attracted to the unbelievably beautiful voices, but because they were driven mad by it and had to find some way to make it stop. Without wax in their ears or being bound to a mast, the only solution available was to drown themselves.

But in her dream, the voices changed from their horrible, screeching, nails-on-the-blackboard collective shriek into something beautiful. They morphed into a song unlike anything she'd ever heard. So beautiful that it hurt her chest and brought tears to her eyes. She stopped and stood there, listening to the angelic voices, marveling that she'd never heard them sing together like that before.

But the meaning of the song was beyond her grasp. She usually heard English when they spoke to her mind, even though she knew they were scattered all over the world and probably each spoke a different language or some form of ancient Greek they could all understand.

Reg listened to the song. Harmonious, rhythmic, achingly beautiful. She felt a vibration in her own vocal cords—a humming, coupled with a desire to raise her voice with them. Reg had never enjoyed singing or been good at it. When music was a required subject in school, she had mostly mouthed the words, lip-syncing her way through the songs. Her teachers got after her for it, until they actually heard her sing, and then they decided she'd better go back to faking it. There were no solos for Reg Rawlins.

Reg awoke with a start, torn out of her sleep. Her body was rigid. Something was clearly wrong, but she didn't know what. She opened her eyes and squinted around the room. It was getting light outside, but she wasn't an early-morning riser. Dawn was still the middle of the night for her. She couldn't exactly get up at six in the morning when she'd been dealing with seances and other client consultations at midnight and the wee hours of the morning. She needed her beauty rest.

She looked at the windowsill, expecting to see Starlight, her tuxedo cat, sitting there looking outside like usual. But he wasn't. The windowsill was empty. He must be looking out the living room window, stalking around the cottage, or having a snack of dry kibble from his bowl.

Though lately, she wondered if he were somehow getting into the food in the fridge during the night. It seemed like she threw out just as much dry food as she added to the bowl in the first place. She didn't let it sit for too long, knowing it would get stale and Starlight wouldn't eat it then.

But did he eat it at all?

"Starlight?" Reg called and made kissy sounds to call him. "Star? Where are you? Come see me."

She listened for kitty footsteps coming toward her or the snort that meant, "Are you kidding? I'm a cat; I have better things to do than to cater to a human being." But she didn't hear anything. The cottage was as quiet as a tomb.

"Starlight?" Reg tried again.

He still didn't respond. She closed her eyes, intending to go back to sleep. He was a cat. Cats didn't come when called unless you had a can of tuna in your hand.

But the silence of the cottage and Starlight's absence concerned her. Starlight usually did come to her when she called him at night. He was as concerned with keeping watch over her and making sure she didn't get into any more trouble than necessary as she was with seeing that he was warm and fed, safe and sound in the cottage, and that his kitty litter box was cleaned reasonably regularly.

When Starlight still didn't return to his usual perch at the window, she sat up and looked around. He had been poisoned once, cursed by Norma Jean out of jealousy for her daughter's affections.

The combination of the siren song and Starlight's absence was too worrying. Reg couldn't go back to sleep until she saw Starlight and confirmed to herself that he was okay. With a groan, Reg rolled over and slid her feet off the bed. She sat on the edge of the mattress for a minute, orienting herself, hoping that Starlight would come strolling in and she could just lie back down and continue with her sleep.

But he didn't.

Sighing, Reg rose to her feet. She took a quick look around the bedroom, but she knew he would not be there. If he wasn't snoozing on the bed or looking out the window, he didn't have any reason to stay there.

Reg yawned and padded out of the bedroom. Her first stop was the bathroom to take care of other concerns, since she knew she wouldn't find him in there. His litter box was in the bathroom, but that was the only reason he would be in there. Or to drink out of the faucet. But that was generally only when she was there to turn it on for him.

Reg washed her hands and walked out to the kitchen and living room area. There wasn't any need to check her office, since the door was shut and she rarely used it. It had become more of a dumping ground for things she needed to store and didn't have any other place for. Starlight liked to sneak in there when she opened the door to inspect the boxes and hide behind the various stacks. Which was exactly the reason she didn't want him in there and kept the door closed.

"Starlight?" Reg looked around the kitchen and living room and couldn't find him.

He wasn't sitting on the back of the couch looking out the window. He wasn't eating from his bowl or sitting on the counter where he wasn't supposed to be.

Reg walked around with increasing concern, looking under pieces of furniture, in dark corners, anywhere Starlight might have decided to hide. Cats hid when they were sick or injured. They pulled away from even the ones they loved and pushed their faces into dark corners, isolating themselves.

Where was he? There weren't that many places in the cottage to hide. She couldn't think of anywhere else to check. She returned to the bedroom, turned on the light, and looked around for him. Under the bed? In the closet? Under the blankets of the bed? Curled up on the dirty clothes that had not quite made it into the hamper? In the hamper itself?

There was no sign of him. Reg returned to the bathroom and bent down to look into the cave of his litter box. Not there.

She walked back out into the front of the cottage and saw Starlight sitting in the middle of the floor. He sat tall and regal, like a statue of Bastet.

CHAPTER TWO

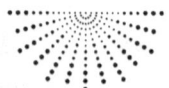

"Where were you?" Reg demanded.

Starlight blinked, first with his green eye and then with the blue, looking at Reg as if she were the one behaving strangely. What was she doing getting out of bed in the middle of her usual sleep schedule calling for him?

"I looked everywhere for you and you weren't here," Reg told him crossly.

He just stared at her.

"Were you hiding? Why couldn't I find you?"

There was no answer. Reg reached out to him with her other senses, trying to get a read on his emotions and thoughts. It wasn't quite the same as reading someone's facial expression or body language, but it was similar.

He wasn't open to her as usual, and Reg got the distinct impression he wanted her to go back to sleep and forget about the whole thing. It wasn't any of her business where he had been or what he had been doing. She was supposed to be in bed asleep.

"I woke up and you were gone," Reg told him crossly. "How am I supposed to go back to sleep when you disappear like that?"

His gaze was unblinking.

Just go to sleep and you'll feel better when you wake up later.

"I don't want to go back to sleep," Reg argued stubbornly,

But she did. She was exhausted and she didn't feel like she had been sleeping very well when she had been dreaming the siren song. It hadn't been that restful stage of sleep she craved. Instead, it had sapped more energy from her. She needed to crawl back into bed, slip under the covers, close her eyes, and go to sleep again.

Starlight finally moved, walking over to her and rubbing against her legs. He led her toward the bedroom door, purring.

Reg looked around the kitchen and living room, getting the distinct impression he was trying to distract her from the question of where he had been and what he had been doing.

But everything was not in its place as she had first thought. In the early morning light creeping through the windows, she could see that things had been knocked down and disarranged on the counter. And in the living room, the throws and pillows were in the wrong places. Not on the floor, like they would be if Starlight had been zipping wildly through the house, chasing imaginary mice and knocked them down. But they were in the wrong places, as if a human had been there, looking through her things, coming up with a new decorating scheme.

"What the…?"

Starlight wound around her legs, meowing and purring, trying to entice her back to her bedroom and the prospect of a few more hours of sleep. She looked down at him.

"Did you do this? Who has been here? Was it you? Harrison?"

Harrison was one of the few entities who could get into her cottage uninvited. He had no problem passing even the strongest wards. Which was fine, because he wasn't there to do her harm, but it was still disconcerting. The immortal had no sense of privacy or propriety, and she sometimes awoke to find him sitting on her bed looking at her or playing in the living room with Starlight while she was sleeping.

Starlight just looked up at her, purring at top volume. *Didn't Reg want to go to sleep? Didn't she want to crawl under her soft, comfy covers, close her eyes, and drift off into oblivion?*

"No, I don't want to go to sleep," she lied. "I want to know what's been going on here."

But of course, the cat had no answers for her. Even when he had appeared to her in other forms, he had never spoken to her in human words. It was all body language and the connection of their minds.

And this time, he didn't have anything to tell her about the state of the cottage or what he had been doing while she was sleeping.

CHAPTER THREE

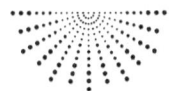

*R*eg was standing at the kitchen island with a cup of coffee, staring off into space and hoping that the caffeine would kick-start her brain and make up for the deficits caused by her lack of sleep.

Sarah let herself into the cottage after a cursory warning rap on the door.

"Good morning, Reg!" Reg's plump, older landlord looked at the watch on her wrist to check to see if it *was* still morning. Which it was, and Reg mildly resented the implication that she had slept that late. She had hoped to sleep through the morning, but she had tossed and turned for hours after going back to bed, trying to figure out what was happening.

Sarah looked around the cottage and raised her brows. "Did you decide to redecorate?"

"It *is* different, right?" Reg agreed, relieved that she wasn't going crazy in thinking that things had been moved around.

"Well, yes." Sarah looked around, evaluating the new arrangement. "It looks very nice," she said tolerantly, though Reg suspected that she didn't like it at all. Because it was a change from how she had thought things should be arranged, or because she wanted Reg to keep everything as Sarah had initially arranged it? It was Sarah's guest cottage, after all, and though Reg rented it from her, that didn't mean she could go around changing everything. "Are you going to keep it this way?"

"I... don't know."

Sarah raised her brows. "Nothing wrong with trying things out a new way," she allowed, though her tone said that there definitely was something wrong with Reg rearranging things without asking her. She patted at her gray hair as if that, too, might be out of place.

Reg looked around the cottage again. Clearly, it hadn't been Sarah who had rearranged things on a whim. And suggesting to Sarah that there might have been an intruder during the night would not make her happy. Best to keep quiet about it while Reg tried to figure out what had happened. If it was just Harrison, then Reg wasn't in any danger. He was her protector; he wouldn't let anything happen to her.

If *Corvin* had managed to get by the wards again, then he would have entered Reg's bedroom. He wouldn't have just rearranged the decor. She couldn't think of anyone other than Harrison who might do that.

"You look tired." Sarah was watching Reg. "You didn't sleep well last night?"

"No." Reg yawned, covering her mouth. "I was restless. Woke up a lot. Didn't sleep very soundly."

"That's too bad. I can make you a tea for tonight. That will help you to sleep better."

Sarah was helpful, but she was not an adept tea maker. She might get all of the beneficial herbs right, but the taste... left something to be desired. When Reg had been served a strengthening tea by Lady Papillon, she had been surprised to find how pleasant and tasty it was. Sarah's medicinal brews always tasted nasty.

"I'm sure I'll sleep better tonight," Reg assured her. "The second night after a bad night's sleep, I always do better. I'll sleep like a baby tonight."

Sarah nodded. "I'm sure you will," she agreed. "Are you ready to get to work?"

Reg took another gulp of her coffee, considering. She knew she was supposed to be helping Sarah to strengthen the protective wards in the yard and cottage each day. Sarah's powers were no longer a match for Corvin's, as he grew in power and hers dwindled. Reg wasn't convinced that adding her intention to the wards actually made them any stronger. But so far, Corvin had not returned to the yard, so maybe their efforts were having an effect.

Maybe he had just been too distracted by his campaign for the leadership of the coven that he had not bothered to test the limits of the renewed wards and charms. And when he did... maybe then, Reg would see just how pitiful her attempts to strengthen the wards were.

As it turned out, she was more likely to ignite the wards than she was to imbue them with power.

"I'm so tired this morning. I don't know if I will be of any help to you," Reg told Sarah.

"I'm sure you'll be just fine once you get started. It's like exercise. You're tired before you start, but then you get a burst of energy when you get into gear."

Reg groaned. The last thing she wanted to hear about was how she should be getting more exercise and taking care of her body. Since she had moved to Black Sands, she'd put on a few too many extra pounds. She'd been thin before that, not eating as often as she should have, so the first few pounds had been welcome and she had not been concerned about them. But those first pounds had brought along a few friends, and then Reg's skirt waistbands started to get tight. She needed to get down to business and focus on eating healthily and maintaining her weight at an appropriate level.

But when was she going to do that? She wasn't the type of person who could turn down tasty, decadent food when it was offered, and the bad foods just kept appearing in her fridge. That wasn't *her* fault. Not exactly.

"Come on," Sarah said briskly. "The fresh air and exercise will do you good."

Reg sighed, took two more swallows of her coffee, and put it down on the counter. She reluctantly followed Sarah outside, and they started to go through the process of renewing and strengthening the protective wards. Reg needed to focus on the process and to remind herself that it was for her own protection. If she wanted to ensure that no one with evil intentions could enter her cottage's backyard, she needed to do her part.

The first ward, a millet bird feeder that hung from the branches of a tree located near the gate, went up in a brief flash of fire and a lot of acrid smoke. Reg coughed and waved her hand in front of her face to dissipate the smoke.

Sarah cocked her head at Reg. "You need to focus, Reg," she reminded her. "You need to learn to put these powers to use in a constructive way. You can strengthen the wards and put power into them without lighting them on fire."

Reg rubbed her aching forehead. "That might seem easy to you, but trust me; it isn't that easy for me. You're not a firecaster."

"I may not have an affinity for firecasting, but I can produce a flame if necessary. The processes of imbuing with power and creating a flame are quite different."

"For a non-firecaster."

"What would Davyn say? Would he let you get away with giving excuses? What does *he* do if you ignite something by accident?"

Davyn was Reg's mentor in firecasting. He definitely did not let her get away with being lazy or ignore her mistakes. He was a tough teacher. A good friend too, but he made her work. She had not been trained when she was younger and that made it hard for her to control her abilities.

"He would make me practice more."

"Well, here you are." Sarah made a motion that took in the rest of the yard. "You have plenty of opportunities to practice."

Reg liked practicing with Davyn because she got to play with fire. He gave her opportunities to expand her abilities and to see what she was capable of, though he kept tight control on their practice sessions and was able to quash any fires that sprang up where they weren't supposed to or burned too hot or too big.

Sarah didn't have that ability. All she could do was stand back and watch her wards burn. She would have to charm new ones, and that took work and effort.

"I'm sorry, Sarah," Reg spoke in a low voice, "I didn't mean to screw up. I know you put a lot of work into these things..."

"Don't worry about that. You worry about yourself. Getting your gifts under control. Do you know what will happen if your abilities grow too fast?"

Reg moved on to the next ward, avoiding the question. She didn't know what would happen, but she was sure it wasn't good. She would have known that even without Sarah's serious voice and the wrinkle lines between her brows.

"Reg?" Sarah persisted. "You need to think about this. I don't want to make you feel bad. I know you're trying, but you need to focus better. Even if it is hard, you must keep working at it."

"I am. I'm here. I'm doing it."

Sarah pressed her lips together. "You have been blessed with a great deal of power, Reg, but that is a dangerous thing. Fire can do a lot of damage. And with your siren powers emerging as well, you need to realize what serious responsibility comes with these abilities..."

"I know that. I'm not using my siren powers and don't intend to. And I'm working with Davyn on the firecasting. You're helping me with this stuff..." Reg pointed to a small wind chime tinkling in the breeze. At least it was made of metal and she could not light it on fire. Maybe if Sarah would make all her wards out of metal, they could bypass the lecture on how she wasn't yet in control of her powers. "I am doing my best. I'm not just sitting around doing readings all day."

Sarah was silent as Reg did her best to feed good intentions and well-being into the wind chime. It was there to do more than just provide the garden with a little music when the breeze blew. It was there to protect her. She needed to give it as much strength and power as she could.

The little metal tubes turned from gray to red and Reg eased back on her efforts, trying to draw on her feelings of gratitude and strength instead of the fire that burned at her core. Sarah watched her, eyes hooded, and said nothing.

CHAPTER FOUR

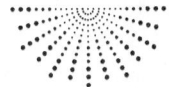

*S*trengthening the wards outside took much longer than Reg had expected it to. Most days, they finished more quickly, but she just couldn't focus. It was a tossup between being totally ineffective and trying so hard to transfer power that she ignited the wards or other nearby objects.

Sarah followed Reg into the house, shaking her head and clucking at Reg's distraction. "You must not be feeling very well today," she said sympathetically. "After you've had a chance to rest and recover and maybe eat a bit of lunch, you need to strengthen the wards inside, too, okay?"

She waited for Reg to look at her and acknowledge that she would, making Reg feel very much like she was back in foster care, promising her foster parents about completing her chores or her homework even when she had no intention to do so.

Yes, of course I'll do it. I just need a little break first.

I won't forget.

I'll do it on my own. You don't need to worry about it.

Reg nodded her agreement. "You're right. I'm just feeling a bit off today. I'm sure it will pass. I'll have a little bit of breakfast and see how I feel."

"Don't forget. You know it is important. You need to protect yourself. You don't want *certain persons* to be able to get into your cottage."

"But they can't, not with the wards in the backyard too. The only way they would have access to the cottage is if I invited them through the backyard. And I won't do that."

"But it has happened in the past. You know you need to have more than one level of protection." Sarah smiled slyly at Reg. "It's rather like birth control. You can't just rely on pills or the barrier method. You need both together to be sure."

Reg rolled her eyes, her face warming. She didn't want to discuss birth control with Sarah any more than she wanted to spend another hour strengthening protective wards.

"I'll be careful," she promised. "I'll take care of it."

"You wouldn't go out in the rain without your raincoat..."

"I get it, Sarah." Reg waved her hands to shoo Sarah away. "Go on. I need to relax for a while now."

Laughing, Sarah went back to the big house. Reg flopped down on her wicker couch and pulled out her phone to see if she had missed any calls. There was one missed call from Marta Jessup. Reg tapped on the number to call her back.

"Reg!" Marta greeted. "You're finally up!"

Reg glanced at the phone and saw that it was past noon. "I've been up for a while. I was just helping Sarah."

"Oh, I see." Marta's teasing tone suggested that she didn't believe it. "Helping Sarah."

"I was. But I'm back now, so what's up?"

"I just wanted to make sure we were still on for dinner tonight after I get off."

"Oh." Reg hadn't checked her appointment book yet and hadn't remembered that they had made plans. "Sure, of course. That's tonight."

"You didn't schedule any clients that will conflict, right?"

Reg didn't get up and walk over to the kitchen island to check the book. "Nope. All clear."

"Good. I'll see you, then. We going to meet at The Crystal Bowl?"

"Yeah. Like usual."

"Okay. I just wasn't sure because last time when Corvin was there…"

Reg grimaced. She did not want to end up anywhere Corvin was. "I'm sure it will be fine. If he's there… we'll get takeout and come back here. How about that?"

The Crystal Bowl didn't exactly serve takeout, but they could ask for their meals to be packaged up, just like they would have done with leftovers at the end of the meal. Reg wouldn't waste leftover food. She'd gone hungry too many times. Food was food. She wasn't going to let it be thrown out.

"That's fine with me," Marta agreed. "It isn't like I want to be anywhere near the guy either."

The revelations of what had happened between Corvin and Marta Jessup years previously had come as a shock to her, and there wasn't any way she was going to be friendly with him or invite him in to consult on any of her police investigations again. It would be a long time before Marta would trust a power drinker or allow him anywhere near her.

* * *

By late afternoon, Reg was starting to feel better and, when she headed over to the restaurant in the early evening, she felt back to her old self. There wasn't anything to worry about. Cats disappeared and hid in odd places all the time. Lying on a bookshelf behind the books. In a cupboard or a space between the fridge and cupboard she didn't think he had any hope of fitting into, much less getting himself out of later. Cats were like liquids, flowing into the empty spaces with boneless contortions Reg would have deemed impossible.

That was all. Starlight had just been hiding somewhere.

And the changed decorations in her front room were nothing to worried about. Bound to be Harrison. He was such a clotheshorse, with such a flamboyant personality, that it wouldn't be at all strange for him to decide the trappings in the room needed to be changed, even when it wasn't his room. Maybe one of the throw pillows had clashed with his outfit.

She told Marta about it anyway. Not as a police report or something she was genuinely concerned about. Just one of those weird things. Marta had met Harrison. She knew how unpredictable he could be.

Marta's dark eyes narrowed thoughtfully. She was a petite woman with a golden tan complexion, a testament to her mother's Asian heritage. "This was after you had been sleeping, and you woke up disoriented?"

"Yes."

"And you didn't feel like you got enough sleep, even going back to bed afterward?"

"No."

"Maybe you were sleepwalking."

Reg shook her head. But when she thought about it, it wasn't such an outlandish idea, even though she had never sleepwalked before that she was aware of. There hadn't been any sign of anyone having broken into the house, no sign that anyone had eaten anything—and Harrison was always very interested in whatever food she had on hand. If he didn't find anything he liked in the fridge, he would produce what he wanted out of thin air. But there had been no crumbs, smears of chocolate, or dirty dishes in her sink other than what she had left there herself.

But why would Reg sleepwalk and change the decor of her house? Was she bored? Upset? Had she been up cleaning or dreaming of rearranging things before the dream of the beautiful siren song?

"I'm not a sleepwalker," she told Marta. "I've never walked in my sleep before."

"Are you sure?"

"Well... pretty sure. I don't remember doing it. Or any of the adults telling me that I had."

"If no one else was in your cottage and things were moved around... then it would make sense that it was you," Marta pointed out. "I've heard of people being able to do all kinds of things in their sleep. Eating, cooking, driving, you name it."

"But I would remember that, wouldn't I?" Reg shook her head. "I'd at least remember that I had been dreaming of redecorating? Wouldn't it have been in my dreams somehow? I wasn't dreaming anything like that."

"Maybe not. People can do things in their sleep and have no idea that they were even out of their beds. You don't remember everything that you dream."

"I just… don't see how it could be that. Other people do come into the cottage. Sarah. Harrison. I know it wasn't Sarah, because she wasn't happy that things had been moved around. But I haven't heard anything from Harrison lately. He could have been over without me knowing anything about it. And he's crazy. He doesn't follow human conventions. It wouldn't occur to him that he isn't supposed to go into someone's house and rearrange their things. He would probably think he was doing me a favor."

CHAPTER FIVE

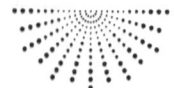

 arta had a few french fries, thinking about it. "It *could* be an immortal," she admitted. "You know more about what they are likely to do than anyone else around here. Most of us haven't really had anything to do with one." She swirled a couple of fries in a puddle of ketchup. "Have you been having a lot of nightmares? I mean... the business with Verity, that was pretty disturbing."

Reg caught herself biting her lip and sipped her drink instead. She breathed deeply, pretending that nothing about what had happened to Verity bothered her in the least. She had to admit that she'd had a few dreams, but she couldn't see why thinking about what had happened to Verity would make her want to redecorate the house in her sleep.

"I haven't been thinking about it *very* much," she hedged. "Sometimes, but I keep busy with other things. I have my business to run and everything... I don't have a lot of time for sitting around feeling sorry for myself. Or thinking about something like that. I didn't even know Verity and couldn't help what happened, so why should I spend time agonizing over it?"

"Well, she *was* burned to a crisp in front of your eyes. Most people would find that disturbing on some level."

Reg rolled her eyes. "Of course it was disturbing. But it wasn't... gruesome or anything like that. It was more like... she turned to stone and then crumbled into dust."

"Oh, not disturbing at all," Marta said sarcastically. "That sounds like a perfectly ordinary afternoon to me."

"But when you say that someone was burned up, you think of... screaming and raw flesh and all that, and the smell. But it wasn't like that. It was shocking, but it was... dry."

Reg shook her head, unable to conjure the words to explain what she had seen and how it had affected her. Ember, her dragon, had only been protecting her. And defending himself and his gold. Verity had been a very powerful witch, and Reg could only imagine what kind of harm Verity could have done to her if Ember hadn't acted when he had.

Verity had been an angry, vengeful woman, intent on getting her retribution on Corvin for having left her decades or centuries before, when she had been pregnant with John Saunders. Though Corvin hadn't known—neither of them had known—that she had been pregnant.

It was a complicated and tragic situation. Corvin hadn't treated Verity well, but he had been trying to protect her from himself and keep her from discovering his true nature. He hadn't told her when they married that he was a power drinker, and it wasn't until after John was born, inheriting his father's curse, that Verity had learned the truth. It had been many years before she had sought Corvin out. Reg didn't understand all of Verity's motives, but believed that she had wanted John to become the leader of the coven rather than Corvin. She would probably have gladly taken the position herself, but the traditional coven was male-only, so there was no way she could be admitted to it, unless someone in authority changed the rules.

So she had groomed her son, preparing him to be initiated into the coven and to build himself up so that he would be able to take over the leadership of the coven in the future. Would they have waited until there was another election and others could challenge Corvin for the coven's leadership, or would John have found a way to remove Corvin some other way once the coven trusted him?

Reg didn't think they would have waited. Neither Verity nor John had shown much patience for the coven's political processes.

"Reg?"

Reg looked across the table at Marta. How many times had her friend tried to get her attention while Reg had been lost in her own head?

"I don't think it's anything to do with Verity and John," Reg said, waving the issue aside. "I don't think I got up at night and redecorated because I was upset about Verity or John."

Marta's eyes were quick and intelligent. "Why are you upset about John?"

"I said I'm not."

"But I never mentioned him. I never even thought about him bothering you. You're the one who brought him up, so you are thinking about him and connecting him somehow to your dreams or being restless in the night."

"No. That's just because you were asking about Verity. John is her son and is the whole reason they were both here so, of course, that's where my mind went. I'm sure it has nothing to do with either of them."

"What is going on with John? Do you know?"

Reg shrugged. "No. I don't have anything to do with him. And I don't want to. He and Corvin are all buddy-buddy now, making up for lost time, and I don't like..." Reg grimaced and tried to think of a way to end the sentence. She couldn't very well say that she didn't like John Saunders. "He apologized for how he behaved while Verity had a hold over him. He seemed sincere. But..."

"You don't think he *was* sincere?"

"I think... Corvin told him to apologize. And... well, when I am around John, I can hear Verity whispering to him."

Marta's eyes widened. Despite Marta's magical upbringing, Reg knew she didn't believe in ghosts. Reg still didn't understand how someone could know that there were real magic and psychic phenomena and yet not believe that spirits persisted after death.

"What does that mean?" Marta asked.

"I don't know. It could mean all different things. Maybe her ghost is attached to him, but I couldn't see her. Or maybe he's just so used to her telling him what to do that he's conjured up an echo in his mind so that he wouldn't be alone. Just like... the voice of his conscience. Telling him to do things the way that she raised him to."

"Yeah, that makes sense." Marta nodded. She probably would have approved of any explanation that didn't involve restless spirits.

"Anyway... I know enough to stay away from power drinkers." Reg ignored Marta's wry smile. "He caught me off guard once, and I won't let that happen again. Being cursed is bad enough. But with a witch like Verity whispering in his ear, even after her death... Well, she was very cunning. She had this whole plan for getting him into Corvin's coven and then taking it over. And now... I guess he's one step closer to fulfilling her dream. He is not a person that I want to be around."

"And what about Ember?"

CHAPTER SIX

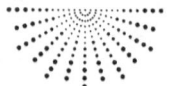

eg blinked and shook her head, frowning at the non sequitur. "What about Ember?"

"I mean… what are you going to do about him? Obviously, you can't have a dragon flying around here, burning people up whenever the whim hits him."

"He was protecting me," Reg reiterated. "Would you rather that I was dead?"

"Of course not. I wasn't there, so I don't know… what could have been done to stop him or deal with it differently. I'm not second-guessing you."

But clearly, she was.

"Ember didn't do anything wrong. He was keeping me safe. I would be dead if he hadn't stepped in."

"Maybe," Marta allowed. "But there were others there who could have helped. Corvin. John. Wilf wasn't far away, and he's an experienced warlock. Quite skilled, despite what you might think of him."

"Corvin and John? Do you think that either of them would have fought Verity? That made it three against one. And Wilf didn't come out of the shop until after everything was over; he wasn't there. Trust me, I couldn't have taken all three of them in a focused attack. There's no way. They are all power drinkers and very powerful."

"Verity wasn't a power drinker," Marta corrected.

"Not by nature, maybe. But she had John feeding her the powers he stole from others, so you can't tell me that doesn't qualify her as a power drinker."

Marta shook her head. "It's not the same thing. Corvin has given you or me extra power in a pinch. That doesn't make us power drinkers."

"Well, no," Reg admitted. But she couldn't understand how Marta could fail to see the difference in their circumstances. Reg accepting a little boost from Corvin when she was in dire need was not the same as Verity grooming her son to feed her his powers to transform her from being a witch with only mild or moderate powers to one whose aura had glowed so brightly with the stolen gifts that Reg could barely look at her. "But Verity was."

Marta studied her, thinking it through. Reg was sure she would argue further, but the other woman eventually shrugged. "Maybe you're right. Growing up in the magical community, I see it as black and white. Either a witch is born a power drinker or he's—she's—not. And Verity wasn't born a power drinker. They are... like a different species. Or they carry a genetic defect. Something like that. They're not the same as the rest of us." Marta took another bite of her fish. "But if she uses someone else to steal powers for her, then *practically*, there is no difference. She is a power drinker."

Reg nodded, satisfied. "And they were all there, against me, and there was no way I could have fought them all. Ember saved me. Just like he saved me when Verity tried to run me off the road."

"Except he didn't kill her when she tried to run you off the road."

"She was just going to keep trying to kill me until she succeeded."

Marta sighed. "I'm not saying that Ember did anything wrong." Though clearly, that was exactly what she had meant. "I'm just saying... how are you going to keep everyone safe from him in the future? He can't be allowed to run rampant around Black Sands."

"He isn't running rampant. He protected me. Once."

"Twice."

"Twice, then. But he hasn't been 'running rampant.'"

"He's getting bigger. He's going to get stronger and more hostile toward humans. He's going to range farther. You don't know what he might do, killing and stealing. That's his nature, you can't exactly tell him to stop or make him sit in a corner."

"He isn't like that. If he was doing things he shouldn't, then I would explain it to him." Reg didn't admit that Ember didn't always do what he was told, even when Reg did explain things to him clearly. He had his own ideas about things, his dragon nature, and the memories of his ancestors. One puny human telling him what he should and shouldn't do wasn't going to make much difference. So what *was* she going to do about him?

"Besides," Reg went on, "I'm not the one taking care of him or training him. That's up to Davyn. I'm just... I visit him and see how he's doing. He doesn't live right in town, so he isn't trying to eat the townspeople. He stays on Davyn's property. Most of the time."

"He won't, though," Marta countered.

"I thought you didn't know much about dragons. You haven't ever seen a real one before. So how would you know anything about their real nature or whether they can be trained? Maybe it's just like with dogs, that they can be loving family pets or trained to be vicious killers. Davyn is not going to raise him to be a killer."

"I've read plenty about dragons, and—"

"But you haven't ever actually had one, have you?"

Marta stopped. "No. Of course not."

"I've seen a lot of movies about girls riding horses and winning championships. Does that mean that I know anything about training horses? That I can enter a rodeo or race, ride my horse to victory, and save the farm?"

"What farm?"

"Whatever farm. They always have to save the farm in those movies."

Jessup shook her head. "No, I don't know how to train a dragon. Or a horse. But I'm not sure Davyn does either. What qualifications does he have to train a dragon? Other than whatever he's seen in movies."

"He's a firecaster," Reg shot back.

Marta was taken aback. "What does that have to do with it?"

"Firecasters and dragons," Reg spread her hands apart, inviting Jessup to see the obvious connection. "They both have the same abilities—the same nature. You should see Davyn with the dragon. They're very… compatible."

"And so are you."

"Yes. That's why Ember comes to help me when I need it. But I'm not the one taking care of him and training him every day."

"I guess I should be talking to Davyn," Marta conceded. "I'll go out there one day and have a chat."

CHAPTER SEVEN

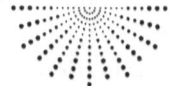

*R*eg was irritated. "Why is it any of your business?"

"I am charged with keeping the peace in Black Sands."

"People, yes. But you don't have any jurisdiction over dragons, do you? Or over how they are trained?"

"I have all kinds of law enforcement responsibilities, including bylaw enforcement."

"You have bylaws about how dragons are kept?" Reg asked in disbelief. Everyone who had seen Ember so far had said they had never seen a real dragon in person before. So how could Black Sands have any laws about how dragons were kept?

Marta couldn't help chuckling at that. "Not specifically, but we have pet bylaws and animal husbandry bylaws. Stuff about keeping exotic pets and allowing other people quiet enjoyment of their properties. There are laws about animals that are deemed to be dangerous. If you have a dog that has bitten someone, for example. So..." she shrugged, "we have a lot of laws that can apply if you decide to raise a dragon within the municipality."

"But he's outside the town limits," Reg pointed out triumphantly. "So those rules don't apply."

"Our jurisdiction extends beyond the town boundaries, and

other laws apply to the unincorporated areas. We can't have people running puppy mills or doing other things that put animals or humans in danger."

Reg pushed food around her plate. "Ember isn't doing anything to harm anyone. And we're not doing anything to hurt him."

"Except that he did incinerate Verity."

"That's *one person* and it was self-defense. My life was in danger."

Marta rolled her eyes. "I think we're due for a subject change. There's no point in us going back and forth on it. I think it's pretty clear that there is a potential for harm, but you're not going to back down on your position."

Reg shook her head and looked away. "No one around here knows how to raise or train a dragon. So you'll have to trust Davyn to do what he can and hope for the best. What are you going to do? Say that Ember has to be sent away somewhere? Where? There aren't exactly any family members that will take him in. Any kennels that will put up dragons. And there are laws about endangered magical species, you know. You have to abide by those too."

Reg had been educated on several aspects of endangered magical species by Julian Sabat, a magical investigator for the Endangered Species Division. Reg still couldn't wrap her mind around it, but she knew that such creatures were afforded certain protections, whether they were dangerous or not, and you couldn't go around taking them out of their natural habitats.

"So... I've been looking into some interesting reports down by the waterfront," Marta said, stubbornly ignoring Reg's words and plowing ahead with the subject change she had suggested.

Reg rubbed her forehead. She was tired after her disrupted sleep of the night before, and Marta was probably right. They weren't going to get anywhere by arguing. "Yeah? What's happening down at the waterfront?"

"There has been a series of attacks on people walking on the beach or frequenting establishments along the waterfront."

"Attacks? What kind of attacks?" Reg's stomach tightened. Hearing about random attacks brought back memories of the draugrs the Witch Doctor had unleashed upon Black Sands. She did not want to face anything like that again.

"So far, nothing fatal," Marta reassured her. "A few minor injuries, people being hit or yanked around. I don't know whether it is an inept mugger, some kind of gang thing, or what. We can't get a reliable description. People never seem to get a good look, and all have different impressions of their attacker. Tall, short, fat, thin, none of them can agree."

"You think it's a mugger?"

"Don't really know. He hasn't taken anyone's money or held them up at gunpoint or anything like that, but he's grabbed for purses—or that's what a couple of women have said, anyway. He hasn't actually gotten them and made off with them, so I have to doubt whether he's really trying to snatch purses, and might just be grabbing for their shoulder to try to get them to go with him or talk to him."

"Go with him where? Does he say anything to them?"

"Nothing coherent. A growl or some muttered words. I've gotten reports of things like 'come here' or 'I need you.' Nothing too helpful, I'm afraid."

"Weird." Reg speared a couple of pieces of pasta. "Do you think it's something... paranormal? Or just... a regular person out causing trouble?"

"I don't have any idea what it is yet. We get all sorts here." Marta sighed. "As you know."

"But you don't think it's anything like... draugrs."

"Draugar? No. These attacks aren't anything like that. Most of those people were killed in their beds. Behind closed doors."

"And you don't think it's... I don't know... werewolves?"

Even though she said werewolves, that wasn't what Reg had been thinking. She remembered being at the harbor with Corvin and seeing two women working together, a mermaid and a siren, trying to lure unsuspecting men to their deaths.

"Werewolves?" Marta laughed. "Where do you come up with these things, Reg? There haven't been werewolves in this part of the country for decades."

"Well, there weren't any dragons around either, were there? That doesn't mean that there aren't any now. I would think they would be able to travel in their human form, wouldn't they? They could get in a car and tootle over to Black Sands whenever they pleased. From anywhere in the country. From anywhere in the world, if they can ride on planes or boats."

"But…" Marta seemed at a loss for words. "I don't know. I suppose they could get around. But they like to hunt in packs, and these have been individual attacks."

"If there aren't many around, then it could just be one lone wolf." Damon had once referred to himself as a lone wolf, and Reg couldn't help considering, if just for a moment, the possibility that Damon was a werewolf.

She didn't know the warning signs or how you could tell if someone could shift form. And she didn't know how many legends about werewolves were actually true. Did they shift when they saw the full moon? Could they change at will? Did they have any control over the process? She thought that werewolves must be hairy when they were in human form, and Damon wasn't a particularly hairy man. But it was modern day, and werewolves could shave or have electrolysis. They didn't have to walk around looking all shaggy.

"Or maybe that's why they aren't giving consistent descriptions of their attacker," Reg pointed out. "Maybe there is more than one of them. They are only describing the one they saw, but there could be more that are out of sight, flanking them or circling ahead to cut them off."

Marta nodded slowly. "Well… that's a possibility. Something to look into. But I really don't think it is werewolves. If it was… we would have deaths on our hands. With big slashes. Werewolves are pretty efficient killers. They wouldn't just be bumping into people or trying to take their purses."

Reg had to admit that sounded more like a human than a wolf attack. Which was a good thing. She wouldn't want it to be a werewolf or a whole pack of them.

But she also didn't want it to be a mermaid or a siren. Especially not a siren.

Her blood pulsed hard in her ears at the thought of another siren in her territory. No one else was allowed to operate in her waters. Norma Jean had given the territory to her. She'd already had to face off against one other siren who had disputed her claim.

Reg didn't want to be territorial. She never intended to hunt in the area, never intended to pull any victim down under the water. Her reaction to the suggestion of another siren in her territory was instinctual, not something that she could control.

"Are you okay?" Marta asked. "You're… kind of flushed."

Reg put her hands over her cheeks as if that would cool them or hide them from Marta's sight. "It's just… warm in here."

"Not really."

"Well, I'm hot."

"A bit early for you to be going through a change of life."

"That's not what it is." Marta's teasing made her feel even more embarrassed and she glanced around to ensure no one was listening in. "Maybe I'm coming down with something. I'm just feeling really warm."

"I hope you're not sick. Sorry. I was just kidding."

"So… do you have any theories of who might be behind these attacks? Is it just some really inept mugger?"

"I guess so. That's all we have to go on right now. No one is getting upset and jumping all over it at this point. The chief thinks it's just… one guy… like you said, an inept mugger. But if it does escalate and there's a death, you know he will have kittens and insist that we catch whoever is behind it. If this guy puts someone in the hospital or the morgue, they will suddenly care about it."

"But until then, you're not getting much help," Reg speculated.

"None. None at all. They're all treating it as sort of a joke."

Reg couldn't see how a series of people being attacked at night could be a joke. They needed to nip it in the bud before it escalated and someone got hurt.

"Do you have any leads? Any clues as to who it might be?"

"So far, the mugger hasn't left anything behind. No personal items, no hair, skin under their nails, fingerprints. It's localized to one area, so we can assume that he lives around there somewhere. And it's at night, so he doesn't want to be seen. Maybe he works days and goes out at night, or maybe he doesn't have a job. If he spends all night out, he wouldn't be able to work at a day job the next morning. He'd be too tired."

"*Is* he out all night?"

Marta considered this, sitting back in her seat and pushing her plate away from her an inch. "Hmm. Maybe not. The attacks have all been after midnight. In the early hours of the morning. Say, between midnight and three. I'd have to check the reports to be more exact."

The same time as Reg was usually up. Seances were best held at midnight and the wee hours of the morning when the veil between the living and the dead was the thinnest. Reg could channel spirits during the daylight, but clients were more likely to feel the dearly departed's presence when they were most suggestible. When they were tired and a bit nervous.

"Maybe whoever it is will give up. He's not having much success. Maybe he will decide it's not worth the bother and he isn't very good at what he's doing."

"Well, that would be nice, but I'm not counting on it. The way I've seen these things go in the past is that they escalate. They don't just decide to stop."

"You wouldn't know about the ones who stop."

Marta stared at her.

Reg shrugged. "If someone tries to mug someone, and it doesn't go well, and they decide it's not worth it, then you wouldn't ever know that. They would just fade out and you wouldn't be hunting them."

"This guy has done more than just try once or twice. He's been at it for a while, and he's not just going to fade into the woodwork."

CHAPTER EIGHT

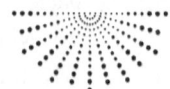

$\mathscr{R}$eg and Marta had finished eating their dinners. They
had finished their coffee and decided not to have
dessert. Reg was eating way too much sugar and junk and needed
to watch her figure, or she would soon be as plump as Sarah. And
Marta, shorter than Reg, had to be even more careful of what she
ate if she wanted to fit her uniform. Reg assumed they would have
bigger uniforms, but law enforcement officers needed to be in good
shape. At least the ones who were out and about like Marta and
not stuck behind a desk all day.

They walked out of the restaurant together, still chatting,
though it wasn't about anything important. They had moved
through the most important subjects of the day and were on to
things like the weather forecast for the rest of the week and
upcoming movie releases.

Reg felt a sudden flush, as warm as she had been when she had
started thinking about another siren operating in her territory. But
this time, she knew it wasn't emotional. It was external. She looked
around, putting a hand on Marta's arm to stop her.

"What is it?" Marta's hand went to her hip where her holster
usually sat. "What's wrong?"

Reg focused on two men who were standing nearby, one of

them finishing off a cigarette. They were both looking at her. Corvin and his son John. Corvin was wearing his cloak, furling out behind him in the slight breeze. He was as handsome as ever, with dark eyes, neatly trimmed beard, and nice physique. And then there was the feeling that Reg got around him. The wave of warmth brought with it the heady scent of roses, strong even though they were standing outside in the open air. His powers were growing. There was a time when she wouldn't have even been able to smell his pheromones when he was outside, or would perhaps catch only a whiff, and then they would be swept away on the breeze. But the scent was strong enough to pull her in, sending her heart beating harder, making her crave being in his arms again. And she had to give up so little to do it…

Marta was pulling on her arm. "Steady, Reg. Don't let him get inside your head." Her face was flushed and her eyes dilated, but she was still fighting Corvin's charms. But then, they weren't aimed at her. Corvin had already taken all he wanted from Marta. Reg took a step to the side, trying to escape the cloud of pheromones.

"Reg Rawlins," John greeted, his voice flat. "Nice to see you again."

"You can keep your distance too," Reg warned.

John flicked his cigarette to the pavement and ground it out with his foot. But it wasn't the stink of cigarette smoke that Reg smelled on him; it was the sweet smell of baking brownies. It was so thick and rich she could almost taste the brownies.

Marta took a deep breath, taking it in. "Nice!" she breathed. "But now I'm regretting not springing for dessert."

John took a tentative step toward her, smiling. Corvin shook his head. "She doesn't have any gifts," he told John, putting his hand on John's chest to stop him. "No point in spending any energy there." He looked toward Marta, his expression apologetic. Because he had said that she had no gifts when she still had some of the residual powers he had left her with? Or because he was the one who had stripped her of the rest? He had been trying to apologize to Marta ever since she had discovered the truth, but she wasn't about to give him even an ounce of forgiveness.

35

Reg wouldn't have either. In fact, she hadn't forgiven him, even though he had given her powers back within a few hours, something that a power drinker never did. Even though he had returned them and saved her life, she couldn't forgive him for taking her gifts from her in the first place. And she wouldn't let him do it again.

Though she had ended up in some compromising situations with him.

That still didn't mean she forgave him.

John's eyes left Marta and turned back toward Reg. "You are looking very nice tonight, Reg."

Reg glanced down at her colorful skirt, poofy blouse, and gold jewelry. Not any different from what she usually wore. It did look nice. She liked the bright, vibrant colors, but they didn't make her glamorous. It was for dramatic effect, not to attract a mate.

"You can turn off the charm," Reg snapped. "You are not going to get anywhere with me. And Corvin can tell you that's true. Do you know how many times he has tried to glamour me?"

John cocked his head to the side slightly. "Maybe he wasn't trying hard enough," he said with a seductive smile. Reg hadn't noticed before just how attractive he was. He didn't look much like Corvin, but she supposed he had inherited some of Corvin's attractiveness and charm.

And the smell of brownies was intoxicating. Reg pictured brownies fresh from the oven, topped with soft vanilla ice cream and hot, thick, chocolate syrup. It didn't matter that she had just eaten. She could almost taste those brownies. A little closer to John. Would his kisses taste like chocolate? Would she be immersing herself into a heady cloud of chocolate, breathing it in like drinking a bottle of syrup warmed in the microwave? She took another step closer to find out.

"Back off," Corvin said suddenly, his voice like iron.

Reg shifted her gaze to look at him. Corvin shoved John back and inserted himself into the space between them. "Just stay away from Regina."

"She doesn't belong to you," John countered. "You haven't taken her."

"She has been mine, and she will be again."

John shook his head, standing firm. "You can't call dibs," he said with an ironic smile. "You've had your chance to win her. Now... it's my turn." He turned his gaze on Reg, sending wave after wave of thick, intoxicating warmth over her, making her cheeks flush hot.

"You swore your fidelity to the coven," Corvin told him. "And to me as your spiritual leader."

John looked at him, eyes narrowed. "That doesn't mean that you have any authority over me. You can't tell me to do what I don't want to do. What goes against my nature."

"You swore to take my counsel."

"So I've heard it. Considered it. And rejected it. Just because you are an advisor to the coven, that doesn't mean we have to do what you say. *Any of us.* Your truth is not everyone's truth."

Corvin's face was getting redder and redder. Reg was worried he was going to suffer a heart attack. Or an aneurysm.

She hadn't known that John had been initiated into the coven. The last she had heard, he was still just a neophyte, someone who hung out with the coven but hadn't yet taken those first steps to be made a full member.

It shouldn't surprise her that one of Corvin's first acts as the new leader of the coven was to have his newfound son initiated. The thought of there being two power drinkers in the coven was horrifying. Reg took a step back away from them, trying to escape the pheromones clouding her brain. She should have been more careful. Usually, the pheromones didn't bother her much outside, but both men were powerful, and getting more powerful by the day. Now that John was no longer feeding his stolen powers to Verity, he was accumulating them himself. With how much Verity had dominated him while she was alive, just how skilled was he in controlling his powers? An immature, uncontrolled power drinker could cause havoc in Black Sands.

"Neither of you is going to lay claim to me," Reg told the two warlocks. "You can't take my powers without my consent, and I won't yield to either of you. It's not gonna happen."

Corvin looked smug. John gave Reg a speculative smile. He knew how close she had been to stepping into his arms with just the effect of his pheromones in the outdoor breeze. Indoors, with him using his other charms... she would have to be very careful. Belatedly, Reg raised a psychic shield around herself. Something she should have done the instant she saw them. She used the shield to reflect the heat still rolling toward her back toward John. He looked uncomfortable, a shadow passing across his face. He took a step back himself.

Corvin looked satisfied that John would not be able to take any further steps. He gave Reg a thin smile. "I guess I will be seeing you around, Regina." He said her name softly, coaxingly, as if the two of them were alone in an intimate setting instead of the sidewalk outside of The Crystal Bowl. His gaze shifted to Marta. "Marta..."

"That's Detective Jessup to you," Marta snapped.

Corvin had always called her by her first name since Reg had first moved to Black Sands. It was a slap in the face, a reminder that Jessup hated Corvin for what he had done to her and her family and would not be quick to forgive, even though it had happened decades ago.

Corvin gave a brief nod of farewell, and he and John moved toward the doors of The Crystal Bowl while Reg and Marta walked away. Marta looked back over her shoulder at the two warlocks.

"Talk about trouble," she commented. "Power is a dangerous thing."

CHAPTER NINE

*R*eg had clients to deal with after dinner and on through the night so, even though she wished she could have gone to Davyn's for a visit and make sure that Ember was okay after her discussion with Marta, she couldn't. That was what came of having adult responsibilities. Suddenly her time was not her own anymore. She could cancel her appointments, but they were her livelihood, and she knew how Sarah would look at her if she acted so irresponsibly, so she did the grown-up thing and honored her commitments even though she didn't want to.

But the next afternoon, when Reg was up and had eaten and dressed, she did get into her car, pausing first to admire the beautiful cherry red paint with painted flames racing down the sides. It was certainly an improvement over the old junker she had driven into Black Sands. Wilf, the car dealer, was a member of Corvin's coven and, while Reg didn't know much about him, she did know that he put his magic to good use in picking out cars for his customers and figuring out exactly what they wanted, even if they didn't know it. Anyone walking into his dealership *was* leaving in a new car, whether they planned to or not.

Reg climbed in and turned on the air conditioner and the

radio. It *was* nice to have a car where everything just worked, instead of having to fiddle with the controls or be forced to choose between the air conditioner and the radio because they wouldn't operate simultaneously.

Hopefully, Davyn would be at his house. Reg hadn't checked ahead, and it wasn't her usual day for a training session with him. He could be at the office, even though it was a Saturday, or he might have taken the weekend off for a trip or just be running errands.

All things considered, maybe it was more likely that he would be away from home than that he would be there.

But if he were gone, Ember should still be there. Davyn didn't take him out anywhere, unless it was to exercise him in an area where there were fewer people around. His house was outside the town limits and he had a big property where Ember could roam, but there were still neighbors.

Ember was getting too big to fit in the car. Reg had noted the last few times that she had let him ride with her that it was getting pretty cramped. In the future, he would have to sit on top or fly up above her. Hard to believe that when he was a hatchling, she'd been able to fit him into her shoulder bag.

As she approached Davyn's property, she could see something gliding above her in the sky. Not an airplane, but Ember, feeling her getting closer and coming out to meet her. What did nonpractitioners see when they spotted him? Would they see a dragon, or would they be glamoured and see something ordinary in his place? An airplane in the sky, a large dog when he was out walking with Davyn or Reg, or maybe a giant lizard. When he had burned Verity up at the car dealership, customers looking out into the parking lot had seen a ball of fire, but none of them had reported seeing a dragon. Would he be invisible to them? Something so impossible that their brains just blocked him out completely? How did it work?

When she pulled into the parking pad on Davyn's property, he stood on the porch watching for her.

"Afternoon, Reg."

"Sorry I didn't call first," Reg apologized, though he didn't sound upset.

He was not as handsome as Corvin. His face was softer. He seemed more ordinary than Corvin. He was still good-looking, but not the type women would swoon over. But then, he wasn't looking for a woman to swoon over him.

Julian walked out of the house, a glass of what Reg assumed was lemonade in his hand. He was blond, with striking blue eyes and an intense gaze. And every time he looked at Reg, he looked like he wanted to ask her for her autograph. He was the investigator in the Endangered Species Division who had investigated Reg, and he was enthralled with her siren heritage and that he had actually known her way back when they were both children in the same foster home. When he had tormented her mercilessly. At least that part of their relationship was over.

"Reg Rawlins. How is everything with you?" he asked, sounding breathless.

Unlike *normal* people who only meant "How are you" as a generic greeting, Julian actually wanted to know everything about Reg's life and whether she was well. If there were anything that he needed to do to protect this rare, endangered creature. She was sure he would be quite happy to lock her into a cage someday. Where he could ensure that she had everything she needed and was pampered and cosseted. It would be a beautiful cage. But it would still be a cage.

"I'm good," Reg told him flatly. "Everything is good, thanks."

Ember dive-bombed Reg, managing to stop just inches from her. Despite the fact that Reg knew he could do this, it still made her jump and shriek a little, her body reacting to the threat even though her mind would have told her that everything was okay if she had been able to think that fast.

Ember flapped slowly, hovering just over Reg, panting slightly while he looked at her with a smug expression. He loved that she reacted with a shriek. It gave him great satisfaction. He gently lowered himself onto her shoulder, but he was much too heavy to actually perch there anymore. He kept flapping his wings to stay aloft so that his weight wasn't on her, and he didn't close his claws around her shoulder.

"You big baby," Reg laughed. She reached up to scratch him under the chin and around the ears like a dog, and he purred and lowered his head to rub against the side of her face.

When he had been newly hatched, his skin had been soft and smooth. Now it was getting rougher, his scales hardening. His face rasped against hers. Reg pushed him back slightly. "Too hard for humans," she protested. "You're going to give me a friction burn."

He let out a puff of fire at the word "burn."

"A different kind of burn," Reg told him. She tried to visualize the red, raw graze that his rough scales would leave, feeding the image to him so he could understand. Ember made a soft cooing sound and pressed his face against hers without rubbing this time. Reg petted and scratched him for some time before he was satisfied and dropped to the ground beside her.

"I should have called. I didn't know you had company," Reg told Davyn, glancing toward Julian.

"It's just Julian. He came down for the weekend. We might do some fishing, but no big plans. Just enjoying some time together."

Reg tried not to give away her embarrassment at the look that passed between the men and the purple hue their auras both took on. It didn't take a psychic to see the feelings the two of them had for each other.

Even knowing how cruel Julian had been when he was younger and the laws he had broken when he had first confronted Reg about what had happened in the Everglades, Davyn couldn't seem to help his attraction toward the magical investigator. He knew that Julian had been broken as a child. That he still was. Maybe he thought he could heal that damage someday. But Reg didn't think anything could ever fix that fractured mind. She had been inside Julian's brain. She knew how disordered it was. The traumas that he had been through early in life had damaged him permanently.

"Come on in," Davyn invited, motioning for her to enter. "Unless you want to sit out on the porch?"

It was already hot and muggy, with flies and other irritating bugs hovering around. Reg didn't have a tough hide like Ember's and didn't feel like being eaten alive.

"Inside is good."

Davyn nodded, and they all went into the house to talk.

CHAPTER TEN

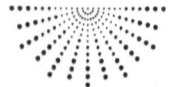

*E*mber went immediately to the big fireplace that dominated the space between the living room and kitchen and was two stories high. It was practically a room in itself, with a door large enough for a man to walk through, big enough to light a bonfire. Ember looked at Davyn, head cocked.

"I told you it's too hot for a fire," Davyn told him. "We have the air conditioner on."

Ember turned and looked at Reg pleadingly. She shook her head. "Davyn is in charge. He already told you no."

Pictures formed in her head of the three of them in front of the fire, soaking in its lovely heat. Davyn and Reg, both firecasters, were unbothered by the heat of a fire, even in the summer. But they had another guest as well.

"Julian would die," she told him, visualizing Julian panting and sweating in front of the fire. Maybe that wouldn't be such a bad thing... but Ember needed to learn about human frailties, one being that most humans could not tolerate heat the way Reg and Davyn could.

Ember went over to the fireplace and nosed at the closed door, sniffing around it. But unlike cats or dogs, dragons had the advantage of nimble claws, and Ember was able to get the fire-

44

place door open by himself. He walked inside and looked back at Reg.

"No fire today," she told him again, voice firm.

He belched out a huge billow of fire and smoke that filled up the enclosed space and hid him from sight for an instant. Then he exited the fireplace and looked at her balefully.

Reg was doing her best not to laugh, but was not succeeding. She knew that she should remain stern and make sure that Ember understood the limits they put on his use of fire. Davyn looked at Reg, and it was obvious he was also trying to keep a straight face.

Reg snorted with laughter. "I guess if he's going to do that, then inside the fireplace is the best place for it." She giggled, covering her mouth with the back of her hand. "Not out here where he could do damage to the decor. Or the house guests."

Davyn shook his head. "I don't have the heart to tell him that he did anything wrong. Maybe he couldn't hold it in."

Julian giggled.

Reg nodded her agreement, unable to speak for a few moments. They all sat down. Ember approached and cuddled up with Reg, putting his head in her lap. He was getting so big. She stroked and scratched. He closed his eyes and rumbled a big dragon purr when she scratched the soft skin around his ears.

"So, what brings you around today?" Davyn asked Reg eventually, in a calm, normal voice.

"Well… I had dinner with Detective Jessup yesterday…"

He shrugged and nodded, waiting.

"She's… making noises about you keeping a dragon here… About him bothering the neighbors or getting into trouble. I said that it wasn't any of her business, but she started talking about bylaw enforcement and laws for pets and exotic animals… she's talking about coming out here to see you about it."

"She can come out here if she wants to," Davyn said slowly. "But I'm not sure that bylaw enforcement will get her very far."

"What if she says that you can't keep him out here, and he has to go away… to a zoo or something?" Reg shook her head. "What are we going to do?"

"They can't put a dragon in a cage," Julian offered, leaning forward. "Besides the fact that it can't be done—if they could build a cage that would hold him—they would be in contravention of all kinds of magical laws."

"They can't put him in a cage?" Reg repeated.

"There hasn't been a cage built that will hold a dragon for long. They are strong and notoriously good escape artists. Dragons need to be able to come and go, to have access to the wilds. You can't keep them inside as pets or prisoners." Julian looked at Davyn, the implication that they had discussed this before clear. "They'll get out. And the more you try to hamper them, the more trouble they will cause. Historically, the only way to keep dragons from human populations was to kill them."

Reg looked down at Ember, who still had his eyes closed and was humming to himself. She tried to keep from picturing anything that would clue Ember in to what they were talking about.

"But..." There was a lump in Reg's throat that she had difficulty speaking around. "They can't do that!"

"No one is going to harm your dragon. He's already been registered," Julian said proudly. "His name and location have been filed with the endangered species division. So if anything were to happen to him, there would be consequences. Severe consequences."

"That doesn't stop people from trying—even succeeding. They aren't going to find out whether he is registered or not. They'll just come here with their torches and pitchforks and ask questions later."

"Not while I'm on the job. Notices are going out to all of the covens and councils. No one will be able to say that they didn't know."

Reg stared at Julian. When they were already concerned about Ember, his behavior, and his safety, it seemed like sending out notices to everybody disclosing his presence was just about the worst idea. "You can't do that!"

"Don't worry. The division will install a gate and No Trespassing sign to keep everybody safe. We know how to protect magical species."

Reg looked at Davyn, waiting for his objections. Davyn just shrugged. He had probably already hashed it through with Julian and knew there wasn't any point in arguing.

"You think a gate will keep people out and keep Ember safe?"

"There's only so much we can offer," Julian pointed out.

"Yeah, exactly. You won't have armed guards here to protect Ember if people come after him. And what if they have guns? What if it is the police or the army? Then what?"

"I don't think the police or army will come after your dragon. They would have to admit that he exists, and do you really think they will do that?"

Reg had to admit that people's ability to preserve the belief that there were no mythical species or paranormal powers and ignore what they saw in front of their eyes was pretty strong.

"Detective Jessup knows that Ember exists. And believes it."

"And what is she going to do? Go to her bosses and tell them? The relationship between magical and non-magical law enforcement is very tenuous. Non-magical law enforcement will tell her she's crazy and put her on leave, and magical law enforcement will tell her that dragons are a protected species. She can't do anything to disrupt Ember's environment. She may think she has some kind of enforcement threat over Davyn… but she doesn't."

That made Reg feel a little better. She looked at Davyn to see what he thought of this.

"I think we'll be okay, Reg," he assured her. "If things go sideways, we'll sort it out. We at least have the benefit of having the Endangered Species Division already in the know. There won't be any delay in finding someone to talk to."

Reg sighed and nodded. She scratched Ember's jaw as he snoozed with his head on her lap. "I have been worried, though… about what he is going to do as he gets bigger. He's already almost too big to get up and down your basement stairs to his lair. And he's flying farther away. He doesn't want to listen to what we tell him… how are we going to keep him safe?"

Davyn sighed and shook his head. "There are so few dragons around, and so little is actually known about them, that we don't know a lot about their habits. Their eggs generally lay dormant for a long time, as Ember's did, so they are hatched alone, with no parents to look after them. I assume they learn from a combination of instinct and experience, like many solitary animals. I don't know how long it will take him to reach adulthood, how big a territory he will need, if he will migrate, how he will find another dragon to breed with when he gets older..." He shook his head again. "Nothing. The little in the literature about their interactions with humans may not be representative of the species. If you look at the records of animals that have become 'man killers'—wolves, tigers, or other animals that have started approaching human civilizations and raiding villages—they are usually animals who are injured, sick, or starving. Healthy predators usually avoid humans."

"So stories about dragons stealing sheep or attacking castles... those might just be sick or injured dragons? But normally, they wouldn't do that?"

"It may be that it was a matter of humans moving into a dragon's territory. If they had given him the room he needed to flourish, there wouldn't have been any attacks. But if the humans start hunting the dragon's prey, then the dragon starves."

"Or had to go somewhere else."

"Until there was nowhere else to go."

Reg thought about that. "But Ember is already living with humans. So does that mean he's going to attack them?"

"I think... he'll need to find other hunting grounds. I don't know how far he will fly to hunt and still come back here. But I don't think he's going to start hunting humans."

Reg was relieved by Davyn's suggestion. She didn't like to think that her cute little hatchling could turn into a man killer. Ember loved her and Davyn. He was comfortable with other people. He was more domesticated than the dragons in storybooks. He'd imprinted on her and she and Davyn had raised him. He hunted independently, but they made fires with him, gave him treasure for his hoard, and talked and played with him. She couldn't see him turning against humans and seeing them as prey instead of friends.

She bent down, putting her cheek on the flat top of his head. "You wouldn't hurt anyone, would you, Ember?"

He stirred and made a purring sound, but didn't wake up.

CHAPTER ELEVEN

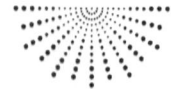

*S*tarlight was not happy with Reg when she got home. She wasn't surprised by this. He usually pouted when Reg came home after visiting Ember. Reg was sure that to Starlight's nose, she reeked of dragon, because he always knew it the minute she walked in the door.

He had been sitting on the couch in a spot of afternoon sunshine, and his head went up when she opened the door and walked in. Then he gave her a look of disgust, jumped down from the couch, and stalked away.

Reg rolled her eyes. "I guess you don't want any dinner," she called after him. He didn't even pause or look back. "It isn't like he's your replacement or something. He's more Davyn's familiar than mine."

That earned her a dirty look. Starlight went into Reg's bedroom and, she assumed, jumped up on the bed or the windowsill to enjoy himself without the burden of her company.

Reg rifled through the fridge for something good to eat and pulled out a few containers of leftovers or takeout. She was going to have to clean out the fridge again. It always got so full, all by itself. It wasn't Reg's fault. Sarah would put food in there because she didn't think Reg was eating healthily enough, or food that Reg thought about and craved would magically appear. Harrison said it was because she called the food to her, and she used the skill he had taught her when she was a child and was in danger of starving if she didn't have some way of getting herself food.

But Reg wasn't sure she believed it. Harrison was obsessed with food when he took on a human form, and she was pretty sure that *he* was the one who was always loading her fridge up with all of her favorite foods. Sometimes she felt like a turkey being fattened up for Thanksgiving dinner.

"Harrison? Can you hear me? Can you come here?" She said the words aloud and looked around to see if he had materialized in the living room. She waited a few seconds, then blew out her breath in exasperation. Trust the guy never to show up when she actually wanted him there.

She closed the fridge door and looked down at the food containers she had assembled on the counter, trying to decide what to eat. She heard a deep laugh coming from the direction of the bedroom.

So he had come, just not to the room she was in. Reg walked over to the bedroom door and looked in to watch the thin, long-legged man playing with the cat on the bed. Harrison wore a pink satin shirt and a bowler hat, and his legs were encased in black and white striped tights. He play-wrestled with Starlight for a few minutes, laughing and whispering to him and getting him to do far more than Reg had ever been able to. Eventually, Harrison whispered something to Starlight and then turned to look at Reg.

"You've come!"

Reg shook her head. "I was already here. You were the one who had to be invited."

Harrison lay on the bed crossways, with his long legs off the side, and Starlight jumped up on his chest, nuzzling his face and licking his ears, which made Harrison squeal. Reg was often disconcerted by Starlight's and Harrison's close relationship.

"I love it when they all crawl over me," Harrison declared. He stroked Starlight's head and back and scratched his ears. "All of them wanting to be loved."

"All of who? Cats? Do you mean when you saw the kattakyns at Francesca's house?" Reg could remember the kittens climbing over him there, and how Harrison had laughed and laughed at how the Witch Doctor—Destine, as Harrison knew him—had sent the remainder of his being into the nine kattakyns, which Francesca had then bound to prevent his being able to form again. The playful kittens had been fun, but it was the idea of Destine being brought so low that was hilarious to Harrison.

"Not just then," Harrison clarified. "*Whenever* the cats crawl all over me."

"Yes, of course. Where else do you go that cats crawl all over you?"

"There are such places in the human world," Harrison assured her. "Places there are many cats to talk and play with."

"Yeah, I guess there are," Reg agreed. Maybe an animal shelter? A cat cafe? Reg had heard that they could be a lot of fun. She imagined being able to go somewhere for tea and be surrounded by playful cats. A good way to de-stress. "Did Starlight tell you he's mad at me?"

Harrison looked at Starlight for a moment, then back at Reg. "Is he mad?" he asked cagily.

"Well, he's not happy with me, anyway. He doesn't like it when I visit Ember."

"Ember is the giant, smoke-vomiting worm?"

Reg couldn't help laughing aloud. "Yes, that's the one." She chuckled. "He's a firedrake. A dragon."

"Ah," Harrison nodded. "Drakes and cats... don't often get along."

"Well, Starlight and Ember certainly don't. He gets upset whenever I go to see Ember. But as far as I'm concerned, he should be happy that I'm not trying to keep Ember here, in the house or garden. Shouldn't he be happy that the dragon is staying with Davyn and I only go to see him now and then?"

Harrison nodded wisely. "Then he would have to be angry all the time."

"Yes, exactly," Reg agreed. She stretched and leaned against the doorway. It wasn't the most comfortable way to be talking to Harrison. "Were you here last night? The night before that?"

Harrison petted and kissed Starlight. "Time is a human construct."

"Were you here? Did you rearrange things in my living room? The blankets and pillows?"

Harrison stroked his long, thin mustache and curled it at the ends by wrapping it around his fingers. "Do you *want* me to rearrange things?"

"No. I don't. I want things left the way they are. But I would like to know if you were moving things around in there. Or if it might have been someone else."

"It might have been someone else."

Reg realized she had asked the question the wrong way. Harrison was so adept at avoiding the real intent of her questions and would never seem to give her a straight answer. His answers were always ambiguous.

"Did you move things in my living room?"

"Perhaps it was Starlight." Harrison kissed him on the top of his head.

"It wasn't Starlight. He doesn't have thumbs. He couldn't have moved things around like that."

"Not in this form."

"Uh… right. Are you telling me he took on a human form just to rearrange my decor? Because he thought it didn't look good?"

"It didn't look good," he echoed. He made a face and straightened his pink shirt. He and Sarah obviously did not have the same fashion and decorating sensibilities.

"So you *did* rearrange things?"

CHAPTER TWELVE

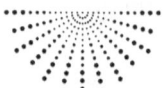

*H*arrison sat up abruptly. "You are hungry," he declared.

Reg was, but wondered whether he was confusing his pronouns and meant that he was hungry. He always seemed to be hungry when he took on human form.

"I was just getting dinner out in the kitchen." Reg turned and walked back to the kitchen to look at the bowls of food. Harrison followed her out and snooped, looking in each of the containers. He apparently liked buffalo wings and started to eat the cold wings with his fingers, standing at the kitchen island. Reg wanted to eat something healthy, but ended up picking up a takeout package of deep-fried Chinese dumplings. She warmed them in the microwave while she looked at the other dishes, then opened the fridge again for something to eat.

"Oh, the milk," Harrison said urgently, pointing a long finger at the carton of milk that Reg didn't remember being there. She took it out and handed it to him.

Harrison took the milk carton from her and, after opening it, took several swallows directly from the carton. Reg shook her head. It was a good thing that she wasn't a milk drinker herself. Though could a human catch a bug from an immortal? She supposed the answer didn't really matter, since she was possibly part immortal herself. Who knew what physiology or abilities she might have inherited from Weston, if he was really her biological father?

"You must observe the creatures of power," Harrison advised her, wiping his chin with the back of his hand.

Reg blinked at him. "You mean Corvin?" she asked, trying to figure out what he was talking about. "And his son, John?"

"It is a dangerous thing, not to be dealt with lightly."

"Umm... no, he's not," Reg agreed. If she had learned one thing in her time in Black Sands, it was that she could not underestimate Corvin or the powers he had. Both those he could use and those that still lay dormant. She wasn't the only one concerned about how he would influence the coven now that he had been elected. She remembered a scripture from one of the times she had been taken to church as a child about bad trees not being able to bear good fruit.

Corvin had helped her in the past. So if he had done good things, he could not be all bad. Yet his gifts and the powers within him drove him to do things that were reprehensible. If he did those evil things, then he couldn't be a good person. According to that reading long ago, a person was either good or bad, depending on their actions, but Corvin had a dual nature that she couldn't put into one box or the other. Maybe that verse did not apply to warlocks. Or at least, to those who were cursed with the hunger and need that Corvin had. No matter how hard Corvin might try, he could not go forever without filling his hunger.

"What do you think about Corvin being elected the leader of the coven?" Reg asked Harrison. "Did you hear about that?"

Harrison stopped eating and looked at Reg for a moment. He rubbed his chin thoughtfully. "He may find it more difficult than he thought," he said eventually.

"Probably," Reg agreed. Corvin had only run for the leadership of the coven because he wanted the power that went along with it. The ability to command and access the power that each of the members of the coven held. He was not thinking about what Davyn had told Reg—that it was the job of the leader of the coven to serve its members. He was supposed to be a spiritual advisor to the other warlocks, not a superior. It would be a shock to him when they started coming to him with their problems. "I don't know if he really understood what all of his responsibilities will be."

"That," Harrison agreed, "and he may have lost his keys."

"His keys?" Reg repeated, mystified. Did Harrison mean actual keys, or did he refer to the authority or gifts that came along with the job?

Harrison nodded sagely. "It is difficult for humans to go anywhere without keys."

"Well, yes. What happened to his keys?"

Harrison looked smug. He shrugged. "They are not anywhere he will find them."

"You stole them? Hid them?"

"Immortals are not concerned with human affairs," he scoffed.

Reg chuckled. "Sure. Not at all. So he's going to have to get all of his keys recut? Or locks replaced?"

Harrison looked through the other containers Reg had taken from the fridge. He opened one of them, revealing a thick, fudgy slice of chocolate cake with whipped cream.

Reg was quite sure that a few minutes ago, it had been a container of leftover stew from Sarah.

"His position also requires a mantle." Harrison slurped and licked the whipped cream from a forkful of cake, and then popped the cake itself into his mouth.

"A mantle. What's that? Like a fireplace mantle?"

Harrison shook his head. "It is… like a cloak. And also like the authority or responsibility to do what he must."

"He has a cloak."

"But that is *his* cloak." Harrison flapped his hands to indicate that it was nothing of any importance. "He needs *the* cloak."

"Oh. So one that Damon had before? And he passes it on to Corvin?"

Harrison nodded. "But… it is also missing."

Reg laughed aloud. "Are you sabotaging Corvin? Because you don't like him becoming the leader of the coven?"

"I think it is called hazing," Harrison informed her primly. "And humans think it is necessary and funny." He lifted his chin. His eyes twinkled wickedly.

Reg giggled. She ate one of the dumplings with her fingers rather than getting out a knife and fork. It was just as good the second day—or was it the third or fourth?—as it had been the first. "I can't believe you did that to Corvin. That's priceless. He must be going wild trying to find his keys and mantle!"

He gave her an affectionate smile, looking exactly as she remembered him when she had been four or five, and he had come to check on her and play magic games with her to make sure she was safe and had enough to eat.

"You must beware," he warned. "Do not let it consume you."

"Corvin? No, I won't. He's not going to get that close to me again." Reg had let Corvin and John get too close to her the night before. She had thought that she could withstand Corvin because she had before. But she had to be aware that his power had now grown. Who knew how much he could pull from the other members of his coven without their realizing it, or what artifacts he might have available because of his new position over the coven. Reg had been told it was one of the most ancient covens in North America. They must have old artifacts that still contained power he could draw on.

And being able to stand up to one power drinker did not mean she could stand up to two. Corvin and John had not been cooperating, but that didn't mean they wouldn't. If they decided that the only way to steal her gifts was to work together… they would make very formidable foes, and Reg didn't know if she would have the ability to do anything about it.

"Things are not always as they seem." Harrison studied Reg closely, his eyes intense. "You must not let your human eyes deceive you."

CHAPTER THIRTEEN

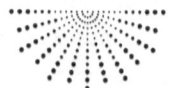

When Reg got up in the morning, there was a series of text messages on her phone from Detective Marta Jessup. She wanted to reach Reg as soon as possible, but Reg had silenced her notifications so that she could sleep. And not be woken up by people who didn't understand her schedule and thought she should be available to them at any time.

She needed her coffee before talking to Marta. And Starlight needed to be fed. Reg had to check her appointment book to see whether Sarah had added anything to it, and then she thought she might go to the store. Except that her fridge was too full to put anything else in it and she needed to clear it out first.

The phone rang as she drank her coffee and considered the problem. Reg looked at the screen. Marta again. Did she know that Reg would be up now, or was she just giving it another try, knowing that, sooner or later, Reg would get herself out of bed and be upright once more?

Resignedly, Reg swiped the screen to answer the call. "Hello?"

"Reg? It's Detec— it's Marta. I was hoping you would be up. I need to bring something over to you to have a look at. Are you going to be home for a while?"

"Yes, but what—"

"Okay. I'll get over there as soon as I can. But it may be an hour or two. That's okay?"

"Well, no. I have things I need to do—"

"I'll get there as soon as I can," Marta promised, and terminated the call.

Reg looked down at the screen in consternation. Just what did Marta have that she wanted Reg to see? And why was it so urgent?

Reg didn't like to be taken advantage of. She didn't like how Marta just talked over her and pretended that Reg had agreed with everything she had said. But she wasn't going to wait around all day for Marta to show up. She would just go ahead and do what she had planned and catch up with Marta later.

If she felt like it.

* * *

As it turned out, Marta showed up sooner than Reg expected, and she hadn't yet managed to get out of the house. She'd had a shower and still had a towel wrapped around her body, and was drinking another cup of coffee to fortify her for her day. When there was a sharp rap at the door, she decided it would probably be a three-cup morning. And that was if she could keep from turning to drink.

Starlight jumped down from the windowsill in the bedroom and walked out into the living area, meowing his complaint about early-morning visitors causing such a disturbance.

"That's right," Reg agreed. "Some people just have no idea they are disturbing someone else. She's up early, so she thinks I should be too."

He *murped* an agreement and rubbed against her ankles.

Reg went to the door and checked through the peephole to make sure it was Marta. It was, so she opened the door. Marta stepped in and looked Reg over as if surprised to find her still in her bath towel. People had to bathe, didn't they?

"I can wait for you to get some clothes on," Marta allowed politely.

Reg rolled her eyes.

"There's coffee on. You know where everything is. Raid the fridge for anything you like. I have to clean it out."

Marta brightened. "I don't know when I ate last." She went to the fridge as Reg headed toward the bedroom. "You always have the best stuff in your fridge."

"I know, right?" Reg agreed. "I can just never eat it all!"

She closed her bedroom door as she shed her towel and dressed, taking her time looking through her wardrobe to find something fresh or that she hadn't worn for a long time. Marta could have her coffee and whatever she found in the fridge, and ponder on the fact that not everyone got up at the same time in the morning.

When she was decent, she joined Marta in the living room. She picked up her mug of coffee and took a few gulps of it so that she would be able to enjoy it before it got too cold.

"So, what's this you have to show me?"

"There was another attack last night. Pretty serious, actually. There was a bit of a dust-up, with a couple of practitioners injured trying to fend off their attackers."

Reg noted the plurals. Not just one attacker and victim this time. But multiple attacks or attackers. It sounded like things were escalating. Not just with increasing violence, but bolder attacks.

"So what does that have to do with me?"

"There was an item found at the scene that I want you to look at."

Did that mean Marta thought Reg had something to do with the attacks? In Reg's experience, whenever a cop wanted to show her something, it was followed by an accusation. Reg just waited without saying anything.

CHAPTER FOURTEEN

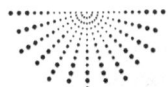

*M*arta set down her cup of coffee alongside a small plate holding a half-eaten cinnamon roll on the coffee table. She had a small, soft-sided briefcase with her, and opened it up to retrieve an object in a plastic evidence bag. She handed it over to Reg without a word.

"What's that?" Reg peered at the thing through the clear plastic, her face twisting into a grimace of disgust. It was a rabbit's foot. A good luck charm. But it didn't look like the fake dyed fur rabbit's feet she had occasionally seen in stores, which had been popular in the eighties. It was longer, with the toes and pad of the foot visible. She couldn't touch it directly, but it seemed hard and dry. Like it was very old. The fur was gray and worn.

Reg looked back at Marta. "A rabbit's foot? A good luck charm?"

"I'd like your evaluation about that."

"About what? Whether it is a good luck charm? It certainly wasn't for the rabbit."

"No," Marta agreed with a low chuckle.

Reg closed her eyes, holding the object in both hands and meditating on it. Was that what it had been used for? Good luck? She had never put any stock in them as a child. But then, the adults in her life had been very vocal about the fact that there was no such thing as real magic and had gone to great lengths to disabuse her of any beliefs in the supernatural. Once she was too old for imaginary friends, they had decided she was attention-seeking and immature and needed to grow up. Immediately. No more fairy tales, ghost stories, or lies about the people she had spent her day with. The ones that she could see or hear and they could not.

"Reg?" Marta prompted, hoping for a quick answer.

"I don't know," Reg opened her eyes. "You haven't given me enough time."

"Sorry." Marta sat back in her wicker chair, indicating that she would be quiet and wait.

Reg made kissy noises and called to Starlight, who was sitting on the kitchen counter watching her. "Star, come here. Do you want to help? Let's figure this out."

Starlight looked at her, his gaze inscrutable. Reg sat still, staring down at the lucky—or unlucky—rabbit's foot, trying to get some sense from it. It would have been better if she could touch it directly, but she didn't ask Marta whether she could take it out of the bag. She already knew the answer. It was evidence. It was going to stay right where it was. She didn't want any of her DNA on it. The last thing she needed was to be the subject of another of Detective Jessup's investigations.

Who had the paw belonged to? Where had it come from? How old was it? Was it as ancient and petrified as it looked, or was it more recent? She had no idea what a fresh rabbit's foot looked like, only those fake ones.

Starlight began to wash, pretending he wasn't interested in what they were doing. Reg looked back at the rabbit's foot and continued pondering its existence, history, and whether it was imbued with powers. Why would Marta have brought it to her unless she thought there was something about it that Reg could divine? It must have a magical history, or Marta at least hoped that it did.

Starlight's curiosity got the better of him and he eventually walked across to the living room, ears pricked and eyes forward, trying to figure out what she was doing. He stopped a few feet away from Reg and sat. He stared at her, unmoving.

"Don't you want to see it?" Reg asked.

He didn't move. He kept staring at her with that unblinking feline gaze. Reg took hold of the rabbit's foot and reached toward him with it, figuring that if she stretched it out far enough, he wouldn't be able to resist taking a step or two forward to smell it. The evidence bag might block most of the smell but, hopefully, it would be enough to interest him, and then he would come closer to Reg, jump up into her lap, and use his power in addition to hers to discover more about the rabbit's foot.

But when she reached the foot toward Starlight, he jumped back and hissed.

Reg was shocked. She wasn't sure Starlight had ever hissed at her before.

"It's just a rabbit foot," Reg explained. He couldn't be that upset about a rabbit's foot. He was a hunter. He would be happy to chase a rabbit, to catch one if it were small enough, so she couldn't understand why he would be offended or frightened by an old rabbit's foot.

Starlight hissed again, staring straight at Reg. She was electrified. Something was really wrong. He was angry with her. She could feel his fury. Reg shook her head.

"What is it? I don't understand."

She looked down at the rabbit's foot.

She had assumed too much when she looked at it. She knew what she expected it to be and nothing she had seen had dissuaded her.

Reg studied it more closely. It looked genuine. She looked at the pad and toes. What did rabbit's feet actually look like? Were they any different from cats' feet? Did the shape of the central pad differ? Was there any way to tell it from a cat or a dog paw?

Dogs' paws differed from cats', of course. Cats had sharp, retractable claws and dogs had thicker, blunter claws that did not retract. And rabbits?

She held the paw close to her face, studying the claws. They were curved, slender, and sharp, like a cat's. Reg looked at Marta, startled.

"What?" Marta asked. "Did you feel something?"

"This is…"

Marta waited, eyebrows up.

"This is a *cat's* paw," Reg breathed.

"A cat's?" Marta shook her head. "Why would anyone have a cat's paw? Rabbit's feet are supposed to be good luck, but I've never heard of a cat's paw being lucky."

"Are they used in any rituals or magic?"

"Not that I know of." Marta shook her head. "Cats were revered in Egypt. No one would have ever considered dismembering one. Who knows what kind of curses that might bring on you."

Reg handled the bag gingerly. She was glad that she hadn't taken it out of the bag and touched it with her bare hands. She could feel Starlight's anger and revulsion more strongly than ever and didn't even want it on her lap. But Marta had asked her to find out as much about it as possible, so she kept it there for a bit longer, reaching out with all her senses and trying to understand why someone would use a cat's paw for a talisman or charm.

It was difficult at first to feel anything but Starlight's grief and betrayal at seeing the paw. She tried to filter those out and focus on the feelings she got from the paw itself. It was cold in her hand. Much colder than it should have been, unless Marta had been storing it in the deep freeze before bringing it over. The toes were dark and hard.

"It's…" Reg searched for words to describe what she was feeling. "It's evil. Not just sad. Not just… a reminder of someone's pet. It has been twisted. Used to… used to ward off some attacker? Used to ward off other cats?" She looked up. "Does that make any sense?"

"No," Marta said flatly, shaking her head. "It was dropped in the most recent attack. But of course there were no cats involved. I don't know what it was used for. Maybe it's just some memento of a taxidermy shop or veterinary lab."

"No. It's not just a memento. It isn't something nice."

Marta considered this. "So… do you have any idea where it came from? Who owns it? If we can find out who these guys are, trace this back to them somehow…?"

Reg considered the paw, trying to picture who had held it, its history, and anything about it. But she could get little more than she had already been able to discern. Evil. Grief. A long, tragic history. But she couldn't see any faces or feel any personalities. She couldn't see its history in her mind like a movie—none of the things she hoped to discern from it.

She shook her head. "No, sorry. I can't tell anything else. I can't tell where it came from."

Marta sighed. "I've only heard of a cat's paw in one usage before. And that's not literal and has nothing to do with using a cat's paw as a ward or charm. It's just from an old fable. Someone being used as a 'cat's paw' is a dupe, a patsy. Someone who ends up doing someone else's dirty work." She shook her head. "As I said, it's nothing to do with this case. Nothing to do with using a cat's paw as a talisman."

"I've never even heard that before."

Reg held the cat's paw toward Marta, but she didn't take it. "Why don't you hang on to it for a while? It's not useful as evidence in the attacks. It can be… misplaced for a while until we really need it, if ever. Maybe if you have it for a while, you'll be able to get something else from it."

Reg reluctantly put it on the coffee table before her so she didn't have to hold it. She didn't want that dark object in her hands or lap. Not if she could help it. She looked over at Starlight, who was keeping his distance and obviously felt the same way.

"What about Corvin? He might be able to tell you about it."

Corvin had been consulting for the police force for a number of years. Reg had seen the relationship work to the police department's advantage more than once. But Marta had cut off that avenue. She didn't want anything to do with Corvin. Which Reg completely understood. But if it would help her to solve the case...

"No," Marta said flatly. She folded her arms across her chest, a typically closed gesture. "He's not consulting on this or any other case ever again. I wish that I'd never started using him. I could have established other relationships in the time since I started police work. I'd be a lot further ahead than I am now."

"But if he could give you a lead..."

"Do you really think that's a good lead?" Marta gestured to the cat's paw. "I was hoping it would be important, but... Someone just dropped it in the scuffle. It's just someone's... I don't know. An oddity. Something their grandfather left them. A charm. Maybe they even think it's a rabbit foot because they never looked at it that closely before."

Reg had to admit that she didn't think it would be the critical piece of evidence that would solve the case. So there was no point in Marta's giving in and bringing Corvin into it. He'd burned his bridges a long time ago.

CHAPTER FIFTEEN

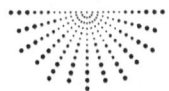

*R*eg slept restlessly. It was a long time before Starlight joined her in the bedroom, which was unusual, and maybe that kept her up longer. Or maybe it was just the events of the day. She kept puzzling over the origin and meaning of the cat's paw and what it had to do with people being attacked at the harbor.

She tossed and turned for a long time before finally falling asleep and, even then, she awoke with a jerk a couple of times and looked around in a panic, so disoriented by the sudden awakening that she didn't recognize her own room at first.

"Just go to sleep," she told herself. "You can worry about anything else in the morning. There's nothing to be concerned about."

But she knew that Marta had been hoping Reg might be able to come up with something to help them break the case. The fact that there was now more than one attacker was concerning.

Reg thought again about sirens. But it wasn't a siren, because sirens would not be hunting in pairs. They were territorial and even family members would not work together.

But she had once seen a siren and mermaid working together. What if that were what they were seeing now? It could even be the same pair; it hadn't been that long ago. Less than a year ago. She hadn't found out about her own siren heritage until after that. Was it possible that it could be so recent?

Maybe the hunting pair was getting bolder now, and the similarity of the attacks was just being noticed.

She should have known better than to start thinking about another siren hunting in her territory. It hadn't been a problem when she had seen them initially. She had felt sickened by the idea of their luring men to the water to drown them, but it hadn't upset her like the thought of a siren hunting in her area did now.

Her heart sped, pumping hard. She heard the rising voice of the siren sisters in her head, her mother telling her that she must protect her territory, that no other siren had the right to hunt there. Reg tried to ignore the voices, silence them, and push them away, but they just seemed to get louder and more discordant, trying to convince her to act.

Reg held the pillow over her head, trying to block the voices out. But since the voices were not audible to her physical ears, the pillow made no difference. They kept wailing in her head.

"I'm trying to sleep!" Reg protested.

"You must use your power," Norma Jean's voice persisted. "You cannot hide from your destiny."

"It isn't my destiny to be a siren. That's only a small part of my heritage. I can choose to be something else."

"You have siren blood," Norma Jean insisted. "You cannot change that. You must use your powers. Assert your territory. Transform! Do not let another siren hunt in your waters."

"I'm not. There are no other sirens here. I was just thinking about them. Thinking about something that could have happened, not something that did. Just let me go back to sleep."

"This rogue siren must be stopped."

"It isn't a siren. It is something else."

"You must use your powers. Rid yourself of any competitors. Stake your claim and anoint the waters."

"I'm not anointing anything."

"It is your fate! Your destiny!" Norma Jean shrieked, "That is the reason you survived. You are strong. A weak siren does not reach adulthood. Now that you are an adult and have felt the pull of the waters, you must take action."

"I'll tell you the action I'm taking right now. I'm going to sleep. It's been a long day."

But that didn't keep the sirens from screeching in her ears until Reg was so exhausted that she fell asleep in spite of it.

* * *

She awoke on her feet. Reg looked around herself in concern and confusion. Where was she? How did she get there?

Light came in the window and her surroundings gradually became more familiar. She was in the cottage. She was standing in the living room, looking out the big window.

"I guess that answers the question about whether I have been sleepwalking," Reg muttered, not happy to have been proven wrong. She could have sworn that she never got out of her bed, and yet here she was in the living room, clearly having a little walk around while she slept. She looked around at the soft furnishings of the room, putting throw pillows and other decorative items back into their correct places. Why would she be moving them around in her sleep? Did she subconsciously feel so out of control that she had to redecorate in her sleep to put her own stamp on the place?

There was movement outside the window. Reg froze, looking out into the garden, trying to pierce through the darkness and see what was out there. Probably just an owl or another night creature that she had happened to catch going past her window. Maybe even something that was a good omen. Elves or another rarely seen magical species.

Or just a cat.

But she picked out movement again, and it was not small. It was not something that slunk along the ground, or that flew up into the trees. It was something large. Man-sized.

Her mind immediately went to the protective wards. She had been trying to get out there every day with Sarah to strengthen the wards and ensure that nothing unfriendly could come into the yard. While it had seemed like it took forever at first, and she still couldn't get through all of them without igniting at least one of them, she was getting much better. She couldn't do it on her own, but at least Sarah was no longer carrying the full burden herself.

Had they missed a day? Had Reg not been paying close enough attention the last time she had strengthened the wards? Was Sarah's magic failing faster than either of them thought?

Reg stepped closer to the window and peered out, trying to get a clear view of what was outside. There was a bright moon. She should be able to make it out.

As Reg strained for a better look, the shape suddenly moved toward the window and hit it with a smack right in front of her face, making Reg shriek in surprise.

CHAPTER SIXTEEN

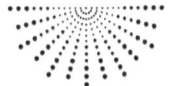

*R*eg fell back from the window, gasping, before she was able to take in that the gargoyle-like face pressed to the other side of the window was Ember.

"Oh! My goodness!" She took a few deep breaths, trying to slow the beating of her heart before walking over to the door and unlocking and opening it. "What are you doing here?"

Ember poked his nose in, sniffed a few times, then entered the house. Reg couldn't believe how big he looked in her tiny little cottage. The last time he had been in there, he was just a hatchling, smaller than Starlight. Now he took up half the room.

"Do you remember this?" Reg asked him. "You were just a dragonlet the last time you were here."

It was a silly question. Ember had the memories of his ancestors. She was sure that the memories of his babyhood were probably lodged in his big brain too. That was a very recent occurrence for him. Reg looked around for Starlight, but decided he must be in the bedroom still. And it was best if he stayed there. She didn't want to see what a fight between the two animals would turn into now.

"What are you doing here?" Reg asked Ember again, as he

turned slowly around to survey all of the front room and kitchen that he could see.

Ember walked farther into the living room, picking his way through it carefully, not swinging his tail as he made a slow circuit around the coffee table.

He saw the cat's paw and nosed at it, snuffling. He snorted and blew out a puff of fire and acrid smoke.

"Gesundheit!" Reg laughed. "Is it dusty? Do you know anything about that horrible old thing?"

Ember raised his head and looked at her. She hadn't been expecting an answer, so she was surprised by the picture forming in her head. At first they were just shadowy figures, but they started to develop as she concentrated on them, trying to use all of her senses to take in the cat's paw, Ember, and the vision all at the same time. She could feel grit under her feet and smell the fishy tang of the waterfront, and the cloaked figures gradually became more clear.

She thought from the body shapes that they were mostly men, but there might have been a few women among them. Somewhere between a half dozen and a dozen of them, all cloaked in black, hoods up so she couldn't make out their faces. One of the figures came into clearer view than the others. Reg could see that his black cloak was edged with red. Something that seemed to indicate his rank over the others.

The *mantle*. The word came into her head from her conversation with Harrison. The leader in this strange coven wore the mantle of his authority. She'd never seen anything like it before. Certainly, she had never seen Davyn wear something so showy when he had been the leader of the coven that Corvin now led. Was that what the mantle that Harrison had hidden looked like?

"Who are they?" she asked Ember aloud. She kept her voice very soft and her attention on the figures, trying to imprint them on her mind and hold on to them.

Suddenly, the leader thrust his hand out, and Reg instinctively drew back, even though she knew it was just a vision. She felt a cold dread emanating from him. Like what she had felt when the Witch Doctor had been reanimating the draugrs. A terrible, sick dread that stretched her stomach muscles tight and made her heart beat harder.

A wave of nausea washed over her.

In his hand, the warlock held the shriveled cat's paw.

Reg recoiled, unable to tolerate the vision any longer, and it vanished. She was left shivering in her living room, Ember looking at her with steady, baleful eyes.

"I don't like that," Reg told him. She could understand why Starlight had reacted the way that he had to the cat's paw. It was horrible. Definitely not the fond memento of a past pet, as Marta had suggested. Something charged with evil. A ward of some kind, intended to keep the forces of good at a distance.

Ember turned his head away from the cat's paw, apparently agreeing with her. Reg was cold. She shivered and gathered her robe around her. Ember padded around the room, eventually ending up in front of the fridge.

"Are you hungry?" Reg laughed as he sat there looking at her expectantly.

Ember nosed at the door. He could, of course, get it open himself, and he surely knew all about how fridges were full of food from living with Davyn. But he waited for her to do it for him. Reg joined him in the kitchen and opened the door.

"There's lots of stuff in here. But I don't know what you should and shouldn't eat. I don't know what's good for dragons."

When he had lived with her, he had mostly eaten bugs, digging in the earth for grubs and small animals, and he had a penchant for the crackers that Reg kept in her handbag for emergencies.

She started going through the containers of food, just as she had when Harrison had said that he was hungry. She focused on meat-based dishes and avoided anything with heavy spices or sauces. As she placed the open containers on the counter, Ember picked them up and emptied them into his mouth.

At least he didn't eat the containers as well.

"This is an easy way to clean out the fridge," Reg chuckled. She would have to wash the dishes that were Sarah's before returning them to her, but she was saved the trouble of scraping them all into the garbage.

Watching Ember, Reg gathered her robe around her once more. Then she looked down at it. She rarely wore a bathrobe. The nights were warm and she slept in a t-shirt and shorts set and didn't usually need anything more than that unless there was a storm or an unexpected cold spell. Or maybe if she had unexpected company and wanted something that covered her more completely. It wasn't like the sleep set was immodest and showed a lot of skin.

When had she put it on? While she was sleepwalking? Had she gotten up, put on her robe, and then sleepwalked out to redecorate the living room?

As she evaluated her state, she realized she was also wearing shoes. She had thought that the grit under her feet had been part of the vision of the cloaked figures, but her floor was actually sandy.

While Ember ate more leftovers from the fridge, Reg pulled out her broom and dustpan and slowly swept up the sand and bits of grass and other detritus from her floor.

Had Ember tracked it all in? Reg lifted one of her feet and examined the treads of her shoe. She couldn't tell whether she had picked up the sand on the bottom from her floor after someone else had tracked it in or had been outside and brought it in herself. Had she been sleepwalking outside of the cottage too?

And if so, where? There was no sand in the backyard or garden. She would have to walk to a beach for that. Or drive. Marta had said that some people actually drove their vehicles while sleepwalking. But wouldn't Reg remember if she had done that?

Of course, Reg didn't need to drive to get to the beach or anywhere else. All she had to do was to focus on her destination and transport herself there using her psychic powers.

The thought that she might have been to the beach during her sleep was disquieting.

She needed to know where she had been and what she had been doing.

She needed to stay in control of herself. She couldn't let herself just wander willy-nilly when she was asleep.

How could she control herself while she was sleeping?

* * *

When Ember was finished eating, belching comfortably, Reg turned her mind to the problem of getting him to go home. She didn't want him out wandering around at night, possibly scaring the neighbors or causing havoc in other ways. He needed to stay closer to Davyn's house, and not come to Reg's for a visit.

"Do you want to go for a drive?" Reg offered, knowing it was the one way to get him back to Davyn's. Ember loved to go for rides in the car.

He lifted his head and looked at her with a pleased, eager expression.

"Yeah? You want to go for a ride?" Reg repeated, hyping it up like she would have to a dog. "Come on, let's get into the car. Let's go!"

Ember left the cottage with her eagerly. Reg looked around the shadowy yard for any intruders or anything else dangerous, but she wasn't really worried. Who would attack her while she was out with her dragon? Only a fool would think that they could do anything to harm her while she was with her dragon.

She took Ember out to the car and climbed inside. She opened the passenger door for him to get in. Ember stuck his nose and head into the car and looked around, contorting his body and trying to figure out how to get it into the bucket seat beside her. But he was clearly too big to manage it anymore. Reg swore.

"Dang it, Ember, I'm sorry." She looked around, then shooed him out of the car. "Let's try this…" She couldn't reach the back doors while still in the car, so she got out and opened one of them for him. Ember didn't seem too happy about this at first but, eventually, he crawled in and nosed around the backseat until he found a comfortable position. Reg rolled down the window to give him lots of fresh air and to let him hang his head out like a dog if he wanted to enjoy the breeze. "There. Fit for a king," she declared. "You comfy?"

Ember seemed to have decided the back seat would suffice.

Reg returned to the driver's seat and pulled out into the street.

It wasn't until she was halfway to Davyn's that she thought about Starlight. She hadn't seen him since she had woken up. When she opened the fridge door, he would normally have been winding around her ankles, begging for a tidbit.

Had he still been in the bedroom? Just avoiding Ember? She felt bad that she hadn't even gone in to say goodbye and tell him she was going to Davyn's. She didn't usually go anywhere without letting him know her plans. Maybe that was silly. He was just a cat, and what did he care about her human plans?

But he was much more than just a pet.

CHAPTER SEVENTEEN

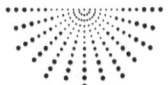

*S*he wasn't sure what to do when she got to Davyn's. She could just let Ember out, tell him to stay put, and hope that he actually would, then drive back to her house.

But she was yawning and having difficulty keeping her eyes open as she drove on the highway toward Davyn's. And she should at least tell him what was going on and that Ember had come to her house.

She didn't like to wake him, but it seemed rude just to drop Ember off. And she would rather lie down on his couch for a few minutes until she was awake enough to drive back home than to go to sleep in her car.

Reg knocked quietly, not really wanting to wake him up, but also not wanting to just walk into his house. She knew that the door would be unlocked. Ember came and went as he liked, so it had to be. Davyn didn't want to keep replacing doors when Ember walked through them, as he had once before.

She was surprised to see movement inside in response to her knock. Davyn approached the door and opened it for her, eyebrows raised. He looked beyond her to see Ember outside.

"Come in. What's going on? Is everything okay?"

"Ember came to my house. I don't know why, exactly, but I

wanted to bring him back here, and make sure that he got settled for the night." Reg followed Davyn into the living room.

"I don't know whether he will stay," Davyn said. "He's often out at night. It's safer for him to be out in the dark than in the light of day when everyone can see him."

"I wanted to make sure he came back here. I don't think he should be coming into town and showing up at my house."

"No, probably not," Davyn agreed.

"I hope I didn't wake you up. Did you hear the car?"

"I thought I heard someone pull up. But I was already awake."

"You don't get up this early, do you?" Reg looked at the time on her phone, which she found in the pocket of her robe. Five o'clock.

"No, not usually for another hour or two. I couldn't sleep, so I thought I would get up for a bit. I didn't want to keep Julian awake tossing and turning."

Reg remembered seeing Davyn's bedroom when he had been missing and she had been looking for clues about his whereabouts. The purple aura around his bed. Julian's deep blush. She pushed the memories away before she started blushing too.

"Do you mind... if I have a nap here? Before I go back home?"

"No. Of course not. I don't want you driving tired. You probably should not have come out here."

"I was okay when I started. But I started to get dozy as I was getting close. I'd probably be okay getting home... turn up the radio and drive with the windows down... but maybe I should try resting for a few minutes first."

Davyn nodded. "I was going to make myself some warm milk. I'll make you one too, and then we'll both see if we can get another hour of shut eye."

"Warm milk?" Reg grimaced at the thought.

"Don't knock it 'til you try it."

Reg sat down on the couch and closed her eyes. Even though she was tired, her brain was still tracking Davyn's movements as he worked in the kitchen and returned with the drinks. Ember had come into the house and gone straight down to the basement, which made Reg wonder whether he had picked up something valuable at her house to add to the growing hoard in his lair.

"Give this a try," Davyn offered, holding out the milk to her. Reg held it in front of her and sniffed the warm drink. Not just milk, but also rum and a spicy, sweet scent.

"This actually smells good."

"It's the best. Even if it doesn't help you sleep, you at least feel much more relaxed and happier after drinking it."

Reg chuckled. She sipped the sweet, spicy, rummy drink and felt her whole body warm as the liquid slipped down her throat. Who knew that milk could be so nice?

They sat for a few minutes, both enjoying the quiet and their warm drinks.

"Were you having a restless night before Ember showed up?" Davyn asked.

"A little. Why?"

"I just figured... I think he's been there a few times, but you normally don't say anything. And because... you look like you have been up for a while."

Reg frowned, not sure what he meant. Davyn gestured at her. Reg looked down at her robe and shoes.

"Your face is a bit dirty and scratched, too," Davyn said.

Reg touched it. Of course she couldn't feel the dirt, but there was a rougher spot of skin under her eye where it was scraped, and the tissue underneath had puffed up. Reg prodded it gently, frowning.

"How did I get that?"

Davyn pursed his lip and shook his head. "I... assumed you would know."

"It's possible that I... bumped into something while I was sleepwalking."

"I didn't know you were a sleepwalker."

"I'm not usually... but I guess I have been lately." Reg shook her head. "I have no idea why. It's weird. Marta says you can do all kinds of stuff in your sleep and not remember it. Even driving and cooking and things like that. But... I would think I would know. I mean… if you do something like that, you should be able to remember, shouldn't you?"

"I've heard about things like that. Did you check the gas in your car? You might be able to tell by the level whether you have been out driving without realizing it. If you are driving in your sleep or doing anything dangerous, you should consider… better security. An alarm that will trip and notify Sarah, or something like that."

Reg didn't like the idea of someone monitoring her, even if it were herself. She didn't want someone watching to see if she were asleep, or trying to take control of her if she were sleepwalking. When she was already vulnerable and had no control over herself. It was a creepy feeling, knowing that her body and part of her brain could be out doing something she wasn't aware of when she was not conscious of it and had no memory afterward. Was that how people with dissociative identity disorder felt? She'd been through the experience of having holes in her recollections before, when she had been possessed by Wilson's consciousness. It was scary not to remember things that her body had been doing without her.

"Do you… think that you walked into something?" Davyn asked, his eyes on her cheek.

"I don't know. Feels like it. Or like… someone hit me."

"But you didn't leave your house, right? And you have protective wards to keep anyone intending harm out of the yard and the cottage."

"I'm sure I didn't leave the house," Reg assured him. But she thought about the sand on the floor and the bits of grass and leaves stuck to her shoes, and worried that she had been out. And not just out in the yard, but several miles away at the beachfront. Where the attacks had been taking place.

"Well, you must have just run into something, then," Davyn said with a shrug. "That will happen when you're walking around with your eyes closed."

"Yeah. I guess so."

Reg swirled the remains of her hot milk around in her mug.

She was feeling sleepy and comfortable. The milk was definitely doing its thing.

"You don't mind if I lie down here and go to sleep?"

"Not at all. I don't want you to drive off the road because you're tired. Sleep all you need to. But things will be noisier in a couple of hours. I'm not sure how long you'll actually be able to sleep."

"That's okay." Reg shook her head. "I'll get as much as I can, and then should be good to drive home."

"I'll head out to work early. I don't know what Julian has planned for the day. He took a few days off. But make yourself at home. Coffee, shower, whatever you need."

"Thanks."

And Ember would be there too. Probably sleeping through most of the morning like Reg. But if anything bad happened, Ember would be just a thought away.

CHAPTER EIGHTEEN

*R*eg slept soundly for several hours. Usually when other people were around, she couldn't sleep. Even having house guests over was disruptive and would throw off her sleep schedule. She supposed she came by her hypervigilance naturally. She had grown up in a home where her needs were neglected and she was frequently in danger from either her mother or the visitors her mother had. And then she was plopped into foster care, never settled for long in one place, often exposed to abusive caregivers or other foster kids who victimized her. That and sleeping on the streets, where anyone approaching her was a potential attacker.

Was it any wonder she found it challenging to settle down and sleep around other people?

But whether it was because she trusted Davyn and Ember to keep her safe, or her sleep deficit, or the warm milk and rum in the early hours of the morning, Reg slept soundly and didn't wake up when Davyn got up and got ready for work. He was gone when she woke up. Julian was brewing something in the kitchen in a machine that ground, boiled, and spit, making a huge racket.

"Sorry," Julian apologized when he saw her sitting up and rubbing her eyes. "I didn't realize how loud it is. It's just background noise. Usually, I never actually hear it…"

Reg yawned. "It's okay. I should probably be getting up soon, anyway. Is Davyn gone?"

"Yeah. A few hours ago."

"Wow. Slept right through it. He said it would be okay if I wanted a shower…?"

"Of course," Julian agreed politely. He looked at Reg for a moment, and she wondered if he was remembering her as a child, swimming in the small swimming pool the foster family had purchased, where he had attacked her and she had turned the tables on him.

Something Reg didn't really want to think about. As polite and civilized as Julian might portray himself now, she knew what a mess his brain was and, like a feral animal, how quickly he could turn.

"I'll be going outside for a walk," Julian said abruptly, turning away from her. "I'm sure you can find everything you need."

"Thanks." Reg was grateful that he would be out of the house. One less thing to worry about.

Julian nodded. He filled his small mug from the hissing machine and made himself scarce.

* * *

Reg was sure she would feel better after a long, hot shower. Her head was still a bit fuzzy, her muscles ached, and her head pounded from the rum. Or maybe from lack of sleep. A nice long shower would help her to relax and work out all the kinks.

There were several showers to choose from, but she took the one that adjoined the master bedroom, which had multiple heads and massage jets. She turned it on to start the water warming up and stripped down.

Reg looked down at her body, then stood in front of the full-length shower mirror, examining herself.

Davyn had mentioned the scrapes and dirt on her face, but he hadn't been able to see anything else, and she hadn't taken any time to look. She'd been too tired and had assumed that she had just walked into something while she had been sleepwalking. After all, if she was walking around with her eyes closed, she would be bound to bump into something and end up with a minor injury sooner or later.

Though if people could drive while sleepwalking, they must have their eyes open and be able to do at least basic navigation. If they were able to successfully drive from point A to point B.

But that didn't explain the rest. She knew she had sore muscles and wanted a nice hot shower to loosen everything up. But that didn't begin to describe the state she found herself in.

There were a number of bruises on her torso. Whoever had hit her—if someone had hit her—had not stopped with a single blow to the face. And there were parallel scratches across her skin in a couple of places. In holding her own hand up to the scratches, Reg saw that the scratches were farther apart than the spread of her fingers. A bigger hand. A bigger person.

She stared at the marks on her pale skin, shaking her head slowly back and forth. "What the heck happened to you?"

CHAPTER NINETEEN

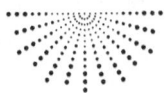

*W*hile Reg was in Davyn's fabulous shower, she thought about the scratches and bruises. And about Corvin and John.

They had to be her first suspects. Both of them had tried to seduce her. Both of them wanted to steal her powers.

But how could either of them have come into her yard or her house?

It was possible, of course. Corvin had defeated the wards in the backyard before, which was why Reg was now helping Sarah to strengthen them every day. But was Corvin stronger than Sarah and Reg together? Had he grown in power that quickly? Was he using powers stolen from his coven? Or had he learned how to access the Witch Doctor's powers that he held but hadn't previously been able to control?

Or maybe he and John were working together, having come to some agreement on how they would split her powers once they had her under their thrall. Verity had been a very powerful witch after being fed John's powers, which meant that he must have been very powerful before giving them to her. Two powerful warlocks might be able to defeat the wards together.

But it still wasn't making sense. She was missing something.

They wouldn't have scratched her. They wouldn't have fought her tooth and nail, but using their charms.

After toweling off and re-dressing in the shorts, t-shirt, and robe she had been wearing when she got there, Reg sat on a bar stool at the counter in Davyn's kitchen and sipped a cup of freshly brewed coffee. She might have to ask Davyn where he had gotten his coffee brewing system. It was complicated and took up a lot of space on his counter, but the finished product was much better than what she brewed using the thirty-year-old percolator at the cottage. She might be able to save herself a lot of trips to the coffee shop if she could actually get a decent cup at home.

As she sat there scrolling through her phone for the latest video feeds, the phone rang, making her jump and slosh coffee onto the counter. But at least it missed the phone.

The name and avatar on the screen showed Reg exactly who she expected it to be. She swiped the call.

"Corvin."

"Regina. I trust you had a restful sleep."

Reg took another sip of her coffee, trying to keep her thoughts fully under control so that he wouldn't be able to sense anything from her.

"I've had better nights," she said flatly. Had they seen each other during the night and she just couldn't remember? Was he mocking her, knowing that she wouldn't remember? Or expecting that she would? Was it a game of cat and mouse, or did the mouse not even know she was being hunted?

"What are you doing at Davyn's?"

Reg bit back a swear. She was still unable to keep him completely out of her mind. She hadn't even been thinking about Davyn, and he still knew she was there.

"None of your business."

"I would not have expected you to spend the night at his house. I thought that his interests… lay in other directions."

"Yeah, they do. So you know that we weren't up to anything. Especially not with Julian in the same house. Now why are you calling me?"

"You were thinking of me."

"You might have crossed my mind. But if I want to talk to you, I'll actually call you. So you don't need to call me."

"I sense you are troubled."

"You can stop sensing anything about me! I didn't ask for your help."

"And yet, you need it. So why don't you reach out to me, Regina? Why don't you ask me what it is that you want to know?"

Reg tried to keep from crystallizing the questions she had, just to keep them vague and unthought. But it was impossible to stop thinking.

"Did we see each other last night?"

"Last night? No. Why? What happened?"

"I thought I was the one asking questions. You weren't anywhere near my place last night."

"No. Certainly not."

"And I wasn't anywhere near yours?"

"Now, how would I know that?"

"You seem to be picking up on plenty of other signals."

"Well, that is true," Corvin conceded. "No, as far as I know, you were not anywhere near my home last night. I certainly never saw you."

"Are you sure?"

"As sure as I could be."

"And what about John?"

"What about him?"

"Did you see him? Or know what he was doing last night?"

"The coven did not meet last night, and I didn't do anything with John. What is this about, Reg?"

"I'm still trying to figure it out. Do you know..." Reg trailed off. She was about to ask him about the cat's paw, but then changed her mind, unsure if she should reveal its existence to Corvin. A powerful evil object? She didn't want him trying to get it into his hands.

"Do I know what?" Corvin prompted.

"Nothing. I'm just trying to figure things out. Have you heard about the attacks on the waterfront?"

Corvin didn't answer immediately. "Whatever has happened," he said slowly, "you cannot fight your nature. You cannot change what you are or your instincts any more than I can."

Reg's heart fell. That was precisely what she did not want to hear right now. She wanted to hear that she was in complete control and could choose what to do or not do, even as far as her sleepwalking went. She didn't want to hear that she was powerless and couldn't stop the instinctual behaviors any more than she could control a reflex.

"What makes you think I did anything?"

"I'm just saying... that we are all born with certain drives or instincts, and that trying to ignore or subvert those parts of who we are... just results in pain. Sometimes to ourselves and sometimes to others."

Reg shifted uncomfortably. "I didn't ask you because I was involved," she told him firmly. "I just wondered... if you'd heard anything about it. Marta was talking to me about it. I thought she might have called you, but I guess not."

Of course, it was nonsense, because she knew very well that Marta would not call Corvin about it. He would be lucky if she ever called him about anything again. His tenure as the special magic consultant to the Black Sands police department had come to an end. He would have to pick up another hobby.

Corvin gave a short laugh that sounded like a cough. "You know very well why she won't call me."

Reg sighed. "Yes. I do."

"Just like you won't call me. Most of the time. Until you do." His voice was soft, caressing. "At least you picked up when I called."

"I probably shouldn't have."

"Just because I have taken over the leadership of the coven, that doesn't mean that you need to avoid all contact with me. I'm still here for you. I'm still the same person."

"You are more dangerous than ever. You have a whole coven

behind you. You can draw on their powers, tell them to do things that would harm me, whatever you want."

"You know that isn't the way it works. As Davyn told you, it is a service position. I serve at the pleasure of the coven. I counsel the members, coordinate efforts, lead meetings and rituals. But I'm not the boss of anyone. Everyone is responsible for their own learning and for making their own decisions. And for their actions. I'm not responsible for anyone in the coven making a wrong choice."

She could see his smug smile in her head. And she remembered the way he had talked to John, ordering him around. He didn't think he had authority over anyone else?

"You can see that it is just an administrative position. So why would you shun me for that?"

"You know that's not why I avoid you."

"I thought you had gotten away from this silly fear that I would do anything to hurt you. You're a strong woman. You have powers of your own. You know that you've been able to withstand any... slips I've had in the past."

"So I should expose myself to more 'slips'? I don't think so."

"I'm not saying that. But it's true. You are a strong woman. Why act like some shy, retiring wallflower? You aren't someone to be pushed around. You are more capable than anyone else I know."

But that still might not be enough. As he accessed more of his latent powers, who knew how strong he might become? Or whether he would join forces with his son in order to bring Reg down.

"You're very nice at a distance."

He whispered in her ear. "You know I'm very nice close up, too," he reminded her. "We have had some very... pleasant interludes."

Reg forced herself to distance herself from him emotionally. She couldn't think of any of those pleasant interludes or the slips. She needed to go on and live in the present, not allowing them to happen again. If she was strong, then she could stand on her own and resist him.

"I don't know much about the attacks at the harbor," Corvin

said, taking on a neutral, conversational tone. "Just what I have seen in the news. Why don't you tell me more about them?"

"I don't really know anything either. Just that people are being attacked... like a mugging... but no one knows what the attacker wants. He hasn't been stealing any money. They were just knocking into people. Sometimes grabbing their purses. But then there was one attack where people were injured. And it wasn't just one attacker. It was more than one person. And more than one victim."

"Well, it makes sense that if they were going to go after multiple victims, they should go in force. Not just one mugger."

"Except they aren't muggers," Reg repeated firmly.

"Okay, they're not muggers, but what else am I going to call them? It doesn't sound like they are serious attacks, either."

"But this time, they injured a couple of people. Not just bumping into them." Reg touched the bruise under her eye thoughtfully. It was still tender and puffy. "The attacks are getting worse. More violent."

"Might just be a one-off because the victims resisted. Most people know that the best thing to do is just to let the mugger have what he wants. Don't try to fight back and risk getting hurt."

"But you don't know anything about the attacks?" Reg asked. "Or the attackers?"

"No. Why would I know anything about that? I have plenty to do without lying in wait on the waterfront."

Reg sighed.

"I would advise anyone who goes to that part of town to be very careful," Corvin said slowly. "There is no predicting what could happen."

Reg wasn't sure whether he was warning her not to become a victim, or not to get caught.

CHAPTER TWENTY

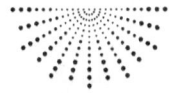

$\mathcal{R}$eg called Marta on her way back home.

"Reg!" Marta answered. "I'm glad you called. Do you have anything to tell me? Something new about that... talisman?"

"Uh... no." Reg had almost forgotten that she was supposed to be trying to get something for Marta about the cat's paw. She didn't even want it in her house, let alone to have to focus and meditate on it. She wasn't sure why she had allowed Marta to leave it there. "Sorry, I haven't had anything else come to me about it. You should probably come and pick it up. I know you can't let evidence go missing. People will be asking you for it."

"Well, no one wants an old cat's paw. It isn't exactly evidence that we can use to identify the attackers. No one is going to be looking for it for a while. I don't think you need to worry about that."

"But..."

"You can hang on to it for a few days. Maybe once you've had some time... something will come to you."

Reg rolled her eyes and shook her head. She knew she wouldn't find anything else out about the relic because she wasn't going to try to. Maybe she would leave it outside in the yard, or put it in her car. She didn't want it in the house and neither did Starlight.

"Do you want to meet?" Marta asked. "I know you don't have anything, but maybe something might come to you if you walked the crime scene with me. Maybe you'll be able to sense what it was that happened there. An imprint left on the scene... something that you see that our forensic guys wouldn't have noticed or cared about..."

"I'm just going home. I have a bunch of chores and things to do, so I don't know if it's a good day..."

It was more the place than the day that was an issue. Reg knew that getting too close to the ocean would trigger her siren instincts, and Marta did not have any powers to protect herself. Though, as far as Reg knew, she was only attracted to men as her prey. Maybe Marta would be perfectly safe. But that wasn't to say that any other men in the harbor area would be. Reg had been able to control her actions despite her siren instincts, and Corvin had told her that she would get better at resisting her impulses over time. But she feared it would get harder instead of easier. The pressure would keep building and the voices would get louder in her head and she would not be able to stay in control any longer.

Maybe that had already happened and she had begun to hunt in her sleep, since she wouldn't let herself do it when she was awake.

"You need to stay home to do what?" Marta asked, her tone teasing. "You need to sweep the floor? Make the bed? I think I know that isn't true."

"You don't know what I need to do."

Marta waited. Reg tried to think of a way to convince her that no, she simply couldn't go to the harbor where the attacks had occurred. She had much more important responsibilities elsewhere. But she didn't, and Marta had a pretty good idea of the shape of Reg's schedule and her responsibilities.

Reg blew out her breath, irritated. "Fine. I need to feed Starlight when I get home and get dressed. I could meet you... a little later in the day. In a few hours."

There was only silence in answer, and Reg glanced over at her phone, which was mounted on the dash so that she could use it without having to hold it in her hand. The call was still active. She hadn't lost the connection.

"Exactly where are you?" Marta asked finally. "You have to go home and get dressed? What have you been doing?"

Reg laughed. "Well, I am dressed. I'm not driving around town naked, if that's what you're worried about. Certain witches and warlocks may attend coven rituals skyclad, but you're not going to get me to any of those types of celebrations."

Marta chuckled. "But you do need to go home and get dressed. So what have you been doing? I thought you had just gone out for coffee, but unless you have to change because you spilled it all down your shirt…"

"No. I was at Davyn's. And no—I wasn't doing anything improper there, either. You guys need to get your minds out of the gutter."

"You guys?"

"You and Corvin."

Marta's voice cooled. "You've been talking to Corvin today?"

"He called me. We just talked on the phone. And I was asking him questions about the attacks at the waterfront, so you should be thanking me. I know that you don't want to have to go around there to question him."

"Why do you think that Corvin had anything to do with the attacks at the harbor?"

"Well…" Reg tried to replicate her previous wandering thoughts to explain how it had come about. "When I was looking at that thing, that cat's paw, then I saw cloaked figures in my mind, the people who had previously owned the paw, and they were all wearing black cloaks; but one guy, he had a black cloak that was edged with red."

There was an intake of breath from Marta. "The leader of the group," she contributed.

"Yeah. I mean, that would figure, wouldn't it? That the leader would have some insignia on his mantle, something to indicate his rank in the coven... or whatever the group was."

"His mantle?" Marta echoed.

"The cloak. Uncle Harrison said a mantle is like a cloak that goes with some kind of authority. That Corvin has a mantle now, and Harrison hid it."

"You're losing me. Corvin has a cloak like that?"

"Well, no. I don't know. I haven't seen the cloak. At the time, I thought it would be a regular cloak, like any of the ones I had seen Davyn or Corvin in before. I mean, they all look pretty much the same to me. Maybe some of them are made from different fabrics or patterns, or by special cloak designer fashionistas, so they are worth more or are like a status symbol..."

"I have no idea," Marta said. "I've never been into any of the deeper magical stuff..."

Reg had gone to a spring equinox celebration with Marta, but that had been community-type stuff, not any deep spiritual rituals. Not that Reg had seen. She knew there had been some prayers and other special circles, but Marta had not participated in any of those.

"Anyway... I just thought... when I held the cat's paw, I saw this leader warlock with the red edging, and I thought that might be like the mantle that Corvin had taken when he was elected leader of the coven."

"A cloak that Harrison hid," Marta filled in, though she sounded like she didn't quite understand what had happened or why Harrison would want to hide the cloak.

Reg didn't know why Harrison had hidden it either, or if it was somewhere that Corvin could find or retrieve it. Harrison just didn't like Corvin becoming the leader of the coven, and that had been his reaction.

"Yeah. I guess. That was the way my thoughts went, anyway. If someone with a special cloak had owned the cat's paw and been involved in the attacks, I wondered if it might be Corvin."

"So you called him to ask him? Why didn't you call me to fill me in on it, so you didn't taint the waters?"

"I... well, I didn't call him. I didn't plan to have anything to do with him. Maybe I should have told you, but my thoughts weren't that well-developed. I was just thinking some things through. He called me."

"Why did he call you?"

"Because that's what Corvin does. He's always calling me when I'm thinking about him. Or when he wants to get together. Or whatever. I can't control that."

"He wanted to get together?"

"No. Well, I'm sure he did, actually, but that isn't why he called. At least, that isn't what he said. He just said that he knew I'd been thinking about him, and so he called..."

"I would not want to have that guy in my brain all the time."

"And you think I do?" Reg shot back. "It isn't by choice."

"I know."

"If I could get him out of my head, I would." Reg pulled over to the curb and turned off her engine. "I'm home. Like I said, I have some things to do..."

"So exactly *what* were you doing at Davyn's that didn't involve hanky-panky?" Marta asked, remembering the previous line of questioning. "You were at his house last night and didn't have your clothes and Corvin thought you were getting... into something with Davyn?"

"Oh." Reg laughed. "It was just Ember. He came over here last night, and I drove him back to Davyn's so that he would be safe. And I was too tired to drive home, so I stayed at Davyn's."

"In your nightgown."

"My nightgown?" Reg repeated. "Shorts and a T-shirt. I wasn't indecent or anything. I'd been sleeping. Ember startled me. If I'd been naked or in a nightgown, I would have dressed first."

Probably. If she'd remembered. She couldn't claim that she'd been at her most astute the night before.

"But I don't want to go through the day wearing the same clothes I slept in. And shorts aren't really my thing for doing readings or seances. I like to dress the part, and no one expects their psychic to be in shorts."

"Okay." Marta laughed. "I think I have the picture now! So why don't you get dressed, and I'll meet you at the harbor in half an hour?"

"Are we really going to do this? Do you think that I'll be able to find anything worthwhile at your crime scene?"

"I don't know. You have in the past, so I'm hoping... yes."

Reg supposed she had walked right into that one. If she hadn't been so helpful in the past or had kept her dreams and gifts to herself, she wouldn't be in the spotlight now.

CHAPTER TWENTY-ONE

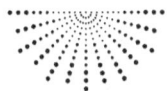

*R*eg didn't know her way around the waterfront district very well. She had been to a few restaurants in that direction and the warehouse that the Witch Doctor had been working out of, and had gotten turned around and lost there once or twice. Not the best track record. But knowing what a danger it was for her to be that close to the water, it hadn't seemed like a good idea to spend time exploring the area.

Marta had given her directions to get to the boardwalk where the latest attack had occurred. Reg was happy that her GPS had directed her there without suggesting any illegal maneuvers or getting her lost. It was always nice when technology worked the way it was supposed to.

"Hey, Reg," Marta greeted, leaning down to the window to see Reg. "Thanks for coming over. I hope this will be a benefit to the case. Who knows? You might find something that will break the case wide open. Just because the cat's paw didn't work out, that doesn't mean it's a total bust. We learned more about it and, now that you're here on the scene, it's only a matter of time…"

She was being pretty optimistic about Reg's part in the thing. More than likely, Reg would find nothing and would go home feeling like a failure for not being able to find anything to break the case like Marta was hoping. Who was to say that there was anything to find?

Reg climbed out of her car and shut and locked the door. "Okay. I'm yours. What do you want me to sniff out?"

Marta looked at her blankly.

"I'm your bloodhound, right? So what do you want me to track?"

Marta smiled. "I wish I could just hand you someone's dirty shirt and have you find them for me. And to prove what role they played in the attacks. Because I kind of need that information as well. They won't just let me lock people up with a 'He's guilty, trust me.'"

She led the way to the boardwalk where the last attack had taken place and walked Reg through it, showing her the direction the victims had taken the day before and where they were eventually attacked.

Reg cleared her throat and looked around. She was breathing shallowly, trying not to take in too much of the salty, fishy air blowing over the water. The boardwalk was gritty with sand, transferred there by hundreds of people who had walked through the sand and then up onto the boardwalk.

"What do you think?" Marta asked, making a gesture to indicate everything around them.

"I don't see anything," Reg said. She shook her head. "There's no kind of imprint I can feel. I don't see or feel any magical artifacts. I don't see or feel anything anyone dropped or left behind."

Marta looked disappointed. "Maybe if you spent a few more minutes..."

"I'm not going to find anything else."

"Well, let's go closer to the water. To where the other attacks took place."

"How many have there been?" Reg asked. She was looking past Marta toward the water. It shimmered in the light, lapping quietly at the shore, and exuded the intoxicating scent of salt and the things that grew in the sea. Was it strange that things grew so well in saltwater? Reg had always thought that watering plants with salt water would kill them. And yet there was such a variety of plants growing in the ocean. All different colors, shapes, and sizes.

CHAPTER TWENTY-TWO

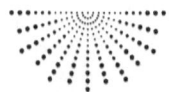

*R*eg didn't hear Marta's answer. She felt the draw of the water. She wanted to dip her feet in it. To swim in it, to skim over it in a boat and under it in a deep dive. Her sense of smell was heightened, and she could smell Marta's sweat, her deodorant, her shampoo, and even the powdery fragrance of her makeup.

Marta turned toward her, suddenly aware of her intense attention. "Reg?"

"Uh-huh?"

"Is something wrong? Did you see something?"

Reg shook her head.

"Feel something? Are you sensing something from the scene?"

"No." Reg stepped back from Marta and breathed as shallowly as possible, resting her hand over her mouth and nose to block out some of the smell. "Just a little overwhelmed."

"Oh." Marta nodded. "It is pretty shocking, when you think about it," she admitted. "Do you need to throw up? Can I get you some water? Tea?"

"I think I should get out of here."

"If you take a few deep breaths, you'll probably feel better.

Then we can go on. I'd really like to get a read on the whole situation. If you can hold out for a little bit longer..."

Reg swallowed. She didn't feel attracted to Marta like when she smelled Corvin's scent. She didn't smell Marta's blood and feel drawn toward her. Maybe she was safe as long as she only dealt with women. Or maybe she was still far enough away from the water, but it would intensify if she got any closer.

If she wasn't close enough to the water's edge for her siren hunting instinct to be triggered, then did that mean it wasn't a siren who had been attacking people on the waterfront? Would all sirens have the same sense of smell and level of activation, or was it very individual?

Of course, there was nothing to say that a siren couldn't hunt farther afield and then bring her prey back to the water. She could decide to hunt rather than wait until she was close enough to the water to be triggered. Reg had previously made use of her siren venom without being on the hunt. She had simply made the decision to use it as a tool.

Reg hadn't talked with other sirens. She had no idea what the others would or would not do. No idea how big their territories were and if there were any chance that another siren was hunting so close to Reg. Though she had said that she claimed the waters, she hadn't had any intention of hunting there. It would have been easy for another siren to remain in her territory or to sneak back into it and continue to hunt there.

"Reg? Are you sure you're okay? Do you want to sit down?"

Reg became aware that she was holding her head. She had been trying to work everything through and resist the siren song growing in her head. It swelled and screeched, but she couldn't tell what any of the words or feelings attached to the song were.

She didn't know how to answer Marta. The policewoman grasped her gently and firmly and took her to a nearby bench. She steered Reg into it.

"What's going on?" Marta asked. "This isn't just a psychic reaction to the attacks, is it? Can you tell me?"

Reg rubbed the spot on her forehead between her eyes, the

psychic third eye position. It throbbed and sent sharp stabs of pain through her.

"Can you… maybe you could get me that tea," Reg suggested. Anything to get Marta away, to keep her from hovering over Reg constantly asking her questions. She needed to be able to communicate with the siren sisters. She couldn't accomplish what she wanted to inside her head. She needed to be able to speak aloud, to hear her own thoughts, every word, individually, instead of muddled together in her head.

Marta promised to find a cup of tea for Reg.

"What kind do you want? Do you have a preference? There's a really good tea house just up the boardwalk from here…"

"Don't care. Anything."

"Okay… well… I'll try to find something good for shock."

Reg nodded. Marta hesitated to separate from her. "Do you want me to have someone sit with you? I can get another law enforcement officer here quickly."

"No. Please."

Finally, Marta nodded and separated from Reg, hurrying to find her a cup of tea. Reg cradled her head in her hands, fingertips pressing in hard.

"Norma Jean," she said firmly. "I only want to talk to Norma Jean."

There was a wail of responses, most of them negative. Arguing that Reg needed to listen to all of the voices.

"Just Norma Jean," she repeated.

Some of the other voices faded out. Reg rubbed her forehead.

"My sweet baby," Norma Jean crooned, drawing the words out with a strong Southern accent. "My sweet Regina."

"That's enough of that," Reg snapped. "I don't need any false front. You never cared about me when I was little. You don't now."

"How could you say that? Of course I cared about you. Then and now."

"You starved and neglected me. You cared more about your drugs and your… relationships than you did about me."

"I was an addict," Norma Jean admitted. "That was not a

choice. I couldn't take care of myself, let alone someone else. But Weston came back. To take care of both of us. He made sure that you survived."

"Harrison was the only one who cared about whether I survived or not. Weston ran away and hid."

"He came back," Norma Jean insisted. "He always comes back."

Reg shook her head, trying to shake off the thoughts and memories. She hadn't called upon Norma Jean to take a trip down memory lane.

"I want to know if there is another siren here," she said. "Is there another siren hunting this coast? Claiming these waters?"

"It is your territory," Norma Jean insisted, her voice a gruff bark, all of the honey and accent gone. "You claimed it. It is your birthright."

"And that means that no one else can be here? No other sirens?"

"No other sirens may hunt there," Norma Jean confirmed. "To do so would be to forfeit her life."

"So you know for sure that no one is, right? No one has decided to give it a try?"

"There is none else in your territory," Norma Jean insisted.

There was a period of waiting, watchful silence.

"Something is hunting here," Reg finally told her.

"On land or water?"

"Land."

"For man?"

Reg paused to think about it. Mankind, yes. But not just the male gender. Not if the attacker was snatching purses.

"Man and woman," Reg told Norma Jean.

"For what? To sate hunger and thirst?"

"Uh… no. I don't think so. They haven't killed. Only attacked briefly… and run away."

"What creature…?" Norma Jean pondered this. "Is it young and untrained?"

Reg remembered how Norma Jean herself had taken Corvin

several times and seemed not to know what to do with him once she had him under her power. Corvin had speculated that maybe her siren blood was too diluted. She was inexperienced, and the instincts were not strong enough to dictate what she should do after immobilizing her prey with her venom.

Was that what was happening at the harbor? Whoever was attacking was too young, inexperienced, or lacked the instinct to complete the kill?

Or did they not want to kill, and had a different goal? To frighten people, to take their money or something else from them? Would the people know if something had been taken from them? If everyone expected a mugger to go for their wallet and jewelry, would they even realize if the attacker had taken something else? Something small and seemingly meaningless?

CHAPTER TWENTY-THREE

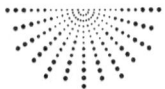

*M*arta returned to Reg and found her sitting there, no longer holding on to her throbbing head, but thinking quietly.

"Hey? Are you feeling better? I guess I was right and you just needed a little time and space to recover?"

Reg didn't bother telling her about Norma Jean or any of the scenarios she had been working through. She took the cup of tea from Marta and raised it to her lips. It was, of course, scalding hot, immediately burning her mouth. She should have anticipated that and protected herself with her firecaster gifts. The harbor attacker was not the only one who was off his game.

"Thanks."

"Did you figure anything out? Have any suggestions of directions for us to go?" Marta prompted gently, trying not to push Reg too hard.

"Tell me about the people who were attacked. Were there any similarities between them? Were they all men?"

"No," Marta confirmed what Reg had guessed. "Men and women. And the couple last night, a man and a woman together."

"Was there anything the same about them all?"

Marta pursed her lips and looked like she was trying to decide how to answer the question. Reg gave her a sharp look.

"You can't call me in to consult and then not tell me everything you know."

"You know that I'm not allowed to tell you everything. There are always things that we hold back so that we know when we get a confession whether it is true or not. I can only tell you the few things you need to know, not the whole picture."

"But then I'm supposed to come here and look around and know the whole picture. Even more than you know."

"I can't help it. I have to work within certain guidelines."

"Which means holding things back. Like who is being attacked."

Marta drew a breath in and blew it out again. She grimaced. "They have all been… practitioners," she revealed.

"They've all been magical?"

Marta nodded.

"And not everyone here in Black Sands is magical."

"Not even the majority. We have a high percentage of practicing witches, warlocks, psychics, and the like… but they don't make up even half the population."

"But one hundred percent of the people attacked have been magical. That can't be a coincidence."

Marta nodded. "Yes. Exactly."

"Someone is attacking members of the magical community… why?"

"We don't know."

"And they aren't stealing anything from them."

"No. They've been very… ineffective."

"Unless they have stolen something, and the victims just haven't noticed it," Reg suggested.

"How could they do that? What would they be stealing?"

"I don't know. If the victims are magical… maybe the thefts are too."

"Like what?"

Reg shrugged. "I don't know. I'm still figuring this stuff out myself. *Could* they steal something magical?"

Marta shook her head slowly, looking baffled. "No... the only ones that I know of who are able to steal powers are those like Corvin, with the curse."

"Could he be the attacker? Him and John?"

Marta sat on the bench beside Reg, thinking about it. She took a swig out of the water bottle she was carrying.

"I guess there isn't anything to definitely eliminate them as the attackers. But..." Her brow furrowed. "That's not the way Corvin works. You and I both know him. He doesn't ambush people. He seduces, convinces, and gets them to give consent. That is very different from what these attackers are doing. No one has mentioned any kind of conversation or charm... no scent of roses. This has been more violent. Not like Corvin at all."

"What about John? And someone else? Maybe he's already consorting with another witch, and she's helping him. He has to feed himself and someone else, so he needs more powers than he is able to steal by himself. He's used to working with a partner."

"Possibly. I don't know anything about the way he operates. I would expect any... you know... power drinker to operate the same way as Corvin does. But John Saunders could be operating in a completely different way."

"He wasn't raised by another power drinker," Reg pointed out. "Corvin wasn't there. He didn't know any others of his kind. His mother raised him. She wouldn't have known anything about how they usually operate."

"Don't assume that. Most of us know how the cursed operate, even if we haven't ever actually met one. Verity would have known."

"And she could have chosen to operate differently so as not to raise suspicions."

"Mmm... I suppose." Marta stared off into the distance, toward the shimmering water of the ocean sparkling in the sunlight. "Do you really think that's who it is? Or are you just throwing out hypotheses?"

Reg didn't answer right away, considering it.

"A hypothesis—" Marta started.

"I know what a hypothesis is. I did go to school, you know. I still remember learning the scientific method." Reg sighed and shook her head. "I don't know. It's the only thing I've been able to think of so far that makes any sense, so it's a good working theory. But I wouldn't make it your only theory."

Marta nodded. "Yes. Exactly. It's as good a theory as any. I haven't been able to come up with any motivation when there was no apparent theft. But maybe they just snatched up a small amount of power... not enough that the victim would notice. And if they did notice, they would think they were just weak because of the shock of the attack. The adrenaline rush and then letdown. If they didn't take a lot, would people even notice?"

Reg shrugged, gazing at the water in the distance.

"Reg? That wasn't a rhetorical question. I'm really asking. Would they be able to tell if they only took a small amount of the victim's powers? I don't have any gifts to speak of, so I don't know the ups and downs of every day... and if you would notice if some portion was missing."

Reg thought back over her various experiences since arriving at Black Sands. Having all of her powers taken away and restored. The various times that Corvin had tried to take her powers by force. His bleeding off her excess power when she had been in danger of blowing up the dwarfen forge and the whole mountain with it. Times when she had tried to use her powers to find an object or reach a particular person on the other side and been unable to. Times she had been exhausted by the use of her powers.

"Yeah, I think so. I mean... I can't always do what I want to when I call on my powers. You've seen that. And other times, I have plenty of energy and can do things I never imagined. It does... wax and wane with my physical and emotional energy."

Marta nodded slowly. She pulled out her patrolman's notebook and jotted down a few notes. "I'll call the victims and see whether any of them have noticed a lack of magical gifts. An unexplained dip in abilities or energy." She sighed and took another sip from her water bottle. "Although the people I have called with follow-up questions have not answered or called me back."

Reg's skin prickled. She looked aside at Marta, trying not to project her sudden anxiety. "You can't get any of them on the phone? That can't be unusual."

"No, of course not. People are cop shy. They don't answer when they see 'unknown caller' or 'law enforcement' on their caller ID. But usually if I call a few times, I can eventually get a person to answer. Unless they're involved in something criminal or have skipped town."

Reg had some experience with that herself, albeit from the opposite perspective.

"So you don't think anything has happened to them."

"No." Marta shook her head. "Why would I?"

"I was just thinking about... when the draugrs were killing people in their sleep. Entering through their dreams. Or how pixies can enter a place to retrieve a possession, even if it is worthless."

Marta shook her head, frowning. "What do you mean?"

"What if they weren't stealing something from the victims? What if they were adding something? Putting something of their own—a coin or a scrap of paper, a receipt—into the victim's pocket or handbag."

"So that when the person goes home, they can follow them inside to retrieve their personal property. Even if the person has protective wards in place," Marta said thoughtfully.

Reg nodded. "Is that possible? I mean... I'm not saying they were pixies, but maybe the same principles can apply to other species or practitioners."

"It seems possible," Marta agreed. "And where one of them dropped something at the scene... it's possible he had meant to put the cat's paw into the woman's bag, so he could retrieve it from her later."

Reg closed her eyes and thought about the cloaked warlocks and their intentions. "I don't think so... I think the cat's paw is valuable to them. I don't think it's just a throw-away possession that they would take the chance of being unable to retrieve later."

"Maybe not, then." Marta turned her wrist to look at her watch. "I'd better get back to my other duties. Especially if I need to go to the victims' houses to follow up with them." She rolled her eyes. "It would be nice if people would just answer calls from the police and cooperate with questioning... Do they really think that I'll be well-disposed if I have to chase them down? Or that I'll just let it go and not bother?"

"They're just scared."

"They have nothing to be afraid of if they just answer my questions."

Marta had no idea what secrets people might be hiding from her.

CHAPTER TWENTY-FOUR

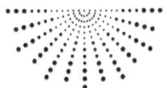

*R*eg finished drinking her tea after Marta left and sat staring at the water for a long time before returning to her car and then driving home. She spent the rest of the morning helping Sarah strengthen the wards, without igniting a single one of them. Progress!

She walked around the garden, pondering and reaching out her senses to try to determine if someone else had been there. Someone who shouldn't have been, but who was powerful enough to get past the wards or had used some trick or loophole to get in. Reg thought she knew all of the exceptions by now, but she was constantly learning new things about magical systems that surprised her. Had Corvin been there? John? Had they been trying to get close to her at night when no one else was around? Or had it been Harrison, someone who was not bound by the magical laws that mortals were forced to adhere to? Or Weston? Were there other species who could come and go as they pleased, even if they had evil intentions?

Reg Rawlins is not happy, a voice observed.

Reg turned around and had to search the greenery for a moment before she saw Forst, Sarah's garden gnome, standing in the midst of the garden, lighting up his curvy pipe. He puffed out a few smoke rings. He had spoken inside her head. He was using his "inside words," as gnomes preferred to do. They were low and awkward using "outside words" to communicate with humans, who normally couldn't hear their psychic transmissions.

I'm not unhappy, she told him. *Just trying to think things out.*

He sat on the bench beside the bubbling pond and motioned for her to join him.

What things be such a powerful sorcerer pondering?

Reg sat down with him. The red peak of his cap fell below the level of her shoulder, and his feet did not reach the ground, but he seemed unconcerned by this. He felt completely comfortable sitting there with her.

I'm just trying to figure out whether someone else might have been in the garden. Someone who wasn't supposed to be here.

Thy wards are strong, Forst told her.

But some people are stronger. Or there may be other ways to get around them.

He puffed on his pipe thoughtfully. *The spirit eater?*

Corvin? Yes. Or his son. Have they been here lately when I didn't know about it? What would you do if you found him here?

I would not challenge him. I would hide.

Forst said it frankly, as if there were no shame in hiding. And for a gnome, perhaps there wasn't. He often hid from sight in the garden, even when the only person around was Reg.

Forst sucked on his pipe. *I have not seen him here.*

Reg felt the emphasis on the word him. *Have you seen someone else? Anyone? Maybe... the long-legged immortal? Harrison?*

Forst shook his head. *Your dragon visits.*

More than once? I saw him the other night and took him home. Has he been here every much?

Only at night, and Forst is not always here in the night.

Reg didn't know where he lived. He did have a wife she assumed he went home to at night. And grown children—a boy and a girl—and six grandchildren, who he was very proud of. Very fertile for gnomes, who normally only birthed one set of twins.

But you were here at night recently? Reg tried to think of what he had been working on in the garden over the past week or two. *Did Sarah make you stay late to finish something? Or to check on the lights?*

Tiny white fairy lights twinkled in the garden after dark, and Reg honestly didn't know how many were man-made lights and how many were fireflies, elves, or other magical creatures.

Forst chuckled and shook his head. *Here to tend the night-bloomers. Moonlight trumpets this week. Very beautiful.*

Oh. Cool. I should come out and see them sometime.

He smiled, cheeks rosy, and nodded his agreement. *To see, you must open your eyes.*

She cocked her head at him, struck by his words. *Does that mean... I came out while you were here? But I was sleepwalking?*

He inclined his head slightly in agreement.

What did I do? Reg asked curiously. She had not expected to find anyone who had witnessed her sleepwalking. She had only been working on Marta's speculation that she had been sleepwalking until then.

Forst raised a brow while he smoked. *Walked around the garden. Checked the protective wards. A long time stood at the gate.*

He tilted his head to indicate the gate between the front yard and the back, which marked the border that an intruder should not be able to cross.

So I was making sure that no one could come in.

He gave a brief bob of the head.

And there wasn't anyone else around? Reg asked. *Corvin or anyone else in a cloak? No one who did not belong here?*

Just Reg Rawlins and Forst. And Ember. The elves and the living things.

Reg breathed a few times, trying to let her anxiety over the possibility of someone else having been in her yard to dissipate. No one else. Just she and Forst. And Reg had been checking, even in her sleep, to make sure that no one could get in where they were not wanted. That helped to calm her down a little. At least she hadn't been wandering around letting anyone who wanted to come into the house willy-nilly.

You fear men in cloaks? Forst inquired.

Well... I don't know. Maybe. If they have a cat's paw and are attacking people in the harbor.

Forst puffed on his pipe, nodding sagely.

CHAPTER TWENTY-FIVE

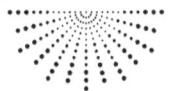

*A*lthough Reg had sworn more than once that she would not call Corvin Hunter for any reason, she had known each time that it was not true and that she would, sooner or later. Probably sooner. Maybe within days or hours of having sworn that she would not.

She couldn't help her attraction to him. That wasn't her fault. His charms made him attractive to women, just as the nectar inside a Venus flytrap attracted bugs. She couldn't change her nature any more than she could change his. And it wasn't her fault they could sense each other's thoughts and feelings. They had been connected ever since he had stolen her powers and then returned them to her. That door would remain forever open to him, at least partway.

Maybe it was her own fault that she wanted to talk to him and that she thought he was the best one to ask for information about the magical culture and history around Black Sands. He was a professor and had done a lot of research into those things and lived through a lot of history himself. Maybe there were other candidates who would be able to help her just as much as Corvin, and it was her own fault that she hadn't sought them out, researching to find someone—anyone—who could answer her questions instead of going back to Corvin.

It was just too easy for her to call Corvin.

He was one of the contacts on her "favorites" screen.

She'd deleted him from it more than once, but somehow he always ended up on it again.

Reg tapped the icon and waited to see if he would pick up or if it would go to voicemail.

After a couple of rings, Corvin picked up. "Regina! It is wonderful to hear from you. I have been thinking of you."

His voice reached right down into her insides. Reg wrapped her arms around herself tightly while she spoke to him on speaker. She was the only one in the cottage, so she didn't have to worry about anyone overhearing them. Except, of course, Starlight. And he hated Corvin. He would probably pout all night after hearing Corvin's voice on the phone.

"Do you have some time?"

"I always have time for you," Corvin purred. Reg couldn't help the flush of warmth that washed over her at hearing his voice.

"Well… great. I wasn't sure whether it would be a good time. You might be… out with your coven. Or trying to find your cloak."

"As you know, most of them work during the day, and our activities tend to be around midnight." He paused. "Why would I be looking for my cloak?"

"Oh. I just heard that you had lost it. I guess you found it again?"

He breathed into the phone receiver, saying nothing. Reg cleared her throat and squirmed uncomfortably. She tried to set up a psychic shield to block him from accessing anything she didn't want to reveal to him. Like that it had been Harrison who had hidden the cloak or that she had seen the red-edged cloak that she thought must belong to him.

"You heard that I lost my cloak?"

"Didn't you?"

"Well, not my cloak exactly, but the ceremonial cloak that the coven leader uses for certain rituals."

"Oh. Right. That was it."

"Who told you that I had lost it?" Corvin paused and, as Reg was about to answer, he spoke again. "Because I don't think I told anyone that."

"You must have told someone," Reg bluffed. "I can't even remember who it was I was talking to. Sorry."

"What is this about, Reg?"

"I wondered what it looks like. This special cloak. How is it different from your regular one?"

"It isn't very different. Maybe slightly older. It has been imbued with the magic from the coven leaders who have worn it over the centuries."

"Oh, I'll bet you love that." the words escaped Reg's mouth before she'd had a chance to think about them. Corvin could suck the magic out of artifacts as well as living people, so a magical object that had been worn by so many practitioners over the years, each leaving behind part of their magic in its fibers, was a windfall. If Harrison hadn't stolen it away from him, he would probably be wrapped up in it now, basking in the warmth of the magic stored in it.

She coughed and tried to cover what she had said. "What does it look like? I mean… is it fancy? Just plain black? I thought maybe it would have epaulets or something on it."

"As the leader of the coven is simply a servant to it, we do not bestow badges, epaulets, or other markers of authority or rank. The cloak is simply a well-crafted black robe with a hood. That's all. You would not think it was anything special to look at."

"No colors or edging?"

"That is a very strange question to ask when I just told you that it was plain black with no markings."

"It's just… I saw a picture of a cloak for a coven leader, but it doesn't look like what you had. It was black, but it had this red edging. Like… I don't know. A priest's cassock or something like that."

"Where did you see this?"

"I don't know."

"Was this a picture in a book or in your head?"

"Uh… it was from Ember, actually. A dragon memory."

Corvin grunted. Reg waited to see if he would offer any thoughts. Even if his cloak was not like the one she had seen in Ember's thoughts, maybe he knew something about it. If it had been around for centuries, then he might know what it was for.

"And you thought it might be my missing cloak?"

"No. I just didn't know if that was what your missing robe looked like. I guess not. Have you ever seen one like that?" she pressed.

"I have heard rumor of such a thing."

CHAPTER TWENTY-SIX

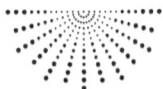

*Y*ou have?" Reg leaned closer to her phone, then picked it up and held it closer to her face. "What did you hear about it? Whose was it?"

Maybe he could help her to find the attacker. Whoever was attacking people at the harbor had dropped the cat's paw, and the cat's paw was owned by someone who might have had something to do with a coven run by a man with red edging on his cloak. Okay, maybe it was a bit thin, when she tried to follow it through to its conclusion.

"This is... not quite in the realm of *history*," Corvin warned.

"What does that mean?"

"It is... myth as far as I know. I have no way of knowing how much is true and how much is simply rumor and speculation. People have been known to let their imaginations run wild."

"Like they did about dragons?" Reg teased.

"I don't think I ever told you that there was no proof dragons existed. I think we have enough stories about them across various cultures to adequately establish that there are, in fact, dragons in this world."

"Aside from the fact that you've seen one with your own eyes."

"The stories about the cloak you speak of... the cloak that you may be speaking of or that may exist in dragon memory… is far more esoteric than that."

"Esoteric?"

"Rare… arcane…"

"What is it, then? What do the stories say?"

"You understand that these are not… verified as being historically true."

"You've told me about fairy tales or myths before," Reg reminded him. "Why is this any different?"

"Because those are at least widely known. Like dragon stories. If they exist across multiple cultures and time periods, then you at least have some indication of a real history behind them. That it isn't something that… someone on Twitter just made up last week."

Reg could see the distinction. "But the story you're going to tell me isn't widely known like that."

"Exactly. It may be one person's made-up story. Like Middle Earth or Narnia. It may just have come from someone's imagination and been passed around to entertain people. A lot of people like to deliberately scare themselves. They read horror stories, watch scary movies, sit alone in the dark listening for ghosts. It's thrilling."

"Sure," Reg agreed. "I do run seances, you know. I've met plenty of people just looking for a thrill."

"I guess you have," Corvin admitted. "The cloak is what the leader of The Cabal of the Withered Paw is described as wearing."

Reg's mouth went dry. She looked around for something to drink, but hadn't brought a glass or cup of tea to the couch. She swallowed, a lump in her throat. "Well, that's dramatic. The Cabal of the…"

"Withered Paw."

"And what is this cabal supposed to be involved in? Taxidermy?"

Corvin chuckled. "I would not mock if I were you. As I say, there is no evidence to support their existence, but there is also nothing to prove that it does not exist. If it does, I would not want anyone to overhear me mocking them."

Reg's stomach gurgled. Not like she was hungry. She put her hand over her cramping intestines and tried to keep her tone light, not buying into Corvin's warnings and her association of the words "withered paw" with the relic that still lay in its plastic bag on the coffee table in front of her. She was glad it was enclosed but wasn't sure how much the plastic would dampen the evil magic around the artifact.

"Okay, then, what do you know about these guys? What is it they're supposed to do that's so awful? Why wouldn't people want to be overheard talking about them?"

"They were a secret society some centuries ago, who were said to prey on magical practitioners."

"For what? Do you mean like cannibals?"

"No. Not cannibals. At least not in any of the versions that I heard. There was talk of torture, possibly through the use of poppets, of abductions and disappearances... generally, anything that would start a panic at the mention of their name."

"Puppets?"

"Not quite. Poppets."

"What is a poppet?"

"It is a doll or effigy used to represent the person you want to control or harm."

Reg processed this, frowning. "A voodoo doll?"

"That would be one form of poppet, yes."

"This cult uses voodoo dolls to torture people and... what? Make them disappear?"

"I don't know if you can use a poppet to make people disappear. Maybe you can if you hide it or bury it, with the right spell."

"And what's with the whole 'withered paw' thing?"

"I don't know. I suppose it sounded ominous. I don't know the significance."

But Ember apparently had. He had immediately associated the sight of the cat's paw with people in cloaks, the leader's edged in red.

"And you don't think these guys really exist? You think it is just a story? To scare people?"

"The best I can tell, yes. Just the kind of thing to repeat around a campfire and creep people out. And maybe you leave a crudely made poppet on the pillow in their tent if you really want to scare them."

"Corvin! You wouldn't do that, would you?"

"This doesn't have anything to do with me. You're just asking me what I know about it. And what I know is that it is similar to the stories about the man with the hook, Bloody Mary, or other tales people—especially kids—tell each other."

Of course Reg had heard such stories. She had lived in a lot of different households where she had been the new girl, and there were always tales to tell about strange happenings or tragic endings to previous family members.

"And you don't think this Cult of the Withered Paw exists in real life? Or ever did."

"Cabal," Corvin corrected. "I don't know whether they ever did. As the tale is told, they are gone now, but it was prophesied—don't ask me by whom—that they would one day return to carry out their evil purposes."

Reg breathed out a shuddering breath. "Creepy."

"I believe that's the whole point."

"Yeah. Freak people out."

"So, does that satisfy your questions about the cloak you saw in Ember's visions? And that fact that it is not my cloak?"

Reg let her mind drift in that direction for a few minutes. Was it possible that Corvin was the leader of a secret cult as well as the public cult that Davyn had led? Reg was pretty sure that Davyn would never have been the leader of the Cabal, but could Corvin have gained control over both of them?

"It isn't me, Reg," Corvin repeated.

"No. Of course not. You have enough on your plate."

"Isn't that the truth," he grunted.

"Is it more work than you thought it would be?"

"In some ways, yes. I knew that it wouldn't be a walk in the park. There are a lot of demands on someone in my position, and it is a very old and prestigious coven. People… watch you to see how you handle things."

"You're always on display?"

"Yes. Very much so. What happens in the coven is supposed to be private ritual and worship but, in today's world, nothing is that private. Everyone has a video camera in their hands. People report things to their friends on the Internet. Or to the world at large, it doesn't even need to be friends."

"Yeah. You should… tell Marta about all of this."

"Tell Marta?" Corvin repeated. "She won't listen to me. She has nothing to do with me anymore. If you want this information passed on to her, I'm afraid you're elected. Even if I wanted to tell her all about it, she wouldn't let me. She'd shut me down."

"I don't know if I'll get all the details right."

"It doesn't matter if you do, since it is nothing more than a ghost story. Why would she be interested in it?"

"Because it exactly matches a case that she is investigating. She called me in to consult on it. And now that I know… I think you should tell her about it."

"You will have to tell her," Corvin repeated.

"All of this stuff about puppets? I'm not going to get it all right. I'm going to forget something."

"Poppets."

"You see? I can't even get that right!"

"I'm sure Marta will know the story of the Cabal herself. You just have to remind her of it. If, as you say, it fits the facts of her case, she will fit the rest of it in. If it doesn't match up, then she can discount it. But of course… it is just a story."

"What if it isn't, and the Cabal has returned, like they always said they would?"

CHAPTER TWENTY-SEVEN

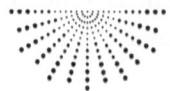

*R*eg left a message for Marta, but she didn't answer or call back. That wasn't unusual. She didn't usually answer when she was on duty unless she wanted something specific from Reg. She might be investigating another attack or have rounded up a few of the witnesses to interview. That could take several hours, so Reg was not concerned.

What Reg *was* concerned about was the food in her freezer.

She had zealously thrown out all of the half-eaten pints of ice cream in all of the fun flavors and anything that looked like it had been in there too long and might have freezer burn. And that meant pretty much everything in her freezer. It now looked nearly empty, and she had no ice cream.

She headed out on a grocery store run. She was sure there would be other things she needed to pick up that would come to mind once she saw them, but she wasn't a list-maker. She was bound to forget some things and get other things that she didn't need. But that was the fun part of going to the grocery store. Lists were tedious, but finding things she hadn't even thought of needing was fun.

She had no idea what she would find when she got there. It was the middle of a weekday, and the grocery store was usually pretty sleepy, with a few tired-looking women pushing carts around the store and the employees stocking shelves, taking inventory, or mopping up spills.

She hadn't known that the store would be the center of activity for the town. It wasn't a holiday and she hadn't seen events published on any of the bulletin boards she pinned advertisements for her psychic business to, or heard anyone discussing it in restaurants or coffee shops. But apparently, she had missed the big salsa buzz.

She supposed that a town like Black Sands could make a festival around anything. There was some town that claimed to have the biggest ball of string, so why not a salsa festival in Black Sands?

The basis for the event seemed to be the release of a new brand of salsa, or maybe a new flavor of an old brand. Or maybe they just had a lot of salsa in the back room that needed to be moved. But there were big banners up in the parking lot, on the outside of the store, and strung across the doors she went in.

As soon as she entered the store, she could smell the delicious, mouthwatering scents of tacos and corn chips, and who knew what other hearty, spicy Mexican foods they were cooking onsite?

A mariachi band was playing *La Cucaracha* in the background. Or maybe it would be more accurate to say they were playing it in the foreground. It was noisy and intrusive, and Reg was afraid when she walked in that the leader of the band was going to walk right up to her. He made eye contact and leaned toward her and jiggled around, but he stayed where he was, allowing her to pass by the bandstand without confronting her.

There was a huge pyramid of salsa jars. It must have taken hours to get them set up, probably by several employees and at least one small crane or cherry picker. Reg didn't think that a ladder would have sufficed. The base of the pyramid was too wide to have set a ladder next to it that would be within arm's reach of the apex.

A few booths had been set up, decorated with sombreros, strings of colorful chilies, and bold, colorful signs advertising their services. A salsa-tasting booth dominated them, twice as large as the others, with salsa, chopped vegetables, guacamole, and baskets of yellow and blue corn chips to sample the salsa in style.

There was a booth demonstrating how to make nachos, which seemed to Reg to be a pretty simple task, and another making a seven-layer dip that might require an advanced degree.

And people were everywhere. School was obviously out for the summer, because there were hordes of children as well as adults. There were even teenagers, taking pictures of each other with their cell phones as they tried on sombreros and ate chips loaded impossibly high with toppings.

The mariachi band switched to something Reg recognized but didn't know the name of.

"Happy Salsa Day!" a senior employee told Reg enthusiastically as he walked by. "I hope you will join in on our festivities!"

"Salsa Day?"

"There are lots of samples. Help yourself. There are educational booths scattered throughout the store. Do you have kids?" The manager looked around Reg, trying to identify whether any children in the vicinity belonged to her.

"No. I'm just... here by myself."

"Well, I hope you enjoy your day! Buy a couple of bottles of Tia Mia's Handcrafted Smokey Salsa to make mouthwatering, authentic Mexican cuisine in your own kitchen!"

Reg bobbed her head up and down, assuring the bug-eyed manager that she would definitely partake in the festivities and take home some salsa. "I just need to pick up a few things first, and then I'll grab some salsa on my way to the till."

He blasted her with a toothy smile. "Excellent! Have a Happy Salsa Day!" He turned his attention to the next person to come in after Reg. She blew out a puff of air and shook her head at the hyperactive hustle. She regretted having chosen Salsa Day for her impromptu shopping trip.

Luckily, the rest of the store was quieter. Both because it was farther away from the lively mariachi band, and because everybody seemed to be sticking to the front of the store to eat the free samples and participate in the day's festivities. There were only a few people who, like she, had arrived thinking that they would be able to do their regular grocery shopping as usual, and not that they would be participating in the full Mexican Tia Mia experience.

Reg decided she would just pick up some ice cream and the one or two things that she really needed, and then she would get out of there. Maybe things would quiet down a bit, and she would not have to run the same gauntlet to get back out.

When she made her way to the checkout lines, she saw the same hyperactive manager shaking people's hands and encouraging them toward the salsa pyramid and table displays. He spotted her and took a few steps toward her, but Reg shook her head.

"I'm just picking up my salsa now," she told him, heading directly toward the salsa pyramid. She would grab a jar and use it as her ticket to get out of the store, having paid the salsa gods their due.

Reg's way was blocked by a line of half a dozen teens with sticks holding aloft what looked like a papier mâché dragon with a feathered headdress and tail. Reg gaped at it as they carried it past her. She was still turning to watch its progress as she approached the salsa display. Children were pointing at it excitedly and racing after it. A baby was crying.

As Reg was looking after the long, sinuous serpent, something hit her from the side, shoulder-checking her so hard that she crashed into the salsa display.

Reg swore and tried to get her bearings to take a piece out of whoever had run into her. But she wasn't finished falling yet, and continued to knock over jars of salsa on her way to the floor.

CHAPTER TWENTY-EIGHT

*R*eg wondered briefly how many jars would break. Well, she wasn't paying for them, that was for sure. What did they think they were doing, building the display so high? It wasn't her fault that they had made it so vulnerable instead of just lining up the jars of salsa on a shelf like everyone else.

There were shouts and screams, which Reg assumed were aimed at the dragonlike papier mâché creature that was still winding its way through the crowds.

There was a low rumbling like an earthquake or a train bearing down on her. Reg finally stopped falling and tried to evaluate her condition and how many jars had broken around her. What a mess it was going to be.

She had only an instant of awareness of her situation before the entire salsa pyramid started to avalanche on top of her. A split second during which Reg realized that there was no way to escape the ton of bottles that were about to bury her.

The rumbling noise grew louder and Reg threw her arms in front of her face and flipped over onto her stomach.

There was no way to stop the bottles. People screamed and shouted, but they kept falling, sliding over one another and rocketing toward Reg's head, back, and kidneys. She held her breath and braced herself.

It seemed to go on and on for minutes on end. Eventually, everything was still.

Except for the crying and babble of the crowd. After a breath or two in which no more jars of salsa fell, several people rushed forward and started plucking the bottles away from where they had last seen Reg. She could hear them a few feet away, calling urgently to each other and digging down through the bottles of salsa, looking for her.

"She's under here!"

"No, I saw. She was over here!"

"Someone should call the police!"

"The fire department!"

Who was more qualified to move heaps of broken bottles? Reg couldn't see how one rescuer would be any more qualified than the other.

She moved experimentally, pushing the jars with her hands and feet, still face-down on the floor, protecting the most sensitive areas of her body.

"Over here, over here! I saw something move!"

The rescuers converged on her, sweeping and pulling bottles away.

A hand closed over Reg's arm and pulled her up. She rose like a swamp creature out of the sea of salsa bottles.

"Ma'am? Ma'am are you okay?" he demanded, hauling her to her feet and shaking her.

Reg tried to pull away from a skinny young clerk with red hair. His eyes were wild and his grip like iron. Caught up in the moment and not thinking about his actions.

"Stop it," Reg snapped at him. "Get your hands off of me!"

"You don't move someone who is injured," one of the other rescuers, a heavyset woman with glasses and curly hair protested. "You're supposed to leave her where she is and make sure that she is safe. What if she has a back or a head injury?"

The young redhead looked at Reg, then back to the heap of

bottles he had dragged her out of, as if trying to figure out how to put her back down where she had been and start over.

"I don't have a back injury," she growled. "Just let me go."

He let go of her suddenly as if he'd burned his hand. "I'm so sorry, ma'am. I was just trying to help. Are you okay?"

Reg looked at herself. She was covered with red liquid and had no idea if she was hurt. Broken glass could have ripped open a dozen holes or pointy ends embedded themselves in her flesh.

But nothing hurt. Not more than a bruise or two, anyway.

"Come over here and sit down." It was the bug-eyed, hyperactive manager who had been pushing Reg to buy the salsa. "We need to make sure you're okay. The EMTs are on their way, but most of us on the staff are first aid certified." He directed her into a lawn chair previously occupied by someone who had manned one of the booths. He reached for her to physically move her into the chair, but she slapped his hands away.

Her knees were a little weak, and she was glad to settle into the chair to catch her breath and contemplate how close she had come to death by salsa.

"You must be cut," the manager told her, grabbing her hands and holding her arms up to examine them for cuts under the soupy layer of salsa dripping off of her.

Reg shook her head and pulled away from him. "Would everybody please stop touching me!"

"We need to make sure that you're not injured."

"Leave me be. I'm fine. I just need to go home and clean up. If you could grab…" Reg looked at the massive pile of broken jars, trying to spot her shopping cart. It had apparently been knocked over and covered up with the avalanche of salsa. Reg patted her side to confirm that her shoulder bag was still attached to her. She would just have to return another day for the needed supplies. She would go without ice cream. Or wish it into her freezer rather than buying it. She just couldn't deal with the spicy smell of salsa that now covered every inch of her exposed skin and soaked into her clothes, all of the people and shattered festivities, and people insisting on touching and moving her and hovering over her to discover how badly she was injured.

"Never mind," she amended. "I just want to leave."

"We can't let you go until the EMTs have at least had a look at you," the store manager protested. "We could be seen as negligent if we don't follow up to ensure you're okay. Injuries that happen in the store have to be properly documented and followed up on—"

"I'm not going to sue you. I want to go home. This was a mistake."

However, Reg could already hear the wail of emergency vehicles and knew that she wouldn't be able to get out of there anytime soon. Once the EMTs and whoever else arrived, she would be forced to stay there for hours while they took everyone's statements. She would probably escape faster if she told them she was injured and needed to go directly to the hospital, bypassing whatever questioning she could.

An ambulance pulled in front of the store, siren wailing and lights flashing. The way that the siren of the ambulance and another siren she could hear nearby vied with an earsplitting, discordant duet reminded her of the song of her siren sisters.

CHAPTER TWENTY-NINE

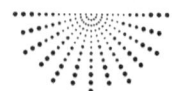

*T*he EMTs took a few minutes to get out of the ambulance, gather together their equipment, and enter the store. Real-life emergency personnel always took much longer than those she watched on TV. Go figure. They also always seemed calm when faced with even apparently serious injuries or illness. The emergency doctors on TV yelled and panicked and were always in a rush, but Reg had never seen that sort of scene replicated in real life.

There was a male EMT, muscular, with glasses, and a woman who was smaller than he and moved more quickly, looking around like a bird, head tilting and turning while she evaluated the situation.

"How many injured?" she asked immediately.

"Just her," the manager said, indicating Reg. "She was right beside it when it all came down. She was buried underneath. She wouldn't let me do a proper first aid evaluation, so I don't know if she's bleeding anywhere."

"We'll take it from here," she said authoritatively. "Maybe I could get you just to walk around and make sure that there was no one else close by or who is experiencing any symptoms. Elderly shoppers having chest pains or anything like that."

The manager's eyes went even wider at that suggestion.

"And you should cordon off this area and start with the cleanup as soon as you can."

The man hurried off to take care of things. The female EMT turned to Reg and looked her over.

"You're a mess, aren't you?"

Reg nodded. "Yeah. I don't even *like* salsa that much."

Both EMTs chuckled. "Not to worry," the woman said. "At least it will wash out easily enough. You'll just need to get sprayed by a skunk to get rid of the odor. Or do I have that backward?"

Reg laughed.

"Let's start with some cleanup," the woman suggested. "I'm Helen, by the way."

"Reg."

"Good to meet you, Reg. Sorry it's not under better circumstances. Though it could certainly be worse." She turned her head to look at the pile of broken salsa jars. "You were actually pretty lucky."

"Yeah. I guess. Though it would have been luckier not to be under it in the first place."

"My partner is Ron," Helen nodded to him. "Why don't you open a few four-by-fours, Ron, and we'll just start with some mop-up here to make Reg more comfortable."

She handed the first opened bandage to Reg, indicating her face. "It's not too bad, but you've got a few splashes there." With the next bandage, she indicated Reg's arms. "I'll just do a quick wipe-down here."

Reg held her arms out for Helen, feeling more at ease with this than the store employee grabbing her arms to look at them. Reg was expecting a few cuts or scrapes on her arms under the layer of salsa, but when the salsa was wiped away, the skin was unmarred. Helen shook her head. "You really are lucky!"

They did their best to remove as much of the salsa from Reg's body as possible, and didn't find any injuries. No big hunk of pointy glass sticking out of her thigh unnoticed, like there would be on a TV show, to be revealed at just the right dramatic moment.

She was not sitting in a pool of blood as she gradually got paler and more tired.

She was, in fact, in perfectly good health. Just a little bruised where the man had run into her.

"Who was that, anyway?" she asked the onlookers. "Who rammed me into the pyramid in the first place?"

They looked at each other, shaking their heads and murmuring back and forth. No one seemed to have seen. Or if they had, they were not volunteering the information.

"Somebody rammed you into it?" a sharp voice demanded.

Reg looked around and realized that a cop was standing there, notebook open, taking down the details of what had happened. She had been oblivious to him. He'd obviously been the other emergency vehicle she had heard, but she hadn't marked his arrival, too caught up in the cleanup being supervised by Helen.

"Yeah. Somebody came along and shoulder-checked me right into the display. Knocked me right over. And then everything came down on top of me."

"Did you get a look at this person?"

"No. I never saw him. Maybe there's something on the surveillance cameras."

The cop looked up at the ceiling and back down again. "Been telling these guys to get working cameras for years."

"They don't work?"

"Never have. Waste of time and money. What's the point in electronic security if you don't spend what it takes to get it working? Nonfunctional equipment doesn't do a thing."

It might deter some shoplifters, but even that was doubtful. Reg had shoplifted earlier in her life—never in Black Sands, and only when in dire need—and a few security cameras would not have stopped her when she was desperate for something to eat.

"Do you want to go to the hospital for evaluation?" Helen asked. "I don't see anything, but with the weight that must have landed on you, you might want to get some x-rays, make sure you don't have broken ribs or a concussion."

"No. Just a couple of bruises. I don't need the hospital."

"Well, being admitted would cost money, so if you don't have any concerns, I won't force the issue. Go home and have a shower and change before it starts drying out in your hair."

Reg ran her fingers through her box braids, now extra-red. They were soaked. She might have to get them unwound, thoroughly washed, and completely redone. Not something to look forward to. Hopefully, she could wash everything out without the added work, but she wasn't counting on it.

"Thanks. I'll do that."

A couple of times during their conversation, Reg had thought that she'd seen something out of the corner of her eye. But every time she turned, there wasn't anything there. Or nothing that she could identify as being out of place. Of course everyone was watching her, so she wasn't wrong to feel eyes on her.

As she turned again, quickly moving and zeroing in on the man standing at the edge of the observers, she found that it was someone she knew.

Corvin.

CHAPTER THIRTY

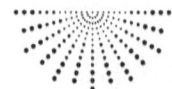

*R*eg scowled. "What are you doing here?"

Hearing Reg's tone of voice, Helen turned quickly to see who she was addressing.

"Shopping," Corvin said in a lazy, unconcerned tone. "It *is* Salsa Day."

"Was it you? Were you the one who hit me?"

He raised his brows, looking affronted. "Why would I hit you? Certainly not. You know that I would do everything in my power to protect you."

Helen was frowning. She looked around for the cop who had just been there, but he must have been interviewing someone else.

"You got a history with this guy?" she asked. "If you think that he might have been the one to cause the accident…"

Reg wasn't sure what to think. She shook her head, but kept her eyes on Corvin. "I didn't see him until now, and I don't think that's the kind of thing he would do, but…"

"Were you here when this happened?" Helen asked Corvin.

He took a couple of steps closer. Too close. Reg knew he would start charming Helen, convincing her that he couldn't have had anything to do with it.

"Stay back," Reg told him. "Go home. Stay out of this."

"Maybe I could give you a ride," Corvin suggested. "I wouldn't want you to be in an accident because you tried to drive while you were so rattled."

"I told you to stay back."

Corvin ignored Reg's repeated instructions, smiling blandly. The paramedics didn't try to stop him despite Reg's words. What if she'd had a protective order against him? She could; they wouldn't know the difference. Would they just let him walk up to her?

Maybe if he had looked threatening instead of mildly concerned about her, they would have prevented him from getting too close. Or maybe not. EMTs were not cops. They didn't deal with violence directly—only the aftermath.

Where had the cops gone?

Reg could smell the heady rose scent of Corvin's pheromones. She was already tired and overwhelmed, but tried to fight back against them. It was a large space rather than an enclosed area, so the effect of the pheromones would dissipate quickly. She should be able to resist him.

Helen and Ron both had dopey looks on their faces. They were not accustomed to Corvin's charms as Reg was. They had no idea how to defend themselves against him or even that they needed to.

Reg looked at Corvin with frustration. "Look..."

"I'll just drive you home, Regina. You'll be fine. You can come back here later when you're feeling better and retrieve your car. It will be okay for that long. You know that you're feeling too light-headed to drive right now."

He said it in a hypnotic voice that wasn't a question, but an instruction. She was too lightheaded. She knew she was too light-headed. Reg tried to resist the suggestion, but her head whirled with the intoxicating perfume and she felt like she was drifting farther away from herself to a quiet, peaceful place where she was safe with Corvin and could trust him to protect her and do what-ever he needed to do to make her perfectly happy and satisfied.

Helen was looking at Corvin with dreamy eyes, her hand on his arm, looking ready to cuddle right up to him. If Reg didn't watch out, she would be the one Corvin took home.

"Hey," she said sternly to Helen. "What do you think you're doing?"

"What do you mean?"

Reg saw movement in the corner of her eye again and turned her head. She had thought it had been Corvin she had seen before, but the movement was there again, just at the edges of her vision, disappearing every time she tried to focus on it.

What was that?

"Regina?" Corvin prompted, studying her and trying to figure out what she was looking at. "Come on, let's get you home and to bed."

"Bed?" Helen echoed, licking her lips and practically drooling over Corvin. Even Ron seemed ready to go with him.

Reg tried to resist, knowing that she shouldn't let his pheromones overwhelm her. She knew that she didn't want to be charmed by him. And yet...

CHAPTER THIRTY-ONE

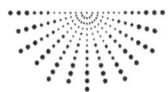

*R*eg," another voice said urgently. Reg startled and turned her head toward him. Davyn stood beside her, lowering the cloak of his hood to look at her. Had it been Davyn hiding in the corners of her vision? She had forgotten about his gift. He used his invisibility so rarely, she tended to forget about it.

Or maybe she just thought he only used it rarely. She wouldn't know if she didn't see him use it. Although Davyn had been the leader of the coven, his gifts were not widely known in the community. Warlocks tended to guard their secrets. It was rude to ask someone what their powers were, and some of them went to great lengths to hide their abilities.

Firecasters were frequently vilified so, even though Davyn had come from a long line of smithy firecasters, his magical firecasting abilities were not well-known. Reg and her closest friends knew, because he was training her to use her own ability properly. What did everyone else think his powers were? Maybe just the ability to lead or to keep things organized.

Even fewer people knew his ability to make himself invisible. Reg had accidentally revealed it to Julian, who had not known about it before Davyn had been abducted. She was still kicking herself for that. She had assumed he would share his abilities with his romantic partner—an assumption she should not have made.

"Davyn." Corvin looked irritated. "Where did you come from? What are you doing here?"

"Looking out for Reg's interests," Davyn said steadily. "Which, as it turns out, you are not."

"Of course I am. She's hurt. She's shaken. She needs someone to see her home."

"Not you."

"Why not? Do you think I can't control myself?"

"We both know that you have not in the past. Leaving Reg with you in a weakened, vulnerable state is not a good idea."

"Does she look like she's been ensorcelled? I'm just going to escort her home."

"I'm fine," Reg told Davyn faintly. Then she tried to strengthen her voice. If she were going to convince him that she was strong enough to resist Corvin's attempts to seduce her, she would have to sound a lot more convincing than that.

Was she actually going to be able to?

"Reg. If you need help getting home, I will assist you," Davyn told her. "Do not get into the car with Corvin. You know better."

"I've been in the car with him before."

"And when you were at full strength, you have been able to resist him. But you can't trust yourself to withstand his charms if you are not. And if he is gaining in strength, you don't know how you might fare against him. With his kind, you can never assume that his strength is the same today as it was a day or a week ago."

Reg's thoughts were muddled, and she didn't want to have to think it all through. She didn't want to argue about it or figure out if Davyn was right, she just wanted to go home with Corvin.

"Just let me go," she told Davyn irritably.

"That tells me that you are not thinking clearly. You can't, Reg. You need to come with me. Clear your head and get back on your feet again."

Reg looked at herself, still sitting in the lawn chair where she had landed. Sitting on a lawn chair inside of a grocery store. What was she doing there?

"How about you go home with that one," Helen pointed to Davyn, "and I will go home with this one." She gave Corvin a sloppy, soppy smile.

Corvin looked down at her tolerantly but, of course, he had no real interest in her, despite the fact that he had thoroughly charmed her. Corvin's only interest was in power, and he found Reg's gifts especially attractive. Having held them briefly once, he needed to get them back. It wasn't just the driving hunger he usually felt for the powers of the humans he lived around. It was something even deeper than that. He had to possess again what he had lost. He probably romanticized it and thought it was a bigger deal than it was. Like a heroin addict chasing that first, life-changing high.

Corvin patted Helen on the back. "I think we're finished here now. You will return to your vehicle."

"I'd rather stay here." Helen salivated over Corvin.

Was that what Reg looked like when she started daydreaming about being in his arms again? Did she get that stupid, cow-like expression on her face and fawn all over him? It wasn't very attractive.

"Umm. Maybe I should go back with you," she told Davyn. "I just wanted to get… I can't remember what I came here for."

Davyn looked around. "Salsa?" he suggested.

Reg laughed. "I don't think I'm ever going to eat salsa again. I never was that big on it, and after this, I think maybe… I'm off of it."

"Guacamole?"

Reg looked around. She recognized that Davyn was trying to get her brain moving. He was trying to make her think, make the connections, and understand the joke, so that she could resist Corvin and pull back from him.

Corvin shook his head sourly at Davyn. "I thought that since you were no longer the leader of the coven, you would stop trying to block me all the time. But you still seem to think you can tell me what to do. You are no longer my spiritual leader. In fact, I am yours."

"If I so choose," Davyn said calmly.

"What?"

"I have the right to choose. You don't have authority over me. I have the ability to choose the spiritual leader I want to follow."

"But I am the leader of your coven."

"For the time being, yes. But I can choose another coven. Or to be a lone wolf."

"You wouldn't do that."

"I have to make the decision about whether I want to belong to the kind of brotherhood that would elect you as their leader."

"Or I could kick you out," Corvin said poisonously.

"Not without cause. Not after I have been there as long as I have. You would have to hold a tribunal. And to find something to charge me with. I don't think you would get very far."

Corvin didn't like this idea. He continued to glare at Davyn but, of course, Davyn was right about how the coven was run. It was an ancient coven with lots of rules and traditions and, even if they had changed the rule about allowing warlocks with Corvin's affliction to join the coven and to become its leader, they had not done away with all of their other rules. He still had to follow the usual protocols of the group, which would not allow him to use his personal agenda to kick people out.

Davyn turned back to Reg. "Now come, you want to get out of those clothes and wash the salsa out of your hair before it sinks in and you have to smell like Tia Mia's Handcrafted Smokey Salsa for the next couple of weeks."

Reg nodded. Her head was still fuzzy, but she knew that Davyn was right and it was best if she let him make the decision, since she was muddled by Corvin's pheromones and other charms. Corvin ground his teeth and shook his head, folding his arms across his chest.

"I'm good enough when you need answers to your questions. You call me up to get help or comfort, get me to boost your strength or to help to moderate it when it gets out of control, but you can't trust me to drive you home. Why do you think I came here? Just for my own health? No, I came here specifically to help you."

Reg looked at Corvin and, despite the pheromones and the closeness of his body to hers, experienced a chill.

Had he really just come there for her?

But how would he have known about the accident she was about to get into? Or had he had something to do with causing it in the first place? She didn't think that he had been the one to run into her. She would have felt his presence if he had. But he could have arranged for someone else to cause an accident, not realizing how catastrophic it could turn out to be. If Reg hadn't been so quick to react when she had realized that the whole pyramid of Tia Mia's Handcrafted Smokey Salsa was going to fall on top of her, the outcome could have been very different.

She met Corvin's dark eyes, but he was doing his best to block her from reading him. His eyes glittered and he turned away from her, rebuffing her.

Like he had something to hide.

Reg put her hand on Davyn's arm to anchor herself to him. She needed to use his strength and clarity of mind to help to pull herself away from Corvin. Once she was out of his presence, she would be able to focus more clearly and sort out what had happened.

Davyn bent over and solicitously helped Reg to her feet, then steadied her, making sure she was physically strong enough to walk with him without toppling over. Reg expected Helen and Ron to object to her leaving. To insist she should go to the hospital. But they were both still under Corvin's control, not even realizing it. Helen had her hand on Corvin's chest, salivating over him, and Ron stood to the side, dazed, gazing over at the handsome warlock.

"Let's go," Davyn said quietly.

Reg went with him, leaving behind the noisy mobs, the EMTs, the store employees, and the powerful warlock who wanted to hold her in his thrall.

CHAPTER THIRTY-TWO

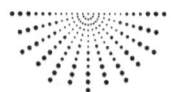

*T*hey got settled into Davyn's car. Reg turned up the air and pointed the vents directly at herself, trying to wake herself from the dream. Or the nightmare.

"That was a close one," Davyn said. He put the car into gear and pulled out.

"I used a psychic shield," Reg told him. "If I hadn't… I'd probably be covered with cuts. That was a lot of broken glass. Or if I got hit on the head with some of those jars that had fallen right from the top…! I got hit by a few of them at first, but got my shield up before the worst of it."

"Yes," Davyn agreed with a nod. "But I wasn't talking about the display falling on you."

"Oh." Reg shook her head and tried to sort it out. "What did you mean, then?"

"Corvin taking you. You were ready to walk right off with him, weren't you?"

"Well… no. I don't think I would have. I was holding my own before you showed up."

"I've watched you with him before. I don't think so. I think you were ready to fold."

"Well…" Reg shrugged. "We'll never know. Because nothing happened."

Davyn didn't say anything, appearing to be focused on the road.

Reg watched out the window a few minutes and then turned to look at him.

"Davyn?"

"That was no accident," Davyn said, answering the question she hadn't even gotten around to asking. "You need to be careful. Watchful and alert at all times, even in a public place like that. I didn't think he would be so bold as to ensorcel you in public, but it's clear he is just as obsessed with obtaining your powers as ever, if not more."

"But why would he be? He's the leader of the coven now. He is gaining control over the Witch Doctor's powers. He can take power from other magical practitioners or objects. Why would he care so much about mine?"

"I don't know. Without being a power drinker, I can't put myself in his shoes. I can't understand what he is thinking or feeling, and I don't want to be able to. But you need to be more careful. More aware that… he may have other people helping him now."

Reg took in a deep breath of the fresh air the AC unit was blowing into her face. "Why would anyone help him? They know what he is. No one who knew that would help him to… to hunt."

"Don't forget about his son. He has a clear ally in John, someone who would not shrink from helping him to feed his powers."

"Except that John wants my powers for himself."

Davyn shook his head. "I suppose I shouldn't be surprised. But the coven is also at Corvin's disposal. He might not be able to tell them directly to help him with his hunt, but he can influence them without them realizing it. And he can lie to them, give them a logical reason to do his bidding."

"Did you see who knocked me into the salsa tower?"

"No. I was there, but I didn't have eyes on you at the time. I'm sorry."

"What were you there for? Were you watching me?"

"I was restless. I felt like I needed to get out. I was drawn to the store and its festivities and thought it would take my mind off things. And then... there you were, and I decided I might as well keep an eye on you and ensure you were okay."

So did that mean that he had gone there to watch over her or not? Reg couldn't decide.

"I thought you had work."

"I did. But I can take a break, run some errands, visit a client, whatever is necessary."

And he had felt it necessary to go to the Salsa Day festivities at the grocery store. Or had felt drawn toward Reg.

"You think other warlocks in the coven would help him as long as they didn't know why?"

"Somebody did. I don't think they could be easily talked into doing anything that might be considered harmful or would encourage him to steal the powers of another. But it wouldn't be impossible. Many of the lower-level members of the coven are... too naive or easily influenced."

Reg thought about it the rest of the way back to her house.

"Are you going to go back there?" she asked Davyn when they arrived at the front of Sarah's property.

"Back to the grocery store? Probably not. Why? Do you need something?"

"No. I just wondered... if you had unfinished business."

He glanced at her and didn't confirm or deny the possibility.

When he had been the leader of the coven, it had been his responsibility to keep an eye on Corvin and make sure he didn't try to do anything that went against the rules laid down for power drinkers. Now that Davyn was no longer the leader, he didn't have to. But he also didn't have to toe the party line and say that the soul-suckers had the right to follow their nature as long as they operated within those guidelines.

It would be interesting to know what his real thoughts were. How his opinions were developing now that he was no longer constrained by the role of the coven leadership.

"Just be careful," Davyn warned. "Stay alert. Don't… be the victim of any more accidents. Use your powers wisely."

CHAPTER THIRTY-THREE

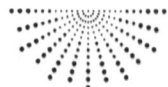

*R*eg didn't have any time to worry about Corvin or the other members of his coven causing more trouble with her, since she had clients coming and needed to focus on her commitments. It wasn't easy to do psychic readings or other work when she was already exhausted by everything that had happened. It had been a long day. She had to rely more on her ability to cold-read clients than on getting into their heads. It was less effort to look at the surface and do all the tricks professional psychics employed. Asking leading questions, making educated guesses, making the occasional wild leap of logic to anticipate what a client needed to hear.

They wouldn't know the difference, and she would make it up to them in the next session.

The following morning, Reg was surprised when she looked at her phone that she didn't have any messages from Marta. Marta tended to text or call Reg in the early morning when she was bound to be in bed, rather than in the afternoon, when she would be clear-headed and ready to work. But for once, there was nothing from her, even in the middle of an active investigation that Reg had been asked to consult on.

Reg had left her a message, and Marta still hadn't called her back.

She had her morning coffee and fed Starlight. After eating, he sat staring at her as if waiting for her to do something. Reg cocked her head at the cat. "What? I don't have anything to do until this evening."

He gazed at her steadily. Reg ignored him and sat down with her phone to browse through her social networks and video feeds to see if anything significant had happened while she had been asleep. Apparently, the world was still running without her intervention.

But she saw from a local feed that there had been another attack at the harbor. She watched the newsreel, frowning and trying to get as much as possible from the sparse information they shared. According to the reporter, "the police could not be reached for comment." While it wasn't likely they would give much information to a reporter while they were still trying to figure out what was going on and how to catch the culprit, Reg thought it was off that there had been no contact with the police. Not just "No comment" or "This is under active investigation" but "Police could not be reached."

She switched to her phone app and touched the entry in her favorites for Detective Marta Jessup.

It rang a number of times before going to voicemail. Reg tapped the back of the phone, thinking about it. Of course if Marta were busy investigating the latest attack, she might be unable to take Reg's call. But Reg would have expected Marta to at least return her call from the day before in the hopes that she had found out something more about the withered paw.

Reg shuddered at the thought of it. It was still lying on her coffee table, and Reg wanted someone to come and take it away. She was glad it was in a bag, but she didn't want to look at it at all or for it to be there in her house. She didn't want such an evil thing in her home.

Starlight jumped up on the couch behind Reg, startling her.

"Oh! You scared a year's growth out of me, you silly cat! What do you want?" Reg scratched his ears and chin, murmuring to him. Starlight rubbed against her hand and face and made a few *murp* noises, encouraging the attention.

"What should I do about Marta?" Reg asked him. "It seems strange that she hasn't called me at all, doesn't it? She didn't return my call or ask if I'd figured out anything else. She didn't call me before I was awake this morning, expecting me to fill her in on the latest gossip. Just... nothing."

Starlight purred and made agreeable noises. Reg sighed. "I am just worried something might have happened to her. You don't think anything happened to her, do you?"

She wanted him to tell her no, to send her soothing thoughts and feelings. But he didn't. Reg couldn't fight the growing sense of unease. Her stomach hurt and felt sick at the same time.

Reg wasn't responsible for keeping track of a law enforcement officer. Of a grown woman. Yes, she and Marta had eventually become friends, but that didn't mean that Reg was responsible for her friend's movements and well-being.

No matter how much Reg tried to convince herself it was true, she couldn't. She searched the web for the main number to the Black Sands police department, deciding to start from there.

She bounced around a little to start with. The phone operator put her through to Marta's line, which Reg already knew she wasn't answering. The operator said she couldn't give out any other numbers or information about an officer's location or well-being. That Reg would just have to wait for a call back from Detective Jessup.

"I think something is wrong," Reg pressed. "She's not answering or returning calls. I've been leaving her messages for twenty-four hours. She hasn't been in touch at all, which is really unusual."

"I'm sure she's just busy with the cases that are under investiga- tion," the operator assured her. "She will get back to you eventually."

"Can you look at her on the computer and tell whether she has checked in at all over the last twenty-four hours? If she's investigating someone and doesn't ever check in, isn't that kind of suspicious? Don't you want to make sure that everything is okay?"

There was a sigh and hesitation from the operator. She tapped away at her keyboard, maybe looking to see when the detective had last checked in, as Reg had asked. Maybe doing something else like looking Reg up in the system to see how much of a pain she had been in the past and whether she had a criminal record. Reg tried to send positive feelings over the airwaves to Marta and the operator, hoping she would find out that everything was a mistake and Marta had just been out of the calling area while she investigated someone who lived outside the jurisdiction. There were a lot of dead spots in the woods.

Eventually, the operator changed her tune. "I'll put you through to Detective Jessup's sergeant," she said. "He'll be able to give you a better idea of when she might be available to talk to you."

"Thank you!"

She listened to the phone ring again and hoped she would not end up in the sergeant's voicemail. Then what was she going to do? Leave him a message? Or look for a way to make a bigger stink so that they would pay attention to her?

"Sergeant Pitts."

"Oh, hi." Reg scrambled, trying to think of the quickest way to get to the point and make Pitts understand that something might have happened to Marta and she was really getting concerned. "I, umm… my name is Reg Rawlins, and I'm…"

"You're one of those crazies," Pitts said flatly. "A psychic."

"Well… yes, that's me."

"Detective Jessup may see some benefit in retaining outside consultants like you to see what shakes loose, but that is not my preferred modus operandi."

"Uh…"

"I'm not interested in any predictions or offers of what cases you could help me solve. That's Detective Jessup's purview."

"Umm, well, that's the thing. I don't know where she is. I've called and left messages for her, but she doesn't get back to me. She hasn't, I mean. Usually, she does, which is why I am getting worried…"

"She has a lot to do with this investigation. I would suggest you wait until her time constraints ease up again."

"It's about that case, though, and she hasn't called me back."

"Maybe she's come to her senses."

"Is she there? Does she work in a bullpen where you can actually see her?" Reg went with the way she had seen homicide departments portrayed on TV, since the police stations she had attended over the years never actually looked like that.

There was silence for a moment, and then the sergeant made another dismissive noise. "Look, Ms. Rawlins—"

"I'm not crazy, and I'm not making psychic predictions. When was the last time she checked in with you? Or reported to you? Whatever it is that they do. Has she given you an update since early yesterday morning?"

"You sound like you're fishing for information on the case."

"No, I'm not. I just want to know that she's okay. That she's safe and everything is fine."

"She's fine, Ms. Rawlins."

"So you have talked to her. Is she there now?"

"No. She's off. Getting some shuteye. She probably has her ringer turned off, so just leave your message for her, and she will get back to you when she is up."

"I've left messages already. Is she at home, then? Sleeping? Not just in a room over there at the police station?"

"At home," Pitts agreed.

"Did she investigate the attack last night? I saw it online. She must have been pretty upset that there was another attack. Was it similar? Was there anything left at the scene?"

"She was not available last night."

"She wasn't on? Then why is she sleeping now?"

"She was exhausted. Sometimes investigators try to put in too many hours and forget that they're not superhuman. I sent her home and told her not to come back until she was fully rested and able to focus on the case."

"When was that?"

"Ms. Rawlins, it's really not any of your business. She will be back on shift when she is able. Until then, let her get the rest she needs. This case has been taking a lot out of her."

Reg could imagine Marta spending too much time on the investigation, skipping sleep for a day or two, wolfing down a sandwich in her car now and then, trying to chase down all of the clues she could, to interview all of the witnesses, looking for the minutest details that might have been overlooked.

"Was she able to talk to any of the witnesses in that case?" Reg asked. "The victims? She had more questions for them, but they weren't returning her calls. She couldn't get them."

"Unfortunately, that is the way of the world, as you are finding out. I'm sure everything will be sorted out soon. Detective Jessup will get back to you in time."

CHAPTER THIRTY-FOUR

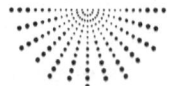

*R*eg felt restless and did not want to be stuck in the cottage all day. On the one hand, it felt unsafe going out anywhere after her experience at the grocery store but, on the other hand, she couldn't stand being cooped up and not seeing anyone except Sarah or her clients. Starlight was good company and she could have called on Harrison to see if he would appear, but she wanted to be with human beings.

Or at least around them. She wasn't sure she actually wanted to have to talk to any of them.

Eventually, she decided that she had to go out. A little jaunt over to The Crystal Bowl for coffee and lunch—though it would count as her breakfast—was just what the doctor ordered. She could get out of the house and be around others without actually having to engage.

All went well, until, sitting at the bar, she turned to look at something that caught her eye outside, and saw Wilf standing by her car.

And he wasn't just standing by it. He was looking around it carefully, touching it, looking underneath the car and, while she watched, he opened the hood, which Reg thought could only be done by releasing the latch from inside the car. She waved at Bill, the bartender, to make sure he saw her put her payment down on the counter and then hurried outside to confront Wilf.

It wasn't unusual for him to be around cars, of course. He was the used car salesman who had sold Reg her car. He had a gift for understanding what a client wanted or needed in a car and was able to put them into one that fit them like magic. And the magic didn't wear off and turn the car into a pumpkin—or lemon—when the buyer got home. It seemed to just keep on working.

"Hey!" Reg shouted as she marched up to her car. "What are you doing?"

Wilf turned toward her, a smile on his face. He beamed at her from underneath his bushy white mustache, not seeming to notice her confrontational attitude.

"Ah, Reg," he greeted, holding out his hand in greeting. Reg automatically raised her hand, even though she had no intention of shaking with him, and he took her hand and pumped it vigorously up and down. "Good to see you, good to see you. I just saw this little lady here," Wilf patted the car affectionately, "and I had to see how she was doing. Still behaving for you? You haven't run into any problems?"

"Yes… the car is still just fine. What are you doing here?"

He indicated the car. "Just checking in. Following up on your purchase."

"You can't just come over here and pop the hood and start… inspecting my car."

"Oh." Wilf sobered. "I'm sorry; I didn't mean to cause any offense. Would you like to bring her into the shop, then, and we can have a quick look to make sure everything is in working order."

"Uh… no. I told you, everything is fine. I don't need you to look at anything."

Reg tried to put herself between Wilf and the car, though she wasn't sure why she bothered. He wasn't going to do anything to sabotage the car right in front of her. And if he did, it wasn't like Reg would be able to recognize what he had done.

But Wilf was in Corvin's coven, and she couldn't trust anyone in the coven. She had to assume that he would do something to harm her or the car if given the chance. Who knew what Corvin may have influenced him to do?

Wilf frowned, his bushy eyebrows almost meeting. "I just want to make sure that you're happy with your purchase."

"I'm happy with it. You don't need to keep following up. Everything is good."

Wilf reached up and shut the hood, pushing it down so it clicked snugly into place. He gestured toward the front passenger seat. "I noticed some scratches on the interior door panel. If you like, we can buff those out for you."

Ember. There was no point in buffing them out until Ember was too big to fit into the car anymore, so he wouldn't be making any more. Then they could fix the damage he had caused. It was like having a great big puppy.

"I'll get back to you on that. There's no point in doing it yet."

"You don't want to let things go," he warned. "You take care of your car, and your car will take care of you."

"I don't think the car is going to malfunction because I got a scratch on the inside of one of the door panels."

"No, but she'll feel much happier if you get it fixed." Wilf patted the car again as if comforting a large animal. "You want to keep it in tip-top shape."

"I'll get it taken care of," Reg said evenly.

"Good, good." He stayed there, hovering, for a moment longer, as if he didn't remember how to say goodbye.

"Did Corvin send you?" Reg demanded.

"Corvin? No. I just happened to be by and saw your car parked here. It is rather distinctive." He referred to the painted flames racing down the sides of the car. It was a beautiful car and well-suited to Reg.

"You can tell him to just stay away from me. I'm not fraternizing with any of the warlocks in the coven. So he can just forget about getting to my powers that way."

"I'm sure he wouldn't ask anyone to do anything to take your powers from you. Just because he is the leader of the coven, that doesn't mean that we are all zombies doing his bidding." Wilf laughed. "We all have minds of our own."

"Yeah, and you think that you're acting on your own, but you're not. He can get inside your mind and twist it up. You don't even know why you suddenly want to... come over and see my car. You just know that you want to."

"I always want to check up on the cars that I have sold. It's part of our fantastic follow-up service."

"It's great... but I don't want you to do it anymore. Just leave me alone. Unless I call you."

"You don't want to wait until you're experiencing serious difficulties."

"Stay away from me and my car."

Wilf gave a shrug of resignation. "Okay. But you're just misunderstanding..."

"I know that Corvin is still trying to get my powers. And the 'accident' at the grocery store yesterday was no accident. I don't want anything to do with any of the coven's members."

"But that would include your friend, Davyn," Wilf pointed out.

Reg squirmed at that. Davyn was different. She knew him better than any of the other warlocks. She knew where his head was and that he wouldn't try to take advantage of her to get the powers Corvin coveted.

"Davyn's different."

Wilf briefed a sigh of relief. "Thank goodness you aren't ditching all of your friendships and still have somewhere to go if you were to end up in trouble."

She hadn't been expecting that reaction from him. She just shrugged and shook her head. "I'm not trying to be mean. I just don't want to open myself up to... to being vulnerable to anyone else in the coven."

"You have to do what you think is best. 'An' it harm none.'"

Reg nodded at the familiar maxim. As long as her choices didn't harm anyone else, she was free to do what she chose.

"Well..." Wilf patted Reg heavily on the shoulder and back.

"You keep me in mind if you need backup for Davyn. I may not be anything like him, but I will not do anything to harm you."

Reg nodded. She watched him go. She wasn't sure that what Wilf said was true. It could all be an act. She felt like he was a safe person, but she didn't know him well enough to be sure. And she couldn't be sure that Corvin couldn't ensorcel him and convince him to do something he wouldn't do of his own accord.

She watched Wilf walk away from her, and the siren chorus started up in her head again, coaxing her to go after him and take him under her thrall. That would keep him from doing anything to her or reporting back to Corvin that he had failed at whatever he had been sent over to do. But once Reg took control of him, her instincts and the siren chorus would insist that she then take him to the water to drown him. And then...

She shuddered and didn't go after Wilf. "He's too old," she told the voices. "He would be too tough anyway."

There was a merry peal of laughter from her siren sisters, and several of them agreed with the assessment.

Reg looked back at The Crystal Bowl. She had planned to spend another hour there but, now that she had paid her bill and run out, she wasn't eager to return and have to face their stares and questions.

Maybe it would be better if she went for a walk. She kept telling herself she needed to get more exercise. It would help to get rid of the belly that she was developing from too much ice cream, chocolate cake, and spareribs.

CHAPTER THIRTY-FIVE

$\mathcal{R}$eg started off down Main Street. Maybe a walk would clear her head as well as burning off a few calories. Was she overreacting to Wilf's presence? To his being close to her car? She didn't want to end up going off the side of the road somewhere because he had done something to tamper with her car. Though she suspected he didn't need to pop the hood of her car to do anything to it. He had an affinity for cars and could probably disable or fix it just by thinking about it.

Not that she could see him doing anything that would end up with her off the side of the road or in some horrific accident. He wouldn't want to see a car damaged like that.

But that didn't mean that he couldn't be influenced by Corvin. Maybe even convinced subconsciously to do something that wasn't in his nature. Certainly, Reg wasn't someone who normally jumped into the arms of every handsome man who came into her life. But Corvin could still make her swoon.

Reg lingered outside of the second-hand clothing store, looking in the windows. She could use some new clothes. Particularly, some with larger waistbands. But she wasn't in the mood for shopping, so she just looked at what she could see in the window and continued on. She stopped in again at Marian's storefront. Marian was another psychic in town and, though she and Reg had initially been rivals and not liked each other very well, they had grown closer and were now pretty good friends, even if they didn't get together to see each other very often. Reg should probably look in on her while she was there.

She hesitated for a few minutes. Maybe Marian was seeing a client. Certainly, she must have better things to do than to visit with Reg, who hadn't bothered to make an appointment or give her any kind of heads-up that she was coming over. It was nice to have visitors, but unexpected drop-ins could be awkward and cause scheduling problems.

Eventually, she decided to go in. If Marian were with a client, Reg would just wave and say they would talk on the phone later. If Marian were alone, she could ask if it was a good time or if Marian wanted to get together later, maybe for dinner. She hadn't ever taken Marian out for a meal, and thought the other woman was a bit lonely. She would probably love to be invited out.

Reg pushed open the door. Bells jingled, and an electronic doorbell rang in the back of the shop in case Marian was farther away.

But she wasn't in the back. She was just at the tea station pouring out two cups of tea.

"Reg," Marian smiled and held one of the cups out toward her. "I wondered who was coming."

She motioned to the table where she did readings for clients and once helped Reg sort out a small problem she'd had with spiders. "You wondered who was coming?" Reg repeated. "You knew you were getting a visitor?"

"I *am* a psychic," Marian pointed out.

Reg had always wondered just how strong Marian's gifts were. While Marian had pointed out more than once how much stronger Reg's psychic and other gifts were than her own, Marian did at least seem to be a legitimate psychic, not someone who was just cold-reading people's facial expressions and making logical deductions.

Marian was wearing a green turban wrapped around her head. Her face was saggy and pouchy and fell into a hangdog expression when she wasn't smiling. Reg didn't know how old she was. She assumed Marian was in her fifties or sixties, but some magical practitioners were much older than they looked. Did that apply to psychics too?

Reg stirred some sugar into her tea. "So... how are you doing? I hadn't planned to come over, so I don't have any special agenda. I was just out for a walk and figured I would stop in and say hi."

"I got a new cat," Marian confided, leaning toward Reg. She smiled, and her eyes sparkled, making her look like a different person. Not hangdog, jowly Marian, but a woman who was happy with the new arrival in her life. Reg had been to Marian's house, and had seen no sign that she even had any extended family outside of Black Sands. No pictures on display. Marian had never mentioned anyone.

"That's wonderful!" Reg did her best to gush. "Tell me all about him. Or her."

"Her. She's a little white cat, very slim and pretty. I got her from the cat sanctuary, and I'm so glad I went there. She's a perfect match. I think she might even be a little psychic herself."

Reg nodded. "Starlight is too. It's nice to have a familiar who can help with some of the more difficult jobs. Except, of course, that half of what he tells me is just how hungry he is."

Marian laughed. "Don't need to be a psychic to understand that!"

"Exactly. Sometimes I wish I understood him a little less clearly."

"But you and Starlight get along very well. You are very suited to each other."

"Thank you." Reg nodded. "Do you have pictures of your new cat? What is her name?"

Marian pulled out her phone and started tapping it. As she looked for the picture, Reg thought of the other cat she had taken to Marian. She had hoped that Marian would adopt one of the nine kattakyns created by the Witch Doctor. Francesca, the white Haitian witch who had bound the draugrs into their cat form, had initially given Horace to a man in Egypt, but bad things had happened to him, and he had returned to Reg in Black Sands.

Horace was pure black like all of the other eight kattakyns, and unfortunately damaged by his experiences in Egypt. So he had not settled into Marian's home like Reg had hoped. Horace had needed a home and Marian had needed a cat, but the match was just not meant to be. The small white cat Marian had adopted sounded like she was the complete opposite of Horace in both looks and temperament.

"Her name is Lara," Marian said, turning her phone around and showing the picture to Reg. "She's such a sweetheart. Very polite and well-behaved."

Unlike Horace, who, like a child who had been abused and neglected, had acted out when placed with Marian. Reg sighed. She smiled at the picture. "She looks very sweet."

"She is," Marian agreed, pleased. "She's everything I need in a cat."

"That's great."

"How is Starlight?"

Reg smiled and nodded. "He's good. I can't complain. Even if he does think I'm a dunce most of the time. It's nice to have someone else in the house. Someone to come home to and to keep me company at night."

"Exactly. And… Horace? I know you eventually found him a new home. Is that working out for him?"

"I haven't seen him for a little while but, as far as I know, he's happy there. I should ask him to come visit me one day soon. I'm sure Starlight would like to see him again." The two cats had grown close. Not just because they had both lived with Reg, but also because of the Egyptian deities they were associated with. Starlight was, if Reg were to believe all she had seen and heard, an incarnation of Bastet, and Horace was paired with the spirit of Merneith, the first female Pharaoh of Egypt. They had known each other in those ancient lives.

Had Starlight seen Horace lately without Reg knowing about it? His disappearances at night might mean that he was traveling with Horace while Reg was sleeping, something she hadn't considered before. The kattakyns had special powers, including the ability to enter houses through people's dreams. Assuming he could take Starlight with him, the two cats might have been traveling all over Black Sands. Or even ranging farther than that.

"Well, you must be very happy with Lara," Reg said, rising to her feet. "I'm thrilled you found a cat that worked out for you. It's so nice not to have to be lonely."

"Can't you stay and visit longer?" Marian asked, also standing up. "We didn't really get the chance to talk."

"Sorry. I should have told you I could only stop for a few minutes. We should do dinner one day. My treat. I'll call you to set it up."

"Well, take care until then." Marian didn't offer to shake hands with Reg. Reg could feel her disappointment and irritation at Reg showing up and then only staying for a few minutes. She had been hoping for a longer visit. She might have a cat at home, but that didn't satisfy all of her social needs.

"I will. You too. And we will get together."

Marian saw Reg to the door.

CHAPTER THIRTY-SIX

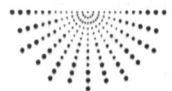

*R*eg walked back to her car, thinking about Horace and Starlight. She had wondered what had happened to Starlight the couple of times she had woken up after sleepwalking. She had looked everywhere in her cottage and been unable to find him. It wasn't a big place and there were few hiding places. She had been sure that he was not there and then, when she had turned around, there he was, sitting in the middle of the floor watching her as if he'd been there all along. Which Reg was sure he had not been.

Horace would explain it. Horace could come and go, and maybe he could transport another cat. Or maybe Merneith, the *sah* that inhabited him, had that ability and had shared it with her host body. Reg couldn't figure out if Merneith was one of the immortals or if she was something different again. Not human, not immortal, but something else ancient that Reg didn't wholly understand.

She found her car right where she had left it and looked around slowly for Wilf or any other warlocks from Corvin's coven. The coast appeared to be clear. No warlock there tampering with her car, watching her, or determined to follow her wherever she went until they figured out how to get into her house.

But why would they want into the house? Corvin wanted in

because he was hoping for another chance to steal Reg's powers. But why would the others want in? Just so they could let Corvin in and he could do what he wanted?

He must have told them he wanted in for some reason other than to prey on Reg. She didn't think that most of the warlocks would have been persuaded to do direct harm.

But maybe she was wrong.

There was, after all, the person who had pushed her into the tower of salsa at the grocery store. He had surely intended her harm. She could have been killed by the display crashing down on her if she hadn't been able to raise a psychic shield in time.

Reg looked up and down the street again for anyone suspicious, then finally unlocked her car and got in. The drive home was short, and she would feel better once she got there. Safe and sound in her own home where nobody could get past the wards.

Hopefully.

She knew something was wrong when she pulled in front of the big house. She sat frozen in her car, extending her senses outward. Sarah was not home. There was no one in the house. But there was someone there who should not be.

"What is it?" Reg murmured. "Who is here?"

There was no answer. She was by herself. No one else was in sight. But she couldn't deny that there was another presence there. Maybe more than one. Was it someone who could cloak himself like Davyn? Come to think of it, was it Davyn himself? He might visit her at home and hide himself from view so that no one would notice him loitering around waiting for her. She looked for shadows within the shadows, wishing, not for the first time, that Sarah didn't have so many big, old trees in the front yard. They prevented Reg from being able to see the gate to the protected backyard. What point was there in wards in the backyard if someone could stand in wait beside the gate so she couldn't even get in?

The leaves rustled in the wind. There was movement; she was sure of it. And she felt more than one presence. Reg didn't dare confront them without knowing who it was or how strong they were. They were lying in wait for her so, presumably, they were powerful enough that they expected to be able to overcome her.

She pulled out her phone and tried Marta Jessup's number.

Of course she didn't answer. She hadn't been in contact for the last day and a half. Why would she start now? Either the case was occupying all of her time, or she had done a very good job of working herself to exhaustion. Maybe she had the flu. Or mono.

What about 9-1-1? Reg stared at the phone screen and then looked outside again, trying to see the men waiting to ambush her. She could still see nothing, only feel them as they waited for her to get out of the car.

There was nothing else to do. Reg called the emergency line. After identifying herself and her location, she explained about there being men lurking in the shadows in her yard and her fear that they were there to harm her.

"Do they have weapons? Can you describe them?"

"I can't see them very well. There are two or three of them. Big guys. But they're in the shadows. I have no idea what they're wearing or carrying."

"We've dispatched a couple of units," the dispatcher assured her. "You don't know who it is or why they would be there?"

"No."

"Do you have any enemies? Anyone who has been making threats to you?"

"I don't know. Does anybody really think that they have enemies?"

"Most people know if someone has been threatening them," the dispatcher said dryly.

"Well, no, I haven't had any threats. Not like that."

"And you didn't set up an appointment to have anyone over? The other possibility is that you set something up and then forgot about it."

Reg looked guiltily in the direction of the trees. That did sound like the kind of thing that she might do. Had she told anyone to come over? It could even be something that Sarah had set up. Reg didn't remember if she had checked her appointment book that morning. Sarah regularly booked people to see her and, if Reg hadn't actually checked to see…

"No. I don't think so," she told the woman. "And if I did, why would they hide in the shadows like that?"

"Maybe they wanted to get out of the sun."

Reg shook her head, looking at the ambush point. Walking to the guest cottage unaware, she would pass that tree, pause to open the gate, and they would jump out at her.

Sirens approached. Reg watched for her uninvited guests to make their escape. All at once, several shapes emerged from the darkest of the shadows. There were only a few quick words or commands shared between them, and then they were running. They split up and went in different directions. One jumped the fence to the neighbor's house on the right, one ran directly toward Reg, and the other peeled off down the sidewalk to the left.

The police cars got there, but not fast enough. Reg got out of her car, shaking her head in disgust. The air was heavily scented with the smell of newly mown grass. "You scared them away with your sirens."

The first cop to approach her seemed unconcerned about it. "Well, that's good. They shouldn't bother you anymore."

"How are you going to find out who it was and charge them?"

He shrugged. "People are very rarely charged in cases like this."

"Well, not if you scare them away!" Reg snapped.

He rolled his eyes and shook his head. "Did you recognize them?"

Reg thought about it. Her heart was still thumping hard, her whole body tense, and she just wanted to haul off and hit someone. Why did the cops have to scare her intruders away? Now she had no idea who they were and no way to keep them from coming back again the next time. She didn't know what they wanted or what lengths they would go to to get it.

"One of them came toward me… I should have been able to recognize him. He was right there in front of me, but…" She shook her head, trying to muddle her way through it, to bring the picture back into her mind with perfect clarity. But the man had been moving fast, and she had panicked, trying to make sure that the windows were up and the door locked and to watch all three of them at the same time to see where they went and make sure that one of them didn't get around behind her to attack her from the other side. "I think… it was someone I had seen before, but he had a hood on, I could only see a little of his face."

Reg pressed her fingers to her temples, rubbing them and trying to squeeze the information out of her brain. Things had gotten so scrambled after the incident with Wilson and she had never been able to sort all of the information she had stored before then. But she hadn't met the members of Corvin's coven until after that. She should be able to remember them all clearly.

CHAPTER THIRTY-SEVEN

*B*ut none of their faces seemed to match that of the warlock who had charged directly toward her. Maybe he was a new member? Someone who lived out of town and hadn't been there the days that she had interviewed the members of the coven while looking for Davyn. But she *had* seen him before; she was sure of it. Too much of his face and body had been obscured by the dark cloak. And maybe he had been using some kind of charm to alter his appearance or befuddle her.

"Well," the cop shrugged, "I would suggest working with a police artist to get a sketch of this guy, but we're just talking about someone lurking in your front yard, not Jack the Ripper. He hasn't done anything other than trespass on your property, has he?"

"No. I don't know. I don't think so. Not yet. But that doesn't mean that they won't come back."

"Get a couple of security cameras so you can get pictures of them if they do. Stay alert. Give us a call if you see anything else."

Reg stared at him. "That's it? That's all you're going to give me? 'Let us know if you see them again?' Aren't you going to… canvass the neighbors to see if they got them on camera? Search for forensics? Fingerprints?"

"Out here?" He looked toward the yard and shook his head. "There isn't going to be anything helpful. Not worth our time."

"They might have... been smoking cigarettes while they waited and left butts with their DNA on them. Or their cloaks might have caught on a branch or nail..."

"Ms. Rawlins," his voice was deep and gruff, but he was impatient rather than emotional. "I told you, there's nothing we can even charge these guys with. It isn't worth our time to do *anything*. Even if you knew who they were, there isn't anything we could do but warn them to stay away from you, that you don't want them trespassing on your property. You did the right thing to call when you felt threatened, but we can't charge them with scaring you or giving you a bad feeling."

It took too long to get rid of the police afterward. Since they weren't doing anything, Reg wasn't sure why they were still hanging around, chatting with each other, occasionally letting her know there was nothing they could do, but that the prowlers probably would not be coming around again. A few times they speculated on why they had been there in the first place. Just for kicks. Mistaken identity. A scavenger hunt. Accidentally going to the wrong house. Reg just wanted the cops out of there if they weren't going to do anything for her, and it was pretty obvious they weren't.

Eventually, they had filled out whatever reports they were required to, had finished their cups of coffee and illicit cigarettes, and reluctantly climbed back into their cars.

What a circus. She might as well have called for a clown car.

Reg let herself into the backyard and let the comforting feeling of the protected place enfold her.

Her home. Her safe, protected home.

But she was still uneasy about the warlocks. If they had been sent by Corvin and had a portion of his powers, it was possible they could get by the wards. They might have devised a way, and she had interrupted them before they could implement their plan.

The police were no good. They figured it was just a run-of-the-mill trespassing charge, and not even that, that it might have just been a mistake. Certainly not anything that posed a threat to Reg's health and safety.

And Marta wasn't even returning her calls.

Reg let herself into the cottage. She still took the precaution of looking around before she unlocked the door. The yard might be guarded by wards, and the warlocks might have run off when the police had shown up, but that didn't mean that none of them had gotten into the yard. It was still possible to fool or overwhelm the wards. Corvin might have sent a warlock with enough power to defeat them. John, for instance. He understood how to use powers that were not his own. Corvin could build him up with some of the Witch Doctor's powers or magical artifacts that he had on hand for just such an emergency. He wouldn't have to brainwash his son into thinking he was helping Reg somehow. If he got John to take Reg's powers and then took them from John…

Forget the whole issue of consent. When had Corvin cared about consent in the past? He had been happy to trick Reg into consenting, to overwhelm her with his charms, or to take what he wanted by force.

Well, John wasn't going to catch Reg off guard. She looked and listened and stretched out her senses, feeling for any hint of another presence in the yard that should not be there. She could sense nothing. She carefully fit her key in the lock and let herself in, then shut and bolted the door behind her.

CHAPTER THIRTY-EIGHT

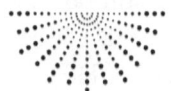

*T*he first item of business was ice cream. Reg wasn't going another minute without good old fudge and salted caramel ice cream. She opened the freezer and saw three pint containers of it lined up in a row.

Sometimes she felt guilty about calling food to her. She thought about the stores she must have called it from and that they would have to deal with the "shrinkage" like any other form of shoplifting.

But sometimes, she didn't care.

The need was great, after all.

Reg could barely even fumble the drawer open to get a spoon out. She had half a mind to rip the top off and start eating it with her fingers. Or shoving her face directly into the opening.

After all three pints had been consumed and Reg was lying on the couch holding her overstuffed belly, she made a call. She knew a security guy. And she knew he wasn't in Corvin's coven. That fulfilled both of her requirements. Damon would keep an eye on things and wouldn't allow any harm to befall her.

"Reg," Damon was enthusiastic and energetic, dispelling her worries that he might be on another job and couldn't give her the time or energy. He sounded right on top of his game.

"Damon, hi. I was hoping you could help me out with something. It would be a paid job, if you can do it."

"Sure. What's up?"

"There have been... some things going on. I don't feel safe here. Not without someone around to watch for intruders and ensure I don't..."

Reg stopped for a moment. She had been about to say that she wanted Damon to make sure that she didn't sleepwalk either. But did she want to reveal that to him? What if there was a remote chance that she had been connected with the attacks at the harbor? She didn't want people to know that she might have left the house during the night.

"Reg? To make sure that you don't what?"

"Just to make sure I don't worry," Reg quickly covered. "I'm so anxious. I won't be able to sleep if I don't find some way to put my mind at ease."

"Ah. Sure."

Reg tried not to think about the fact that one of Damon's gifts was his ability to know whether someone was telling the truth. Would he sense that she had been about to say something else? She wasn't lying about worrying and needing someone to calm her down. That *was* why she had called him.

Sometimes, she didn't know whether she was telling the truth or not.

"You want someone over there right away?" Damon asked, businesslike.

"Yes. If you could. It would be you, wouldn't it?" Reg confirmed, unsure of Damon's use of 'someone' instead of 'me.'

"Yes, it will be me. I can rearrange other things."

At times like that, she wouldn't have minded the ability to tell whether someone was telling the truth or not. Did he have other things that he had to rearrange to be at her side, or was he just saying it to make her feel like she owed him something? She was grateful to him whether he had something else going on that he had to reschedule or not.

"I'll be there as soon as I can," Damon assured Reg. "Until

then, keep your door shut and don't open it to anyone. Pretend you're not even home. All of your wards are intact? And there's no one there already that you know of?"

"The police already chased three guys off. I can't feel anyone else. So I don't think so. But..." Reg looked around her cottage, "they could come back anytime."

"You had the police there?"

"Yes."

"You must really be worried. I won't be long, then. Just long enough to throw a few things in a bag."

"Thanks, Damon. I appreciate that."

"Don't open the door to anyone without the code word."

"What code word?"

"Uh... the name of the fairy."

"What? What fairy?"

"You know which one. Don't open the door to anyone, even me, without that name."

"Okay," Reg agreed, puzzled. "I won't."

After she hung up, she looked at the door to verify that all the locks were in the right position. It was locked up like Fort Knox. No one could get in unless Reg opened the door for them, and she wouldn't open it for anyone but Damon. And then only if he gave her the code word.

As if to prove her reassurance wrong, there was a meow beside her, and Reg, looking down and expecting to see Starlight, grumpy because she hadn't stopped to feed him, saw Horace.

She sat up straight.

"Horace! What are you doing here?"

He sat back on his haunches and yawned. One of those cat yawns so wide it looked as if he would swallow his own head. He snapped his mouth shut and looked at her with a long, slow blink.

"How are you?" Reg asked him. "And where is Starlight? Does he know you're here?"

Horace licked his lips. Reg reached her hand out to him but did not pet him. She let him sniff her hand until he was satisfied and rubbed up against her. Reg scratched his ears and stroked his head.

"How's that? How are you doing, huh?"

We are one, Horace-Merneith's voice was in Reg's head. *And you, Reg Rawlins?*

Well, things have been a bit crazy here. I guess… I'm just fine. I am waiting for a friend to come over and help me, so if you do not want to be seen…

Who comes? The tall one?

Not Harrison. At least, not as far as I know. He's like you; he can pretty much come and go whenever he likes. I am waiting for Damon.

Horace blinked a couple of times but made no sign he knew who this was.

"What are you doing here?" Reg asked. "Did you come to say hi or to get Starlight?"

Another long, slow blink.

It appeared she wouldn't get an answer to that one.

"Have you been taking Starlight away from here? Is that where he is when I haven't been able to find him?"

If he is not here, you cannot find him here, Horace-Merneith purred.

That's true. Are you taking him somewhere else? Can you do that?

We can do many things.

I don't like you taking him away from here without telling me first. Can you at least give me a warning that he is going to be gone? That when I wake up, he might be somewhere else?

He might be somewhere else, Horace-Merneith confirmed with a tinkling laugh.

Where do you go when you take him?

There are many beings in need of help. We must all help to provide sanctuary.

Well, that's nice. Reg nodded. She didn't know what rescue mission they were on, but it sounded good. She couldn't find fault with Horace-Merneith and Starlight helping out people. Or cats. Horace-Merneith hadn't said which it was they were rescuing. And maybe they were even referring to other creatures. Fairies, elves, dogs, who knew?

CHAPTER THIRTY-NINE

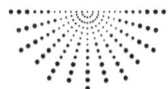

*T*here was a knock at the door, which made Reg jump. She turned to look at the door, her heart in her stomach. It had to be Damon. Only someone who did not intend her harm could enter the yard, and Sarah would not have bothered to knock first. She would have just tried the door.

Reg turned back to Horace to warn him of Damon's arrival, but Horace was gone. Which was probably for the best. Then Reg didn't have to tell Damon the whole story of who Horace was and how he had gotten there and the unique way she communicated with him, unlike her interactions with other cats. And then to explain his mysterious appearances and disappearances. It was a bit much to explain all at once.

Reg walked over to the door and looked out the peephole. She never could see very well out of those and wished she had a doorbell cam instead. The fact that Damon was wearing a black cloak did not help. He could have been anyone.

"Who's there?" she called through the door.

"It's Damon."

Reg put her hand on the first lock, then paused. "What is the password?"

"Calliopia."

Reg let out a sigh. Of course it was the name of the fairy that she had worked with Damon to save. She twisted the deadbolt open, unlocked the other locks, and let Damon in. He nodded to her.

"Good job remembering to ask for the code word."

"Well, you did tell me like ten minutes ago. I'm not that forgetful."

"No, but you still might have decided it was unnecessary." He slid his hood down. "There are those who are remarkable mimics. You think you know who you are letting in and then... it turns out to be someone else."

Reg remembered Hope, the woman she had let into her home, thinking she was a guest of Sarah's. She had been very adept at transforming her features to fool Reg. She'd had no idea who Hope really was.

"Yeah. I hadn't thought about that." Reg shut the door and turned the locks, though she felt silly doing it now that her protector was there. He would keep out any intruders.

As long as they were not stronger than he was.

Reg grimaced at this unwelcome thought.

"So..." Damon motioned to the living room. "Do you want to sit down and give me the lowdown on what's happening here?"

Reg sighed and sat back down on the wicker couch. Damon took one of the chairs.

Reg told him about her concerns that Corvin and members of his coven might be out to get her. It sounded crazy and paranoid when she said it aloud, but Damon didn't question it. He just listened and nodded as she explained it to him. He looked at the cat's paw still on Reg's coffee table and didn't pick it up or touch it.

"You think that Corvin might be the leader of the Cabal of the Withered Paw?"

"I don't know... I think it's possible. Couldn't there be a public coven and a secret coven at the same time? And some members might cross between them? I know Davyn wouldn't have been the leader of the cabal, but Corvin might already have been. Or it might have been a position that he had the option of taking up when he took the mantle of the leadership of the mainstream coven."

Reg shuddered when she said *mantle,* thinking about the vision of the cloaked figures, including the one with a cloak edged in red. She was glad, looking at Damon and talking to him about the story, that he was wearing a pure black robe and she didn't need to worry about whether *he* was really the leader of the cabal.

"I never even believed that the Cabal of the Withered Paw was real," Damon confessed. "I thought it was just a story to scare kids. I guess this means that it was real and is back." He pointed to the cat's paw on the table. "But it could also just be a prank to make people think it was. You know, like parents making 'Santa footprints' in front of the fireplace to reinforce the myth of Santa Claus. It doesn't prove that the cabal is back or ever existed in the first place."

Reg eyed the relic. "But I can feel its evil. And Ember could remember the paw and the cabal. If he can remember it, then it must exist."

"Or he remembers the legends as well. Maybe dragons tell their children scary stories before bed."

Reg opened her mouth to protest that dragon mothers were long gone before their offspring hatched, and that Ember's memories were actual memories of his ancestors. But Damon wasn't looking for dragon lore. He was interested only in what could be proven, and she couldn't prove that Ember's memories were true any more than she could prove that the cat's paw was an authentic magical relic or that the cabal had truly existed and was back.

"It might exist," Damon said, cutting through Reg's whirling thoughts. "Or someone might be pretending that it is. Either way, it makes no difference. Whether it is a resurrection of the original cabal or a group of people who are determined to pursue the objectives of a fictional cabal, the result is the same."

Reg thought about that. It was true. Even if it were just a group of warlocks who had decided to reenact a fictional cabal, they were clearly willing to go to significant lengths for the sake of authenticity. The icky cat's paw imbued with power. Attacks at the waterfront. People hiding in her front yard.

"Do you think they know you have the paw?" Damon asked. "Is that why they were here to ambush you?"

Reg's stomach turned over. She was beginning to regret the three pints of ice cream.

"Do you think that they would do that? Attack people in real life? It's not just a game?"

Damon scratched his short beard, considering. "There have been actual attacks. But no injuries. They weren't trying to hurt or kill the victims. They had another motivation."

"There were a couple who were hurt when they resisted."

"But I don't think that was their objective, do you?"

"I don't know. What were they after? Corvin said that they tortured or kidnapped practitioners with puppets."

CHAPTER FORTY

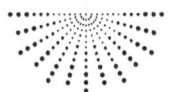

*P*oppets," Damon corrected. "It's difficult to know what their motivation or objectives were. It is a *secret*, after all. That's the whole point. There were a number of different theories, but it was only ever speculation. Anyone who was in the cabal was sworn to secrecy, and I can only imagine the punishments or consequences that would be in place if they told what they knew. The punishments for discussing secret organizations are usually quite… gory and terrifying. The whole point is to scare anyone from saying what they know."

"And this new cabal, it could have the same goals or something completely different. If there is no way to know what the original group was trying to do, then these revivalists could have anything in mind."

"Except that, as you say, they don't appear to have violent intentions."

"But before… they didn't torture people in person anyway, did they? They used their voodoo dolls."

Damon considered this, steepling his fingers and leaning back in his chair, eyes closed. "No. You're right. But then… what is the connection between the attacks and the cabal? Is there one? Or are you only assuming that there is one because the attacks started at the same time as you came into possession of *that*?"

"It isn't just the timing. Marta said that only practitioners were being attacked. And the cat's paw was dropped by one of the attackers. So it *is* the Cabal of the Withered Paw that is responsible for the attacks."

"Or that one, anyway."

Reg nodded. "At least that one. Or two. It was two people who were attacked, I think."

"Why would they attack people instead of using poppets?"

Frowning, Reg pulled out her phone. She scrolled through her contacts list and tapped on Francesca's name. After a few rings, Francesca answered.

"Hello, Reg. What are you up to tonight?"

Reg loved the Haitian accent. It made Francesca sound so exotic and mysterious. She tapped the screen to put the call on speaker so Damon could hear it too.

"I'm just doing a little bit of research. I thought you might be able to tell me... how do you make a voodoo doll."

"*I* do not make a voodoo doll," Francesca told her coldly. "I am not a Vodou practitioner."

"I didn't mean *you*. I just meant... a person. How is it done?"

"Effigies are not common in Vodou. And they are not like you see them in Hollywood."

"Okay. But if someone was making effigies or poppets... for some kind of ritual... how is it done? Do they have to be made out of something the person owns?"

"There is a stronger connection between the person and the effigy if it can be made from something the person owned. Or perhaps... something from their body, such as hair or nail clippings. The more strongly you can connect the doll with the target of your spell, the more effective it will be."

"That's all I wanted to know. I've heard stuff before, but... I know you can't believe everything you see on TV. I wanted to get it from someone who would know."

"Regina," Reg knew from the warning tone in Francesca's voice what she was going to say before she said it. "This is a very powerful kind of magic that you do not want to get involved in. Someone who is not experienced should not be dabbling in making an effigy."

"I'm not. I just needed some background."

"Be careful. The witch who uses this kind of magic can be very dangerous."

Reg terminated the call and looked at Damon. His eyes were open now and he was staring at her. "So you think the attacks were designed to get something from the victims. Not to hurt them directly, but to get something personal to make a poppet. And then to use the poppet…"

"If they use the poppet to torture them or whatever it is they are up to, then they have an alibi. They can be across town, on surveillance cameras, when… whatever it is… happens to the victim."

Damon nodded his agreement. "It would be nice to know what they are doing. Why go through all of this, risking being caught 'mugging' someone? Accidentally injuring something directly? Why would they be so concerned with hurting someone remotely?"

Reg nodded, sucking in her cheeks. She had a feeling that Corvin would know. But of course, if Corvin were the leader of the cabal, then he knew all about it. He had been the one to do the research and figure out how to resurrect the group and how to use the ancient magic they had previously employed. Maybe he'd come across an artifact—even the cat's paw—that had taught him what he needed to know.

He was not the one to go to with more questions. Even though he had denied being the leader of the cabal, she could not trust him.

"Have any of the victims of the attacks… been retargeted?" Damon asked. "If they've been hurt or killed, or the victims of other crimes, then maybe we're on the right track. That they were being set up for a remote attack… of some sort."

"I don't know. Marta was going to follow up with them to ask them some more questions, but no one was taking her calls or calling her back. And then... I haven't been able to get her. She hasn't been returning my calls. I even talked to her boss, and he basically told me to back off, that she was off duty taking a rest and would call me when she got around to it."

"When was that?"

"That I talked to him? Uh... I think it was this morning. It's been such a long day; it feels more like three. And I haven't seen her or been able to get ahold of her since I talked to her yesterday morning. It's been... usually, if she asks me to help with a case, she's all over me. Calling me to find out if I've figured anything out yet. Harassing me. But it's been quiet, and I've called her a few times and she just doesn't respond. I know her boss said she would call me back and just to leave her alone, but I'm worried something might have happened to her."

"If that was this morning, then maybe he has a different opinion now. He would expect her to report in, and if she didn't respond to *his* calls..."

"I don't think I want to talk to him again. Getting through to him the first time was hard enough, and he'll be home now. The switchboard operator or whatever she is won't be there to put me through now. And if he has an answering service, they won't put someone like me through to him at home. The mayor, maybe, but not some psychic worried about the well-being of an officer who's just sleeping around the clock to make up for the sleep she lost during the investigation."

Damon grimaced. "That's probably true. Nobody is going to think that it's anything to worry about. They'll think they wouldn't bother calling a psychic back either."

"Even though she's the one who brought me into it to start with."

He nodded. "Well... give her another call in the morning, and if she still doesn't answer or get back to you, then try the boss again to see if he's starting to get concerned, or whether she's been in to work and just hasn't bothered to call you. Maybe something has broken in the case and she's just really busy with it."

"I hope so. It would be really good if she's made progress

without me. Maybe she doesn't even need any of this stuff. Maybe she's already got it all figured out."

Damon nodded. He looked around. "Do you have anything going on tonight? Clients coming in? We should talk about protocols before anyone shows up."

Reg shook her head. "I canceled tonight. I didn't want anyone showing up here after the intruders… If anyone is still hanging around here, I wouldn't want them to get in with legitimate clients, or to attack them or something. Though most of my clients don't have any powers," Reg added as an afterthought. Most of them were non-practitioners who weren't even sure they believed in psychic phenomena.

Reg could remember when she didn't believe in psychic phenomena.

"That's a good plan," Damon said. "I'd rather not have to be responsible for anyone else's welfare or to have more people around here than I can keep track of at one time. So just let me know how you want to handle this. If you want to do something on your own and I'll hang out and keep an eye on things, or you want me to do something with you."

Reg could see herself sitting on the couch with Damon, watching TV, eating a bowl of popcorn, nice and relaxed and unworried about what might be going on outside the house.

That was Damon's other gift. Or the only other one that she knew about. He could put visions into her head. And it could be pretty disruptive, because she couldn't tell when it was a vision he had put there and when it was real. She knew it was a vision this time because of the time jump. She couldn't remember him moving from the chair to the couch beside her, or remember making popcorn or picking out a movie to watch together. Had those memories not been missing , she would have believed what she saw.

She'd told Damon before not to put visions in her head without consent or warning. But he didn't seem to be able to control it the way she thought he should. It was ingrained in the way that he communicated, like someone who talked with his hands. Damon might be able to resist for a while, but then it just happened again.

She shook her head and extricated herself from the vision. "I can put something on TV," she agreed. "But if you want popcorn, you're on your own. I've had too much to eat already."

Damon nodded agreeably. "Whatever you want. If you have other plans, you can go ahead and ignore me. I'll put myself in a chair facing the door and stay out of your way."

"No, it's okay. I think we're safe here... but I needed someone else here. Just to be sure..."

"I think it was a wise move."

CHAPTER FORTY-ONE

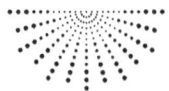

*A*t some point, Reg had drifted off without realizing it. She woke up with her head lolled over to the side in a position she would regret later. She scrubbed her eyes with her fists and looked around. Damon was still awake, watching her with amusement.

"Oh. I never fall asleep this early," Reg said, rubbing her eyes again and squinting at her phone.

"It sounds like you've had a rough couple of days. Why don't you go to bed, and I'll keep an eye on things."

Reg yawned and groaned and stretched. "Yeah. I'd better. Sorry, I wasn't planning to fall asleep so early."

"No problem. You're not here to entertain me. I'm here to guard you."

Reg stood up. She stayed still for a moment, making sure she was steady, then headed for the bathroom and, after that, bed. She looked around the bedroom, frowning.

"Starlight? Are you here? Where are you?"

He wasn't sitting in the window and she hadn't noticed him in the living room or kitchen when she had gotten up.

So Horace had taken him away again. Reg didn't know whether to be happy that Starlight wasn't underfoot or in any danger from the harbor attackers, or disappointed that he wasn't there to keep her company. She wasn't completely alone. But she wasn't going to ask Damon to cuddle up with her on the bed like Starlight would.

Tonight, Starlight was off protecting creatures in need. From what kind of danger, Reg didn't know.

She flopped into bed and pulled the covers over her head. She tossed and turned for a few minutes and then drifted off back to sleep again.

* * *

It seemed like only a few minutes had passed when Starlight's plaintive meows reached through to her conscious mind, pulling her out of sleep. She knew that sound. His dish was empty. Or at least, he didn't want to eat whatever had been sitting in his dish all night and wanted something better. Apparently, Horace had not taken him out for dinner after their nocturnal adventures.

"Okay, okay, I hear you," she told him as she approached the kitchen. She didn't stop to think about Damon being there. That part of her brain hadn't woken up yet. She fumbled around getting Starlight some fresh food, then, after putting his dish on the floor, leaned back on the counter watching him and rubbing her eyes.

She gradually became aware of a coffee cup sitting on the kitchen island. She had not left it there. And the messenger bag that Damon had brought with him and left beside his chair. Everything seemed to be where it should be, except for Damon.

Reg craned her neck to see the bathroom door, but it was open and he was not there. He wasn't anywhere. Reg looked down at Starlight. "Did you and Horace do something with Damon?"

Starlight looked up at her with a questioning trill, then continued eating.

The front door was no longer locked. Reg had left it with all of the locks secured, and none were in the locked position any longer.

Damon wouldn't have left her alone there.

He was there to guard her. He wouldn't have just wandered off.

But he might have gone outside to look at something if he had heard a disturbance or seen someone or something that should not be there.

She hadn't even thought to warn him about Ember, who might have come by at night to see her again.

Reg opened the door tentatively. "Damon? Are you out there?"

She expected to see him walking around the yard, checking the perimeter. Or sneaking a smoke. But there was no sign of anyone in the part of the yard she could see from the cottage door.

Reg's stomach clenched and she felt sick. Where was he? He wouldn't have gone anywhere without telling her first, even if it were an emergency and he got called out to another site his men were at. So where was he? He wasn't in the cottage. He wasn't within sight of the door. He could be around back. He could be checking the gate between the front and back yards to make sure it was still secure. That was where the intruders had been hanging out, so it would make sense that it might be a weak point.

He would be back within ten minutes. It wouldn't take him longer than that to look at whatever he needed to and return to the cottage. He obviously hadn't expected her to wake up while he was gone, or he would have waited for her and had her lock the door behind him until he returned. He had only intended to step out for a few seconds.

Reg walked back into the house and around the interior, looking out each of the windows to see if he were in the back or another position she couldn't see from the doorstep. He might even have gone to the big house to ask Sarah about... something. Reg couldn't think of what. But Damon was the one who knew security, and it was Sarah's house so, if he had a question about the cottage security or the wards in the yard or inside, she would be the one to ask. Especially since Reg was sleeping after a long, hard day and he didn't know how long she would be out.

But she couldn't see him anywhere, and he didn't return to the house within ten minutes. Reg got dressed without a bath or shower and put on her shoes. At the door, she stopped with her hand on the doorknob.

Was she really going to act like the hapless victim in a horror flick who left the safety of the house to find out firsthand how her companion had been horribly and gruesomely killed?

She took her hand from the door and relocked each lock. She looked out the peephole and then out the living room window, figuring that Damon would show up as soon as she locked him out. That was the way it always worked, wasn't it?

But there was still no sign of him.

Reg gulped down a cup of coffee that was way too hot, trying to jump-start her brain. How was she going to find Damon and safely get herself out of the situation? There was obviously something going on. He wouldn't have just left her alone for no reason.

The simple solution was to call him. Wherever he was, whether in the front yard or somewhere farther afield, he would have his phone with him. She calmly pulled out her phone and fumbled with it until she could find his contact listing and tapped on his face to put the call through. It rang half a dozen times before going to voicemail. So much for that.

She messaged him in case he was in a situation where he couldn't draw attention to himself by speaking but could answer a message.

Where are you?

She waited. No info tag appeared to indicate that he had read her message. There were no dots in the corner of the screen to show that he was typing something back.

There was no response. It was like her message had just gone down a black hole.

Or he was occupied with something else and couldn't be bothered to look at his phone when it buzzed.

Reg looked out all of the windows again, feeling like she was stuck on an island surrounded by shark-infested waters, too dangerous to step into. She needed someone to rescue her.

She looked at her phone again and tried Marta. She wouldn't still be asleep. She would be back on the job again, even if she had slept for twenty-four hours straight. Her sergeant couldn't tell Reg that she was still sleeping.

But the call to Marta also landed in voicemail. Reg looked

around, hoping for inspiration. She left a message this time, something she rarely did anymore, asking Marta to call her back. But she knew that Marta would never get that message. Something had happened to her. There was no way she would ignore all of Reg's calls for two days and not call her back to see if she had figured out something about the cat's paw or something else related to the harbor attacks.

Reg couldn't stand to get passed around at the police station again until she could find Marta's boss, so she didn't try to reach him again.

She tried another number. This time, it was answered on the second ring.

"Reg. Hi, how are you?"

Reg breathed out, glad she wasn't the only person left on the planet alive. "Davyn. Umm… I need some help. Are you busy?"

"Define busy. Define help."

"There's been some trouble the last few days. I asked Damon to come and stay here last night for security to make sure no one could get in. And this morning… he's gone. No note, no sign of him in the yard, that I can see, but… I'm afraid to go out there and check thoroughly, in case someone or something *did* get him and is still out there waiting for me."

Davyn didn't answer immediately, processing this. "Sounds like a bad horror movie," he said eventually.

"I know. And I know from watching those that if I don't want to be the next victim, I'd better not go out there by myself."

"And from personal experience."

"Well, yes. That too." There had been a few too many times when Reg had just plowed ahead, thinking that she could handle something or not anticipating the danger ahead. This time, she was being cautious. Maybe she was actually learning.

"Okay. I'll be over there shortly," Davyn promised. "You're going to stay inside, right?"

"Yeah."

"Don't open the door for anyone else—"

"Even if I know them," Reg finished. "I won't. Should we have a password?"

"I don't think we need a password, do we?"

"If some siren, shape-shifter, or immortal comes around here in your form…"

"Okay. How about—"

"Don't say it out loud. How about the place in the mountains?"

"The place in the mountains?" Davyn repeated blankly.

"Where we went. And things… happened."

"Oh. Okay. I know where you mean."

"Good. See you soon, then. Don't be too long. I'm going nuts trying to watch out all of the windows here."

"I'll send Ember on ahead. If he isn't already on his way over to you."

It hadn't even occurred to Reg to call on Ember. Her thoughts went to him now, immediately touching his mind, even though he was miles away. "He's coming now."

Davyn chuckled. "He'll keep you safe until I get there. See you soon."

CHAPTER FORTY-TWO

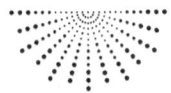

*R*eg felt better knowing that Ember was winging his way over to her. She wished she could fly. She had always thought it would be so freeing to get out into the open air without anything to hold her down and just fly free.

She had been surprised when Sarah had shown her the crude drawings of sirens that had been drawn on a rock in the yard, part of a spell. Back before they had found it necessary to make it as tight as Fort Knox. The thing that had surprised her most was that the sirens were not depicted with mermaid tails, but as bird women. The head of a woman on the body of a partridge or chicken shape. They looked ugly and ungainly. But they had reminded her of her dream of being able to fly. Even as a small child, she used to have dreams of flying, and it had seemed so natural. It wasn't hard to figure out why she dreamed of a way to escape the life that she had with Norma Jean or afterward in foster care. If Reg had been able to shift into a bird shape and fly away, she would have.

The other thing about flying was that it was fast, and it wasn't long before Ember landed with a flurry of flapping wings outside Reg's living room window. She felt safe enough with him there to unlock and open the door.

"Ember!"

He bounded over to her with a snort of flames, and Reg was glad he didn't try to land on her shoulder. He was much too big for that now, even when he flapped his wings to stay aloft so that his whole weight wasn't on her. Instead, she put her arms around his neck and cuddled, letting him nuzzle her while she scratched his ears, jaw, and all of the places he liked her to scratch, purring with delight.

Starlight was back home from wherever he and Horace had been, so Reg withdrew after a moment, not wanting Starlight to get too jealous about all of the attention that Ember was getting. She wondered fleetingly where Starlight had been. Were they rescuing cats in Black Sands? Someone in trouble back in Egypt? She hadn't yet had a chance to inquire and didn't know if either cat would let her know any details. Cats and immortals could be challenging to deal with. They liked their secrets and seemed to delight in ambiguity.

When Reg withdrew from Ember, he took it as a signal that he was on guard duty and needed to get the lay of the land. He sniffed the air, and then the ground around where Reg was standing. He wandered off, following some scent trail, and began working his way in what appeared to be a random path around the yard and garden. Reg had no doubt that if there had been anyone in the yard who shouldn't be there, Ember would have immediately discovered him and attacked. Ember had hatched in that garden, and he would instantly know if anything was out of place.

Reg was a little embarrassed that when Davyn arrived, she was not locked inside the cottage awaiting his arrival as they had discussed, but was sitting on the front step watching Ember snuffle around the yard.

Davyn looked her over. "The forge."

Reg stared at him blankly. "What?"

"I'm supposed to give you a password, am I not? To prove that it really is me and not some shape-shifter? The dwarfen forge. That's where we went in the mountains."

"Oh yeah." Reg chuckled, embarrassed. "Right. Of course."

"You feel better with Ember here?"

"Yeah, I really do."

"No sign of Damon?"

"No." Reg rubbed the third eye position between her eyebrows as it pulsed with pain. "I'm really worried about what might have happened to him. And… I'm worried something has happened to Detective Jessup too. She's not returning my calls and it's been a long time. She would want to know if there were any developments in the case, but she hasn't called me and hasn't returned my calls. I don't know what to do about it."

"How long has she been missing?"

"Umm… a couple of days. Only her boss said she wasn't missing yesterday, just that she was off duty and getting caught up on sleep."

"That sounds like a good thing."

"Yeah, but I don't believe it. And I don't believe that she's been sleeping for two days. Even if she did go home to sleep, even if she was really short on sleep, she wouldn't sleep for that long. Eight or twelve at the most, not the whole day. She would call me back. She's really concerned about this case."

"What case is this that she's working on?"

"The attacks down at the harbor. She had brought me something they had dropped and wanted me to think about it, see if I could get any impressions of it. She would want to know whether I have."

"They?"

"What?"

"Something *they* dropped?"

"Yeah. It was more than one person. At least in the last attack, there were two attackers, not just one."

"I don't think the police have revealed that tidbit."

"Maybe not. But there were. They attacked a couple, so it was two against two."

"Before, they have only attacked one person at a time, so they only needed one attacker."

"Right," Reg nodded in agreement.

He studied her face. "And you think you know more."

"I know some more... but not everything. And I don't know how much of what I know—or guessed—is right."

"And you hired Damon because... you thought they might come after you here?"

Reg nodded. "I was attacked at the grocery store. Well, you know that because you were there. And then there were people here at the house waiting for me, and they scattered when the cops showed up, so they weren't exactly sticking around to give a legitimate reason for being here."

Davyn sighed. "We should take a look around. See if we can find any clue of what might have happened to him. But we're staying together."

"Yeah. No need to worry about that," Reg agreed. "I'm not going to be breakfast for whatever is out there."

Davyn looked at his watch and didn't correct her to tell her it would be lunch, so it must still be pretty early.

"Let's do it, then. Ember!" Davyn clicked his tongue to call the dragon. "Come help us. We're looking for a man who was here." Davyn looked at Reg. "Do you have anything of his?"

"Uh, sure. Of course."

CHAPTER FORTY-THREE

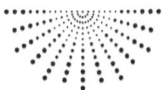

*R*eg went back into the house and opened up Damon's messenger bag. She found a toiletries kit and took it back outside with her to show to Ember. He sniffed it and immediately tried to use his claws delicately enough to grab the zipper tab to open it. Reg pulled it back. "Oh no, you don't, you little klepto. You don't get to see what treasures he has inside. We're looking for Damon. The man who owns this." She visualized Damon as clearly as she could and held the toiletries case up to her nose, breathing in the scent of Damon and his usual deodorant and cologne. The picture sharpened. She could almost have reached out to touch him.

Ember snorted and looked around. He sniffed the air and headed toward the gate to the front yard. Which Reg had to admit she had been expecting. If Damon were in the backyard or Sarah's house, they would have found him by now. He was somewhere else. And that meant he'd either gone out the front gate or the back. The front gate was the one they usually used. The back one was hidden behind a screen of trees and shrubbery. There was a clear path to it, but the vegetation was cleverly arranged to make it almost invisible unless you were actually following the path.

Reg paused before leaving the backyard. That was her safe

place. If someone else had been there, she would need to increase the strength of the wards, but she wasn't going to run away. For once, she had a place where she belonged, and she wasn't going to give it up any time soon.

She took a deep breath in, and let it out slowly. Davyn and Ember both turned to look at her expectantly. Reg nodded. "Let's go."

They walked out the gate. Reg could feel the loss of the safety of the magical charms, like taking off a coat when it was still cold outside. Ember took a few steps into the front yard and looked around. He didn't put his nose to the ground to pick up the trail again. Reg looked around. Damon's big truck was parked right behind her car at the curb. She walked toward it, not knowing what she expected to find. Damon asleep in the front seat? He could have gotten into the truck to get something out and then fallen asleep, couldn't he? She couldn't imagine what he would have gone back to the vehicle for, but it was a possibility.

"This is his?" Davyn asked.

"Yeah." Reg pointed to the Knight Security logo on the side of it, in case Davyn didn't trust her recollection of the vehicle Damon normally drove.

He nodded his agreement. He looked around grimly. "If he isn't in the house or the yard, and his truck is still parked here, then where is he? He didn't tell you that he was going to talk to anyone? Check anything out?"

"He left while I was asleep."

"That doesn't make sense."

"I could understand it if he needed to go check on a job that one of his men was working on if it was really urgent and impor-tant. But he would have woken me up or left me a note. As it was, he left the door unlocked. All I could think about was that... maybe he heard a noise outside or saw something he needed to investigate. And so he left the cottage and... something got him."

"Or someone."

"Yeah. That's what I meant." Reg was thinking too much about all of those horror movies. Why had she ever watched them as a kid? Because she wasn't allowed to? Because her foster mothers always told her they were too mature and scary for her and would give her nightmares? So, of course she had to break the rule and see what she was missing. And she had filled her head with pictures of monsters and horrors and now they were all coming back as she worried about what had happened to Damon when he had gone outside and left the yard.

He would have been careful, yet he had apparently been snatched. Just like Marta. Just like the witnesses that wouldn't return her calls. Everyone who was involved in the case was disappearing. Except Reg herself.

She shuddered and walked closer to Davyn, wishing he would take her and hold on to her. They had never been intimately involved. But they were friends, and Reg wished she had someone to hold on to.

He touched her shoulder briefly, but then moved on, looking around the front yard as if there might be some clue there as to what had happened to Damon. But whoever had taken him was long gone. Reg should have guessed that from the cold coffee.

She walked over to the place in the trees where the trespassers had been hiding the day before. She hadn't taken the time to look for any clues while the police had been there. She had just retreated to the cottage. She assumed that if there were anything to find, the cops would have found it, even if it was just a cigarette butt or footprints in the dirt.

But who was she kidding? It had not been a top-priority call. The police didn't call in forensics to handle every little prowler call. Reg didn't have anything to show that it might be related to the Harbor attacks. They might have paid attention if she could draw a line between them, but she couldn't. They'd probably just had a smoke, a laugh at her expense, and gone back to their patrols.

But however little effort they had put into it, they surely could not have missed what Reg found there.

CHAPTER FORTY-FOUR

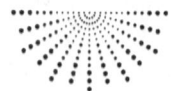

On the ground under the tree, dappled with a bit of sunlight that was able to push its way through the trees, was something that initially looked like a burlap sack or a dead animal. She felt immediately sick, worried they had done an animal sacrifice to invoke a spell. Maybe that was what had attracted Damon's attention. He'd gone out there to stop it and walked directly into... something awful.

But as she got closer, squinting at the small object and trying to make out the details to make sense of what it was, she saw it wasn't anything dead. Not an animal, after all. And not a burlap sack, though it had been sewn out of something like burlap, only with a finer weave. The stitches that held it together were large and crude.

It had a form. A head atop a body, four limbs stretching out from it.

"Davyn?"

Davyn didn't come immediately. He could probably tell from her voice that it wasn't urgent. She hadn't found Damon knocked unconscious—or worse—under the branches of the tree. But he joined her a minute later and cocked his head as he looked at the object.

"What is it?"

Reg was surprised. She had assumed that he had seen one before and would be able to identify it immediately. "I think it's one of your poppets."

He opened his mouth to correct her and then realized she'd said it the right way. He leaned closer to examine it, then bent one knee to get down close enough for a good look.

"Yes. I think it's you."

"Me? That's not me!"

It didn't have any clothes, for one thing. If they wanted to make a poppet of Reg, it should have a brightly colored skirt, not just bare legs and body. And maybe a scarf around its head, her usual "business attire."

There just wasn't anything about it that screamed "Reg Rawlins."

Well… except that it had dark red yarn hair. It wasn't done in box braids, but the way it was arranged around the doll's head was not unlike how the braids fell around hers.

Reg didn't like the expression stitched into the cloth doll's face. It looked like she had sucked a lemon.

"Do you think… that it's safe to pick it up?" she asked Davyn.

He nodded. "I don't see or feel anything that would indicate it is dangerous or that you would trigger some curse by touching it."

Reg hesitated at that, her hand hovering over it. She didn't particularly like Davyn's answer. He had said that he thought it was safe, but then suggesting danger or a curse made her think twice about what she could risk if she touched it.

"You think?" she asked uncertainly, needing reassurance. "You think it's safe, right? And you would know, you're an experienced warlock. You've been around for a hundred years, all that?"

He smiled. "I could be wrong. But I don't think I am."

"Well… great." Reg still considered it for a few minutes and didn't touch it immediately. Davyn didn't think it was dangerous. It didn't look dangerous. There weren't any runes or candles around it, anything that indicated to Reg that it was part of a spell. However, she knew it was impossible to tell just by looking at an object whether it was charmed or cursed. She hovered her hand over it, but couldn't sense any evil intention. If anything, she felt a warming reaction. As if it were friendly, intended for her, and she should take it home and find a place for it.

Maybe it was just a friendly gift from an anonymous admirer.

Reg allowed her fingers to close around it.

Nothing bad happened. Reg tried to monitor both her environment and her own reaction to it. Physical, mental, emotional, whether it did anything to her powers. But it didn't harm her.

Reg was able to examine it more closely. She took it out from under the shadows of the trees to the sunny part of the lawn and looked at it in the light of day.

The face seemed a little more cheerful in the sunlight. Maybe it had just been a strange smile that had made it look so unhappy while lying on the ground. It looked like something that a six-year-old might have made, and Reg wondered fleetingly whether she had made it herself as a child and Harrison was returning it to her from wherever she had lost it in the past. It might have been her own attempt at a comfort object, a little friend like herself to keep her company when she was cold, hungry, and afraid.

Ember trotted over and sniffed the doll. He didn't react negatively either and, like Davyn, he immediately associated it with Reg. It was definitely made to represent her, however crudely it was made.

"Well, there's nothing else to find out here," Davyn concluded. "But I think the situation is worrisome enough to warrant calling the police. He obviously did not go home or to one of his other work sites. He would not have left his truck here. He was hired to stay with you and protect you, and his disappearance is alarming."

Davyn's tone was grave. Reg wondered if he were remembering when he had been kidnapped. If that was the right word for what had happened to him, trapped in a cold, dark void between worlds. He hadn't talked about it much. Reg was the one person that he could have spoken to about it. She was the one who had gone there to find him, had found a way to get him out. No one else had been there. They could try to describe it in terms that humans could understand but, unless someone had actually been there, there was no way for them to understand exactly what Davyn had gone through.

She should probably encourage him to talk about it. She had often been pushed into talk therapy as a child. She'd often been told how important it was to bring the traumas and secrets out into the light of day rather than hiding them. It was the only way to heal.

Only she had never found it particularly healing. She preferred to bury it. To leave it behind her, part of the past that she didn't ever have to revisit. That was what she wanted. And maybe that was what Davyn wanted too. She could respect that.

Reg turned toward the gate. Back to safety. Was she going to call the police about Damon? Did she really want to call them twice in a row and have some cop telling her that she had to wait twenty-four or forty-eight hours to report Damon missing unless she had something compelling to indicate that he had been kidnapped or harmed? What proof did she have? Maybe she needed to get one of those doorbell cameras. So that next time she would have some evidence that something had happened in the yard.

Though she wasn't sure she wanted to chance catching Ember on video. The police might think she was some kind of prankster if they saw the young dragon on video.

Reg just wanted to get back inside where it was safe and to find a place to showcase her new doll.

CHAPTER FORTY-FIVE

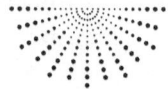

*R*eg stopped with her hand on the gate, making Davyn and Ember come to a sudden halt behind her.

"Something wrong?" Davyn asked.

"Yes. I think there is."

"I mean besides Damon being missing. We're going to do what we can about that situation."

"No… this." Reg turned back toward him, showing him the poppet again.

"Yes. What about it?"

"It *wants* me to take it into the cottage."

Davyn raised his brows skeptically. "It wants you to?"

"Yeah. It does. It's nice and comforting and warm and it wants me to take it home and put it in my house."

Alarm registered on Davyn's face for the first time. "It does?"

"Yeah. I'm thinking… that's probably not such a good idea."

Davyn looked back at the gate, the physical representation of how far the magical wards protecting the yard and cottage extended.

"Right now, you are protected. If you take this object beyond that barrier… perhaps not."

Reg nodded her agreement. "Maybe I should have Sarah take a

look at it. See if she can sense anything about the spell that is on it."

"I think you've probably divined everything there is to be divined. That it has been charmed in some way that you would have an affinity for it and want to bring it into your house. Whoever left it here did not do so lightly. They wanted you to pick it up and take it home."

"So that they can get into the house?"

"Maybe. I don't know. A pixie can bypass protective wards to retrieve something that belongs to him. The same kind of magic may have been placed on this doll. Maybe taking it in will open up a passageway behind you, allowing the maker in as well. Or maybe the poppet will work on you some other way. Make you want to stay in the cottage with it and not go back out again. Cloud your mind or judgment in some other way."

Reg walked back into the shade of the trees. There was a lump in her throat as she looked at the spot where she had found the doll.

"I don't want to put it back."

"No. But I think you're right. You need to."

Reg reluctantly laid it down on the ground. It hurt to have to leave it behind, but that just told her how strong the spell placed upon it was.

Crouching beside her, Davyn passed his hand through the space between Reg's hand and the poppet, muttering a few words Reg didn't understand.

"What was that?"

"A severing spell. You reacted quickly enough that there is hopefully no harm done. You can just leave it here and not be affected by it."

Reg swallowed hard and nodded. "Good."

"Now, let's go back in. But first—how about a fire?"

Reg blinked at him. "Now?"

It wasn't even one of the days that Davyn normally mentored her. And it seemed like a very odd time to suggest one.

"Fire is purifying. I would like to be sure that we have done everything we can to make sure you have shed any spell that might be on that poppet."

"Okay. What do you want me to do?"

"Just a fireball to start out with. Routine warm-up."

Standing straight, Reg held her hands up in front of her, as if holding a soccer ball between them. She moved her hands around, kindling a small ball of blue flame between them. Davyn walked her through a few of her usual exercises. Nothing difficult or out of the ordinary.

"Extinguish it," Davyn prompted, pushing his hands together as an example. Reg brought her hands together, reabsorbing the ball of fire.

"Is that it?"

"No. I want you to let it come back out. Not through your hands. Or not just through your hands. Through every pore in your body, so that you are engulfed in flame from head to toe."

Reg looked at Davyn, her mouth open. She had never performed that procedure before. It sounded quite advanced. "Are you sure?"

He chuckled. "Of course I'm sure. Do you think you can do that?"

"Of course."

Reg stood still, closed her eyes, and let the fire exude from every pore. She felt powerful and centered. While she had meditated with a small flame before, she had never done anything like this. Her fire danced over her skin. She could feel it laughing, almost hear it singing.

"Okay," Davyn said. "Pull back gradually. Let it sink back into you. Nothing sudden; just let it melt back inside."

As reluctant as Reg was to obey, she breathed deeply and tried to do exactly as Davyn said. Just let it melt back into her until she could no longer see or feel it. She took a few more cleansing breaths and looked at Davyn. His eyes were shining.

"I forget how good you are," he laughed. "We've worked so hard on self-control and in mastering each individual step before advancing on to anything more difficult that I completely forget how naturally firecasting comes to you and how powerful you are."

Reg's cheeks heated in a way they hadn't done when she had been engulfed in flame. She smiled in pleasure at the praise.

"How do you feel?" Davyn asked.

"Incredible. It's... like that perfect high you hear about the first time someone tries coke or heroin. Everything just feels right, and clean, and perfect."

"Good. I think it's had the effect I was hoping for. Let's go inside before someone calls the fire department."

Reg laughed and followed him into the yard.

Everything seemed to be more brilliantly colored and more exquisitely detailed than she'd ever seen it before. She'd walked through the yard and garden many times before, but it was like she was seeing it for the first time. And every branch, stem, and bud was perfect. Reg felt a shiver of pleasure. The world was an amazing place. And here she was, living in it.

"You're going to float right away," Davyn chuckled, putting his hand on her arm as if to anchor her to the ground. "You'd better stay down here with us mortals for a while!"

"Why would I want to?"

"It's the way we're made. This will fade over time, and you'll realize you're just as mortal as the rest of us."

Reg hadn't shared with everyone the possibility of her immortal parentage. Maybe she was mortal, and maybe she wasn't. Who could tell?

"Let's go in," Davyn indicated the cottage's front door. "Unless you've had some insight about what happened to Damon while in your... elevated state."

"No. But let's ask Starlight."

CHAPTER FORTY-SIX

*R*eg and Davyn entered the house, and Ember stuck his head in. Reg wondered whether he had noticed how much smaller the house was getting as he was growing. It had to be disconcerting for him that he'd been able to fly around the room as a hatchling, but now getting in the doorway and moving around the rooms without knocking things down was something of a challenge.

After rubbing against the doorjamb and backing in and out a few times like a cat trying to decide whether to go outside, Ember finally decided that he was going in as well. Reg shut the door behind him. She didn't worry about locking the doors this time. If someone thought that they could take on Reg, Davyn, a dragon, Starlight, and possibly Sarah if she noticed that something was wrong or came over to talk to Reg or Davyn, then they deserved what they got. It would take a half dozen warlocks to match them, and only if a couple of them were pretty powerful.

Starlight was not in the living room or kitchen and did not come out to see Reg or Davyn. And Reg knew exactly why. She headed for the bedroom. Starlight was sitting on the windowsill and did not turn around to look at her.

"Quit pouting," Reg told him. "I want to talk to you. Come on out and talk to me and Davyn."

His ear was back, indicating that he was listening to her but, otherwise, he gave no sign. He didn't move, staring out the window as if watching the most thrilling movie ever.

"I know you can hear me. And I could just come over there and pick you up, you know. I can shut the doors so that you don't have any choice but to sit with us and listen to what we have to say."

She couldn't make him communicate with her, though. She couldn't force him if he decided he wasn't going to.

"Look... I could *really* use your help. We need to understand what is going on with the harbor attacks and people disappearing. And I think you and Horace might have some idea about it. Won't you come talk to us about it?"

He cocked his other ear back and turned his head very slightly. He still wasn't looking at her, but it was a little closer.

"It would help us so much," Reg coaxed, trying to appeal to his ego. "You're the only one I can think of that might be able to show us what is going on. The humans are just going to keep running around chasing their tails and never figuring it out."

He looked directly at her.

"I know, humans don't have tails. It's ironic."

He stared at her for a long time, green eye and blue eye unblinking.

"The humans have no idea," Reg repeated.

She could feel his somewhat angry response. The humans *did* know what was going on. Because it was humans who were doing it.

"Well, the humans we are working with, the ones who are trying to stop the attacks, they don't have any idea. They are as helpless as kittens."

Starlight finally conceded, jumping down from the windowsill and marching past Reg back out to the living room area where Ember and Davyn were waiting. He arched his back and hissed at the sight of the dragon, who now took up half the room. Ember blew back a stream of fire at him.

"Hey," Reg growled. "No fire in the house!"

Ember hung his head, but he still watched Starlight with a gleam in his eye. He was glad, she supposed, to be so much bigger than Starlight now. The cat who had once seemed his equal when he was a hatchling of just a few days old was now so much smaller.

But Starlight still had a few tricks up his sleeve. He might be a cat, but he wasn't *just* a cat. Things were not always as they seemed.

"So…" Davyn looked a little amused by Reg's suggestion. "You're hoping that Starlight might be able to help us."

"I think he can," Reg agreed. She sat down on one of the chairs and faced him. "Star… you've been going out at nights with Horace. You haven't been here when I've woken up from sleep-walking."

He cocked his head slightly, looking at her. Waiting for her to ask a question, or just not ready to reveal anything yet?

"Horace-Merneith said that you had been helping creatures in need," Reg said, filling Davyn in at the same time as she tried to establish the facts with Starlight. "I thought… I wondered who you were helping. Is it… are you helping other cats or people?"

Starlight put his ears back and looked at Ember. Reg looked at Ember, surprised at Starlight's reaction. Ember hadn't done anything that Reg had seen. He was just sitting there, in the space near the door, as compactly as possible.

"What is it?"

She caught flashes of a vision from Ember. Sleek cat shadows running through the streets at night. They were all black silhouettes. She couldn't see their colors or markings. Starlight might have been one of them, or it might just have been generic cats. Something that Ember had seen or imagined? Did he already know about Starlight being out at night?

"There are more cats," Reg mused, thinking about the picture. "Are you helping with a feral cat colony? I know that people have programs to try to limit the number of outdoor cats. It's dangerous for them out there."

Starlight's aura was both irritated and seemed to affirm her words. So maybe that was what Starlight and Horace had been doing. Helping unfortunate animals who didn't have proper homes. But how could they help? Other cats couldn't exactly give the street cats a home. Starlight had not brought home any stray kittens to try to convince her to adopt. Cat colonies could get quite large. For that kind of rescue, they would need to involve the Humane Society or some kind of cat sanctuary.

"Oh. Marian said that she got her new cat from a cat sanctuary. I just thought she meant the pound, but… is there a cat sanctuary? Somewhere different?"

Confirmation flowed from Starlight.

"I've heard of one outside the town limits," Davyn said. "I don't know the actual name of it. I've only ever heard it referred to as 'the cat sanctuary.' It must have a name. Anyway, I've heard they do good work."

"You haven't ever thought of getting a cat?" Reg asked.

"I never thought that I would have a familiar. I didn't have any particular affinity for any animals. It has been quite a revelation to have a fire drake." He looked over at Ember, smiling. "That's not something you can usually just pick up at the Humane Society."

Reg chuckled. Everyone she knew of who had seen Ember so far had said the same thing—that he was the only dragon they had ever seen. That they didn't even know that there were still dragons in the world. They were a very rare magical species. Not extinct, obviously, but definitely on the endangered magical species list.

Reg saw the lithe, shadowy forms of cats in her mind again and looked toward Ember. The vision changed and clarified; she could see the remnants of ancient buildings, trees silhouetted in the moonlight, and cats. Lots of cats.

She held on to the vision, studying it, trying to learn as much as possible from the picture.

"Is that the sanctuary?" she asked. "I thought it would be… all kennels in modern buildings. Maybe a playroom to get them out of their cages and have some exercise and socialization. This looks very… ancient and magical. Are all of the cats… er…" She tried to think of the right words. The word that Marta used for the people in Black Sands who had magical gifts was "practitioners," but Reg wasn't sure that would apply to cats. Did cats practice magic? Or did it just... flow through their veins? Starlight had very strong gifts, she knew. Even Sarah had been able to see that he had a very strong psychic aura when Reg had first brought him home. Were all cats more or less magical? Or was it only a percentage of them, like with humans?

"Are all of the cats... gifted?"

Starlight's cocked head and body language seemed to affirm this.

"I guess that's where I should have gone when I was looking for a cat." As soon as the words were out of Reg's mouth, she realized her mistake and covered her lips with a gasp. "I mean—that didn't come out the way I intended—I mean, if I had known that there was a cat sanctuary nearby with cats that were all magical, I would probably have gone there instead of to the Humane Society. But that would have been the wrong choice, because then I would never have found you."

Starlight glared at Reg. Her cheeks flushed in embarrassment.

"I'm sorry! I didn't mean that I should have gone somewhere else. That would have been awful."

She remembered finding Starlight in the cage at the pound. How sad and alone he had looked. Little did she know what a powerfully magic creature he was and how his spiritual life extended all the way back to Bastet. Why had he been in that cage when he could have been free, helping the other cats or living at the cat sanctuary himself?

"Were you just waiting for me there? Did you know that's where I was going to go, where we were supposed to meet?"

Starlight walked over to Reg and rubbed against her ankles. Reg bent over and picked him up. "I'm glad you were."

He purred and butted against her chin with his head. She was forgiven for her slip-up.

CHAPTER FORTY-SEVEN

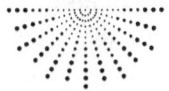

*R*eg's phone rang. She pulled it out and looked at it, feeling like she had traveled back a long distance. Or across time. In the time that she had been talking to Starlight and Ember, she had forgotten that technology and the rest of the world existed.

Looking at the face of her phone was like waking up.

She looked at the name and then had to wonder whether she was, in fact, still asleep. Maybe the whole thing was a dream, from the time that she had woken up to find Damon missing. Maybe he was still home and there was no poppet and no cat sanctuary.

The name on the caller ID was Marta Jessup.

"Marta!" Reg swiped the call to answer and barked her greeting at the same time. "Where are you? I've been trying to get you for two days!"

"I know, Reg." Marta sounded strange and far away. "I've been chasing down some leads and haven't been able to get back to you. And I'm still on the run and can't put this down to deal with anything else. Do you think I could come by your house and pick up the... you-know-what?"

"The cat's paw?" Reg asked. "Yes, please do. I want to get it out of the house. It's creepy."

"Is it okay if I come straight over now? I need it for some testing. If you could just bring it out to me at the curb…"

She really *was* in a hurry. Marta usually had time to at least come into the cottage and have a cup of tea while they discussed developments or just gossiped.

"Does that mean you have a lead? On the Cabal of the Withered Paw?"

"I hope so. But I'm going to need that thing for testing."

What kind of testing did she need to do on an old, petrified paw? She supposed there might be some contact DNA from whoever had owned or handled it last. But that wouldn't really lead them anywhere unless they already had a suspect or the individual had a criminal record with his DNA on file.

"Okay. Just let me know when you're here, and I'll bring the paw out."

When she terminated the call, she looked at Davyn. He was staring at her, his eyes wide and his skin pale.

Reg looked around her for what might have upset him and shook her head, not understanding. "What?"

"The cat's paw? The Cabal of the Withered Paw?"

"Oh." Reg realized with embarrassment that she hadn't told him anything about the cabal and that she was afraid they were involved in the attacks and of taking Damon. She should have filled him in on all of the details. "Yeah. I guess I didn't tell you about that part of it."

"About the cabal being involved in any of this? Yes, you might have neglected to do that."

"Sorry. I was worried about Damon, and it doesn't make any difference who might have taken him. Does it?"

"It would still be nice to know. I can understand why we need to take extra precautions with security if this has something to do with that ancient cult."

"So you know about them, huh? I guess you would. You're part of this community. I didn't know how many people even knew that they existed."

"Everyone in these parts knows the tales. But most do not believe that the cabal exists. It's more like…"

"Santa Claus."

"Yes, I suppose," Davyn agreed. "Something that everyone has heard about and had some fun with, but no one believes that they are real. Except—I do."

"Believe in Santa Claus?"

"Believe that the cabal exists."

That startled Reg. Even Corvin had acted like he didn't believe they could be back, that they would start up again despite the evidence of the cat's paw and the attacks.

"You believe that they exist? Do you think that they could be back?"

"What was that phone call?"

"Marta Jessup. She wanted to know if she could stop by to get the cat's paw back."

"To get it back?"

Reg looked over at the coffee table. She realized that she had put Damon's bag down on top of the table, covering up the cat's paw. She lifted it off to reveal the relic. Damon drew back automatically. Then he leaned forward to have a better look.

"Where did you get it from? How long have you had it?"

"A couple of days. Marta brought it by to see if I could feel anything." Reg shrugged. "You know, who the owner was, what its purpose is. If there is anything that I could divine from it that would help her with her case."

"Which is?"

"The harbor attacks. This paw was dropped by one of the attackers during the incident."

"Can I pick it up?"

"Sure. As long as you leave it in the bag, I don't see what harm you could do. Or what harm it could do."

"You have this in your house, and you wonder why people are trying to get in here?"

Reg shook her head slowly. "I never said I couldn't understand it." Though, truth be told, she had not directly connected the attack at the grocery store or the intruders in her front yard with the cat's paw. She just knew that she was being attacked and threatened.

"How long have they been trying to get this back?"

"I've only had it for a couple of days. I wasn't really thinking about it. There's been... other stuff going on too."

"Well, it's good that you're getting it out of the house. You should be much safer with it gone."

"So you believe in the cabal?"

"As the leader of a coven like this... you hear things. Things that other people may never be privy to. And there have been... whisperings that the cabal had reformed."

"Corvin acted like I was crazy to believe it could be around. Like the stories were just invented to scare children."

"You talked to Corvin about it?"

"Well, he was the only one I could think of." Reg scratched her burning ears as if he might not notice how red she was getting. Why had she not gone to her mentor instead of a dangerous warlock like Corvin? "He's... you know... a professor, and he knows about magical artifacts. I thought he might know something about the cat's paw. Its origins. Who the current owner was."

"And he told you not to worry your pretty little head over it."

Reg grimaced. "More or less."

"It didn't occur to you that if this cabal was back again, he might be very likely to be involved in it himself?"

"Well, yes, once I knew about it. Before I asked him, I didn't know anything about it, so I couldn't expect him to be its leader if I didn't know it existed."

"Do you think he's the leader of the cabal?"

Reg swallowed. "I thought he might be. Or at least... that he might have something to do with the cat's paw. Because of..." Reg looked over at Ember. "Well, when Ember came here that one night, the night that I brought him back to you..."

Davyn nodded. "Yes."

"And I asked him about it, and he showed me a vision of a man with a black cloak that was edged with red. And Harrison had been talking about hiding Corvin's mantle, so I thought… maybe that was the one he was talking about."

"Harrison hid Corvin's mantle?"

"Yeah. But Corvin said that the one for your coven was just pure black, no red on it. Then he told me about the cabal and the red-edged cloak."

Davyn looked at Reg steadily. She wasn't sure what else he was expecting. "Do you still think that the red-edged cloak might belong to Corvin?"

"Well… yes, it's possible. I don't know. It isn't like he always tells the truth. He could be the leader of your coven and the secret cabal, couldn't he?"

Davyn sighed, leaning back. He put the paw back down on the coffee table. "I would hope not. It isn't like there isn't enough to do in the coven without adding a second, secret coven on top of that." He shook his head briskly. "I don't see how someone could take on both positions at the same time."

"He could have someone else run one of them. A deputy. Someone he trusted."

"Maybe his son?"

"Maybe." Reg paused. "But I don't think Corvin trusts John. Or that he should."

"I certainly wouldn't," Davyn agreed.

"Maybe John is the one who is looking after the cabal, and Corvin is looking after your coven. Corvin in the black cloak, and John in the red-edged cloak."

It fit together nicely. But they needed more than a theory that sort of worked.

"Marta said that there is a break in the case. That was why she wanted to come here to get the cat's paw. And I'll be happy to have it out of here."

"I'm sure you will. I don't imagine Starlight has been too happy about it."

Reg shook her head. "He really reacted to it negatively when Marta first brought it."

"I'll bet. I hope she has something concrete that she can use against the cabal, whoever has resurrected it, however it is being run."

Reg's phone buzzed, and she saw a text from Marta.

"There she is! I'll just run this out to her."

218

CHAPTER FORTY-EIGHT

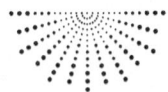

*R*eg was still holding Starlight when she reached over to pick up the cat's paw, which was a big mistake. Starlight yowled and hissed and was gone from Reg's arms, leaving them deeply scratched, blood welling to the surface. Reg swore a few times before she could get herself under control. Starlight had dashed off to the bedroom, and she wouldn't be able to get him back out any time soon. And she didn't have time to convince him she was sorry now. She needed to get the relic to Marta, and then she could try to make up with her cat.

"I'll be right back," Reg promised Davyn, and dashed for the door.

"Uh—Reg!"

She ignored his call and ran out to the front yard and toward Marta's car, pulled over at the curb.

"Ember, stay here. Guard the house," Davyn snapped.

She heard the cottage door slam. Davyn had apparently decided he needed to follow her for safety. She let him trail behind her. By the time he caught up to her, she would be finished with the handoff and heading back to the cottage. It would be as quick as a relay race.

Reg darted up to the car. Marta had not rolled down the window, so Reg jerked on the car door handle to open it and hand the cat's paw to Marta.

And that was her final mistake.

* * *

Reg awoke much later, groaning. Her head pounded and she knew that she hadn't woken from a regular sleep. Her whole body hurt. And more than her body. She felt like her brain and inner self had been beaten up too.

She was disoriented, unsure where she was even when she pried her sticky eyelids open and looked around.

There was a groan beside her. Reg turned her head to look at the man to confirm that the voice and the life force she could feel next to her was Davyn.

"Davyn? Are you okay?"

He groaned again. But in a moment, he acknowledged the question. "I'm in one piece… you?"

"I'm not sure yet." Reg wasn't sure she could feel all of her limbs. Maybe they had chopped something off, and sent it to someone they hoped would pay a ransom to save her having anything else cut off. But she was pretty sure the usual protocol was to start small, maybe an ear or a finger.

She blinked hard, trying to get tears to bathe her dry eyes. Had they been open while she had been unconscious? It felt like she hadn't blinked in hours. Maybe even all day. She couldn't help groaning again.

"What happened? Where are we?"

"I don't know. We were at your house," Davyn recalled.

Reg tried to remember, but everything was fuzzy. They had been at the cottage. She, Davyn, Ember, and Starlight. And then what?

"But where are we now?"

"I don't know," Davyn said patiently. "I don't know any more than you do yet. Something happened. We were at your house and now we're here. I don't know where here is or why."

"Is there anything to drink?" Reg's mouth and throat were almost as dry as her eyes.

She could hear Davyn stirring beside her.

"Can you sit up?" Davyn asked. "It will help you to get your head straight faster."

Reg didn't think she could. She was too muddled even for that. Davyn nudged her. "Come on, Reg. We're not tied up. You can sit up."

"Why would I want to?"

"So you can be ready when they come back."

Reg didn't like the sound of that. She eventually opened her eyes again and tried to figure out where she was. But she couldn't see much, and eventually decided that she'd better do what Davyn suggested and sit up. Her whole body was bruised and exhausted. She wasn't even sure which way was up. But eventually, she managed to sit up.

It helped ease the disorientation. She could see which way was up and down and the rest of the small room they were being held in.

It wasn't much. Bare and cell-like. She and Davyn were on the floor. There was no bed, no furniture at all, but a wooden chair in one corner. Not even one chair each. Not that Reg felt like she could get up to sit on a chair yet anyway, but if you were going to kidnap two people, you should at least provide them with two chairs.

"Were we kidnapped?" she asked Davyn, not sure where that had come from. Did she actually know what had happened? Did he?

"I… maybe. I can't be sure," he admitted. "I don't remember what happened. But considering that we seem to be locked in this empty room together… I would say so."

"We don't know the door is locked."

"I'm sure when we get around to trying that, it will be. But I'm just going to sit here and rest for a bit longer."

"How could they kidnap us? Weren't we careful?"

Davyn laughed.

Reg was offended. They *had* been careful, hadn't they? She had called Davyn for help. The two of them should have protected each other. And Ember had been there too. How did you capture two people in front of a dragon? Ember always came to Reg's aid, so where was he now? Could he not sense her because she had not been conscious? Now that she was, she should reach out to him, and he would come and help her. They hadn't made a cage that was dragon-proof yet. That meant he could break out of—or into—any prison.

But she was too mentally exhausted to reach out to him. It would have to wait until later.

"Marta was coming to get the cat's paw," Reg remembered.

There was no response from Davyn at first. He just sat beside her, breathing. He was probably just as exhausted and disoriented as she was. "Did you give it to her?"

"I don't know. I don't remember."

"If we didn't, then she knows by now that something happened to us," Davyn reassured her. "She can report it to her superiors... or whoever it is supposed to go to."

"We were in a car."

"Mmm." He considered. "Yes, I think we were."

"Why were we in a car?"

"We must have been going somewhere."

Reg growled, frustrated that she couldn't seem to dredge anything up, and Davyn was either having the same problem or was being intentionally unhelpful.

"Okay then, how about this one? *Where* are we?"

They again looked around the bare room, looking for clues about where they were. It was an interior room with no windows, so she didn't know if it were day or night or have any visual clues as to where they were. If she had watched where they were taken while in the car or had listened to the various auditory clues like they did on TV thrillers, it had been pointless, because she could no longer remember it. But it was there, so maybe it would return to her in a few minutes.

Or a few hours.

Or a few years.

How long had they even been there?

CHAPTER FORTY-NINE

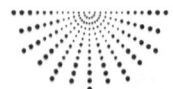

*D*avyn. Davyn!" Reg Reached over and shook Davyn's arm when she resurfaced and realized they had both fallen back asleep sitting up against the wall. More time had passed. How much was anyone's guess. "Wake up. We have to figure this out."

Davyn stirred and rubbed his eyes. He didn't open them. "There were two poppets," he said drowsily, like he was talking in his sleep.

"Two? No, there was just one, under the tree, where we found it. I remember that."

"But in the car, the was another one."

Reg was about to deny it, but a fuzzy recollection came back to her. Looking up to the front seat of the car to see who was there and seeing two poppets, not just one, sitting on top of the little sunglasses tray in the dash.

"Two poppets. Yeah. I guess... one for me and one for you."

"Why? What are they doing?" Davyn mused.

"They've obviously been stabbing them with needles," Reg said. "I'm so sore. I feel like I was thrown down the stairs. Or my poppet was."

Davyn grunted. Reg assumed he felt the same way.

Reg leaned her head against the wall, resting, waiting for her strength to return.

She must have fallen back asleep, because she next woke up with the opening of the door.

She blinked and looked at the figure standing there, trying to sort everything out. She recognized the skinny young man, but couldn't remember where from.

"Who are you?"

He blinked at her. "Chevy."

Reg frowned. She was pretty sure she had never heard anyone called Chevy before. "Like the car?"

"No… like *Chevalier*. But I'm not putting that on my name tag."

On his name tag? Reg studied his pale face and red hair, trying to put it all together. He could see she was having difficulty.

"From the grocery store?" he prompted her. "You've seen me at the grocery store."

"Oh! You're one of the clerks. You were there when I had my accident."

"Yeah." He smirked. "I was there when you had your *accident*."

She saw it all in a flash. Someone slamming into her, pushing her into the pyramid of salsa jars. Had that been him? He had intentionally pushed her into the display. She could have been badly injured or killed. And then afterward, he had grabbed her and jerked her out of the pile, potentially exacerbating any injuries she did have. She glanced aside at Davyn to see if he were awake and taking this all in. His eyes were open, but his expression was vague and she didn't know if he was getting it or not.

"Were you trying to kill me? Why did you do that?"

He just smiled and shook his head. "Why would I do that?"

"I don't know. I don't understand what's going on here. Why are we here? Why are you holding us hostage?"

"It takes time. You cannot rush magic like this. It needs to grow and mature. We need to wait until it's time. Then we will act."

"We? Who is we?"

He cocked his head slightly. "The cabal."

"*You* are in the cabal?"

"I *am* the cabal. Me and a few others." He snickered at her. "People you wouldn't even consider. People you overlook all the time. You don't even see them around you."

Davyn stiffened beside Reg, and she could feel his worry and anger over this revelation.

"I thought it was Corvin," Reg told Chevy. "Or maybe John Saunders."

"They already have a coven. They have settled for something inferior. Why would I settle for mediocrity? They haven't had to work for their powers. They don't know what they could achieve if they really put their best efforts into it. But they don't have to. They can just take power directly from whoever they want." His eyes shone at the thought of having such a gift. "And so... they don't. They agree to be bound by rules and ethics of the less powerful population, to limit themselves voluntarily. Why would anyone do that?"

Reg swallowed. Her head was so thick. She felt dense not being able to take it all in. She felt as if she were coming down with the flu. Headache, body aches, swollen glands, and such fatigue. She could lie down in bed and go to sleep for a week.

"But you're trying to increase your powers naturally," she suggested to Chevy, trying to understand what he was saying. "Through practice and learning..."

He looked at her and laughed. "Why would I do that? Why would I be like all of the rest of you? Don't you know that there is another way? That *you* can do what Corvin Hunter and his kind do without having to deal with the hunger that goes along with his curse?"

"No, I can't," Reg said immediately. Though she knew that Corvin had fed her power in the past and that she had, in fact, pulled power from others without their knowledge. She could pull some strength from others, but that didn't mean she was going to. It wasn't right. She knew how much of a violation what Corvin did was. And most of the practitioners she knew didn't have anything approaching the ability to do what Chevy suggested.

Chevy entered the room and shut the door behind him. He crouched to talk to Reg, bracing his arm against his knee. "Don't you know that there are spells and enchantments that will allow you to access the powers of others? Anyone can do them if they are dedicated enough. But people are ignorant or block themselves, thinking they can't. They don't fully commit to building their powers to beyond what they could ever achieve with 'practice and learning.'"

"What are you talking about? Black magic?"

"There's no such thing as black magic."

Reg had been told this before, and she hadn't believed it then. Witches and warlocks were supposed to promise not to use their powers to harm anyone, but they didn't all honor their covenants. And those like Reg or Damon who were not part of any coven or organization did not make those promises in the first place. Though Reg still felt bound not to harm others with her gifts.

If she could help it.

There had been times when she'd had to defend herself or others, or times when she had not been in control of her powers or even known they existed. Sometimes… things just happened.

But she would never intentionally hurt someone or take their powers without a good reason.

Chevy didn't seem to have any such scruples.

Reg tried to reach out her senses to make contact with Ember, but she was still too tired and muddled to do it.

Chevy laughed, apparently sensing her attempts to overcome whatever drug or potion he had given her or spell he had cast.

"Feeling a little weak at the moment? How would you like that to be the normal state of affairs? How would you like to feel this way all the time?" he asked, taking apparent delight in the thought. "And what if there were no voices, no powers, no special gifts? If you were just… like a normal, everyday mortal? How would you like that?"

Reg had felt that emptiness and hollowness before. The loss of her powers, of the voices in her head, the thoughts of the living and dead around her. She couldn't understand how anyone could live with that appalling silence.

"What you are doing is wrong," Reg told him sternly. As if by being stern, she could convince him to give up this enterprise he had set in motion. "You can't kidnap people and steal their powers."

"You're so persistent, did you know that? You're annoying. You and your friends. You keep getting in my way. Showing up at the waterfront with your familiars when you should be sleeping. I don't know how you have hidden the others, but I will find out. When I take your powers, I will know everything you do, and I will be able to retrieve all our other targets as well."

CHAPTER FIFTY

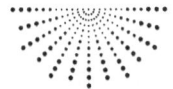

*R*eg tried to hide her surprise at his words.

So the people who had disappeared—the victims of the attacks, Marta, Damon, and whoever else—had not been taken by the cabal?

They were hidden from the cabal, which meant that there was another force at work.

How much else had she missed?

"You will never find out where they are from me," she told him flatly. Which, of course, was true. It wasn't in her brain. She couldn't reveal it to him through any means.

"You think that you can keep it from me? You won't be able to. We will find out where our enemies are. Now that we have this back," Chevy brandished the cat's paw, "*they* can't stop us!"

Though Reg knew that the cat's paw had been made for an evil purpose, she didn't have any idea what it could do, other than repelling cats.

"I don't think that old relic is as powerful as you think it is," she said lightly. "It doesn't really seem to do much."

He laughed. "That goes to show how much you know! They obviously haven't told you much of anything. They're like that, you know. Hold their cards very close to their chests. Don't let anyone get a peek at anything. They're keeping you in the dark. I didn't think our little bluff about giving the paw back to Detective Jessup would work." He smiled proudly, admiring the horrible cat's paw. "But you brought it right to us."

It hadn't been Marta on the phone or in the car at all, it was all just a ruse for the cabal to get the paw back.

"It's not going to help you," Reg persisted, as if she knew what she was talking about.

"We've studied the records of the ancient cabal. We know what brought them down in the past. We knew we would have to battle the creatures. As long as we have the withered paw, they don't have a chance. The cabal would never have fallen if it had not been taken from them by a traitor. A turncoat."

Reg wished he would quit brandishing the paw like it was some sort of wand or weapon. The poor creature that it had been taken from...

Reg blinked, suddenly making a connection. She tried to keep her expression masked to prevent him from seeing the light bulb going on as she connected his use of creatures to hers.

Cats.

Was he talking about fighting the cats? That the ancient Cabal of the Withered Paw had previously been brought down by cats?

She knew from the day that Marta brought the paw to her for examination that it repelled Starlight. He wouldn't get anywhere near it. She had thought it was simply because it was from another cat and he didn't like the idea. Just as she had been panicked by the sight of human skulls in Tybalt's lair.

But was it more than that? Was the *power* of the withered paw the fact that it repelled cats? Not just the idea of it, but its magical properties?

"The cats are still smarter than you are," Reg tried. "They will still find a way to defeat you, just like the last time."

"Not this time!" Chevy shouted. "They can't!"

"Why do you think you keep losing it? If it was so important to you, how did you lose it in the attack at the waterfront? Do you think it was just an accident? It's cursed so that you can't even hold on to it. No matter how much you want to defeat the cats, they are going to get the upper hand." Reg chuckled. "Or rather, the upper paw."

Chevy's jaw worked as he ground his teeth, trying to control his anger at her. Even though Reg recognized his fury at being taunted, she couldn't stop herself from poking at him. That had been her trouble as a kid, too. Even though she recognized the anger, realized that the man was a danger to her, she couldn't help needling him. Pushing him closer to the edge. When she pushed him far enough, he would lose control and, as much as she feared his response, she knew that he would be most vulnerable when he lost control. When he stopped thinking things through and simply reacted in anger.

"You are wrong," he told her, teeth gritted, leaning forward so he was right in her face. "When the spell is ready, I will take everything from you—your powers and gifts, your memories, everything that goes along with them. And then I will know where the sanctuary is. We will be prepared to do battle against them. They will not be able to touch us as long as we have the paw, and we will walk in and take what is ours. Each person who waits there for us is ripe for the picking. All of those powers, just waiting. It takes time for the spell to come to fruition but, when it does, you will not be able to stop me."

The sanctuary. He was looking for a sanctuary where, apparently, the people the cabal had targeted were being protected. She thought first of the ancient temple ruins she had been to while looking for Davyn when he had disappeared. She had gone there to talk to the coven, who were there for some kind of ritual. But the temple was not a sanctuary, was it? It was only ruins, barely visible lines in the ground where the foundations had been. No one lived there or could be held there for any length of time. Not humans and not cats.

The only sanctuary she had heard of was…

"The cat sanctuary," Reg murmured.

Chevy flinched. He quickly covered up the reaction, but Reg had seen it.

"Yes, the cat sanctuary," Chevy spit out. "Don't pretend ignorance with me. I know you're working with them. I've heard about your cat. I've seen him. The little black and white tux with mismatched eyes." Chevy's own eyes blazed. He looked truly demonic, but Reg wasn't going to let him see how he intimidated her. She stared back at him, keeping her face expressionless.

"The cat sanctuary is just a place for rescued cats," she told him with a shrug. "If you think it's some kind of cat battalion..." She laughed and shook her head.

He slapped her.

Reg stayed still as a statue, not backing down. Davyn, next to her, moved sluggishly, still weak and wobbly, thinking he could take on the strong and capable young man. He fell over on his side, grunting in pain as he landed.

Reg's face stung. But she continued to stare at Chevy as if he hadn't even touched her. It had woken her up. Sharpened her mind. The adrenaline was flowing now, affecting every part of her body, readying her for the battle ahead.

"You *know*." Chevy raged. "Just a refuge for poor neglected animals? The cat sanctuary was not built by humans to protect cats. It was designed by the cats as a haven for human victims!"

Reg's brain was whirling, trying to put all the pieces together and understand the whole picture. Horace and Starlight had not been rescuing cats, but humans. The very humans that the cabal had targeted. Somehow taking them between the time they were attacked and when the spell the cabal wove against them using the poppets matured. So that the cabal was prevented from achieving their goals. They could not steal the powers from people who were given sanctuary by the cats.

"And the cats will keep them safe," Reg told him. "You'll never defeat them, even with your old relic. Isn't it ironic that you can't steal their powers because you aren't powerful enough?"

He slapped her other cheek, then stormed out of the room, shutting the heavy door behind him. Reg listened to the door click shut and studied it. She had no doubt that it locked behind Chevy. But what kind of lock? Reg had been practicing manipulating locks ever since she had first arrived in Black Sands, when she had needed Sarah to rescue her because she and Corvin had not been able to defeat the locks and spells in the trap they had sprung.

Davyn was struggling to get back into an upright position. "Reg? Are you okay? I'm so sorry. I wanted to help, but I'm so weak…"

"I know. I don't know what they've done to our poppets, but it's really doing a number on me too. But we can't wait. When their spell is finished, if they can steal our powers from us…" She got a hard, hot lump in her throat. She couldn't face the loss of her gifts. Not again.

"We'll figure something out," Davyn promised, working against the wall to get himself back into an upright seated position. "We'll put our heads together and come up with something."

Two firecasters together would be a hard duo to beat. They could burn the whole building down around them. No need to unlock any doors, they could just ignite the whole thing and walk out of the burning ruins to safety.

But she still wasn't sure where they were. It might be a storage room in the back of the grocery store. There might be a lot of innocent people in the building who would be in danger if they just burned the building down.

Reg tried to reach out with her senses to find out how many other people were in the building. She could usually establish that very quickly. But despite the adrenaline rush and her desperation, she could barely sense Davyn's heartbeat beside her.

So how were they going to get out? If Chevy and his cabal kept her and Davyn in their weakened state until the spell was developed enough to use it to steal their powers, what opportunity would they have to escape?

CHAPTER FIFTY-ONE

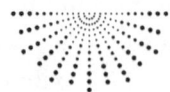

*R*eg tried to find some strength within her. Davyn seemed to be even weaker than she was. Maybe they had been more worried about him and put a stronger spell on him or given him a second dose of drugs, if they were using more conventional methods.

"Keep talking to me," Reg told him, not wanting to be left alone with her own thoughts. The two of them had to work together to find a way out of the fix they were in.

"We'll figure something out," Davyn assured her, slurring slightly.

"Then stick with me. Don't fall back asleep."

As Davyn's breathing settled into a long, even pattern, she felt alone and abandoned. How could he just fall asleep and leave her to her own devices? She couldn't figure this out all by herself.

The voices in her head were more muted than usual. She would have been worried that Chevy and the Cabal had already taken some of her powers if he hadn't told her they had to wait until the spell was ready. She focused on the voices. Her first instinct was to close her eyes to focus on them better, but she was too afraid that, like Davyn, she would fall asleep. She needed to stay awake and alert as long as possible to find a way to escape.

The siren wail strengthened. For once, she welcomed it instead of trying to shut it out. Ember could draw on the memories of his ancestors. Reg could draw on the consciousness of her siren sisters. She wasn't alone if she could hear them.

She pictured her situation, painting it as vividly as she could to the sirens. They hated each other, competed for territory, and would never live any closer to each other than they had to, but her sisters would not let Reg die a pointless death or have her powers stripped away from her.

Help me, Reg told them. *Yours are the only voices I can hear. What am I going to do?*

He cannot hold you, the discordant voices wailed, *break the shackles.*

Reg looked at her arms. *There are no shackles.*

It's figurative, Norma Jean's voice broke away from the others' impatiently. *You must leave.*

I can't leave. I can hardly move. I can't stand up. I'm just... weak as a kitten.

She should have picked another word. The cats were what was holding the cabal back. They were strong. She was as weak as a human, not a cat.

Transform. You have the power. Transform yourself.

More useless encouragement. She had just told them she didn't have the power.

Please help me.

It is within you. You must use your power.

"I can't!" Reg protested aloud, frustrated. "They've suppressed all of my gifts. I can't do anything."

"What?" Davyn murmured from beside her. "I can't do what?"

"The sirens. Why are they so useless? If I could get out of here, don't they think I would?"

Davyn rubbed his forehead. "What did they say?"

"Transform. Transform, use my power. It sounds like some stupid motivational speaker. 'You have the ability to transform your life! You have only to choose! Imagine and you will become!'"

"Transform," Davyn murmured. "Yes!"

Reg turned her head to look at him. "Not you too."

"Sirens are said to have the ability to shift."

"Shift what?" Reg shook her head. She needed to shift her brain. That's what she needed. And to shift her body right out of there.

"The ability to shift into other forms," Davyn straightened and his voice strengthened. "But you haven't ever... changed your form?"

"Changed my form? You mean like a shape-shifter?" Reg shook her head. "Sirens aren't shape-shifters!"

But after she said it, she remembered an encounter she'd had with Mrs. Agnes, another siren, who had appeared to Reg in the form of Eostre until she had been commanded to abandon her disguise and had again appeared to Reg as the little old lady she had originally met. *Sirens could shift?*

"But what good would that do me here?" she demanded. "It isn't like Chevy is going to be confused if I disguise myself as someone else. If he comes in here and Eostre is here instead of Reg, he's not going to be fooled."

"Eostre? Why would Eostre be here?"

"Never mind. I just don't see what shifting into someone else, into some sort of disguise would help."

"Not a human," Davyn said. "Maybe... as a bird, you could escape?"

"A bird?" Reg remembered the crudely drawn bird-woman pictographs she had seen when someone had left the remains of a curse in her yard after people in Black Sands had found out that she was part-siren. Reg had been confused at the thought of sirens being portrayed as bird women when she thought they lived and hunted only in the waters. She still didn't fully understand it, but assumed it was because of their beautiful voices. Or what the sailors purportedly heard as beautiful voices. Beautiful songs, birds—it all lined up.

But she couldn't actually turn herself into a bird. Could she? Could she turn into a bird and fly away? If she waited by the door until Chevy opened it again, and then just flew out, and was gone before he had any idea what had happened...?

That wouldn't help Davyn, of course. How would she get Davyn out of there if she was in the form of a bird?

"I don't know about that." Reg shook her head. "And I don't know how to do it. Do I just think about the form that I want to shift into? Wouldn't I know if I could do that? Wouldn't I have shifted into something else as a child when I was pretending to be something else?"

"I don't know how it works. This is... very ancient stuff. The sirens don't share details about their magic. If you can hear siren voices now... then you should ask them."

Reg sighed. She rubbed her temples, sending her thoughts out to the other sirens once more. *What form can I take? How do I do it? I need a crash course.*

The siren song grew louder, both more discordant and more melodic at the same time. All of the voices singing and speaking together, over top of each other, separate and yet together. If Reg tried to listen to one voice at a time, it grated on her nerves and she quickly lost the thread. She had to pull back and listen to them all simultaneously, not trying to make sense of it, just letting them all wash over her and sort themselves out later. It was no wonder siren song was said to turn men mad.

Pictures formed in her head, at first dark and obscure, but then became psychedelic colors and shapes that looked like a mess until they blended together and turned into something meaningful.

Reg saw all the options in front of her like a buffet. Another human form, in all their many varieties. A bird, soaring up and away from all the trouble, singing her heart out. A fishtail like a mermaid, flashing through the water. Cutting through it like a silver blade. Cool and refreshing and so dangerous to the men she would pull into the water.

And another form. Reg saw it growing and reshaping in her mind. Air, water, and fire. She had her choice. Reg swallowed, watching it, letting it embed itself in her mind.

How do I do it? She asked the sirens. *I know what I want to be. How do I shift to that form?*

She listened to their song. She couldn't hear any individual words anymore. It was a chant, an immersion, something amazing that was too big to explain. Reg rubbed her head, trying to integrate it all into her brain. She might not have genetic memories like Ember, but she had something. Maybe the siren song could be just as useful.

But she had to become one with the siren circle. It wouldn't help her to sit on the outside, asking how to be on the inside. She had to give way, to surrender to them. And everyone had all been telling her not to. To be careful, to know her limits, to beware of power. She had been told over and over again to hold back and stay in control.

Reg couldn't. She had to let go. She had to let it all loose, even if she didn't know what she was doing and what the result would be. Her fire could incinerate everything. With her psychic skills, she could break in and ravage a human mind, breaking it so it was never the same again. She could steal, feed herself, transport herself and others over great distances, all kinds of terrible things.

And she had been told not to. She knew it was dangerous.

Reg swallowed her fears. She pushed away all of the warnings. The only person there with her now was Davyn, and she was trying to save him. She couldn't even heed *his* warnings. He didn't understand her. He could only understand the firecasting, and even then, he had told her she was more powerful than he was. She only needed to learn how to control it and wield it as a tool, carefully, with precision. She had to think before she acted. Just like with everything else.

The sirens didn't ask her to think. They only asked her to sing.

CHAPTER FIFTY-TWO

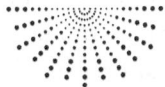

$\mathcal{R}$eg started to hum.

She had always been self-conscious about her singing. She heard her screechy voice and the complaints of schoolmates and foster children who had covered their ears and asked her not to sing. The music teachers who had told her to just move her lips and not to use her voice.

There had been no solos for Reg. Though she had never wanted a solo. She wanted to sing in a choir, to raise her voice with others. And now she wanted to be part of that beautiful discordance she had heard from the other sirens.

She hummed louder. Davyn stirred beside her, letting out a groan, and Reg did not turn to see whether he was covering his ears.

She didn't care what Davyn thought. She was trying to save his life and, if he complained about that afterward, she would deal with it then. She knew what it was like to be stripped of her powers, and she wasn't going to let that happen to someone else if there were anything she could do to prevent it.

Sing, sing, sing!

At first, she could only hum, her mouth tightly shut. Keeping her voice to herself even while she tried to sing with the others. But they kept encouraging her, pulling it out of her. Even Norma Jean, who she had always resisted. Siren mothers and daughters did not have comfortable relationships. They were too territorial. They forced their children to be independent from as young an age as possible. Because otherwise, they would not survive. They might not be like the species who actually consumed their young, but they would kill them in an instant.

But Reg and Norma Jean were far apart, each in their own territories, and that brought harmony of a sort. A different relationship from what they had ever had before. Not in the past life, when Norma Jean had died when Reg was so young, and not in the new timeline, when she had not, and Reg had been removed from the home and not reunited with her until adulthood. Now they were both adults, both women, both equal.

As Reg continued, she gradually obeyed the calls of her siren sisters to open her mouth and let out her voice. Davyn twisted uncomfortably beside her, letting out growls of protest.

"Reg, you're going to rouse everybody in a five-block radius! They're going to come in here and kick you until you stop."

She ignored Davyn and his increasingly violent protests. She knew what she needed to do and, if she were going to save them, she had to do it the right way. A whisper or low hum would not do it.

In full-throated song, she started to feel different. The fatigue she had been burdened with lifted. The brain fog cleared away. Her limbs began to regain their strength.

She was *powerful*. She was *siren*. She was...

Reg got to her feet. The song was swelling, and swelling, and swelling. She felt like she would tear apart with how big and beautiful it was. How had she never known that she could do this? She *could* sing. Not like any human who would ever be on *America's Got Talent* or any other version of the sing-off. The humans who heard enough of her song to think it beautiful were the ones who would be driven mad by it.

She stretched her arms out as wide as they would go, opening up her rib cage and feeling everything growing and expanding. She took up more space. Her muscles grew and swelled with the music. She could no longer control the direction of the music. It was pulling her along now. The siren sisters were leading her, showing her the way. It was no longer *her* song, but *their* song.

"Yes, yes, *now!*"

Her screech of triumph was swallowed up in a roar that shook the whole building. The door opened, and Chevy stood there, staring at Reg with eyes popping out of his head.

She wasn't looking up at him this time. He wasn't across the room from her. He couldn't menace her anymore. This time, she hulked over him, and he immediately cowered, looking for an escape. Reg opened her huge jaws and snapped at him, intentionally missing by a hair's breadth. And then she blew fire straight up in the air, since if she let out that satisfying belch of fire toward Chevy, he would be burned to a crisp. Her fire raced along the ceiling, spreading in every direction. Reg looked sideways at Davyn, evaluating whether he would be able to take strength from her fire to boost his own energy.

Davyn's eyes were wide, but he knew not to fear her. He had seen her fire. He had not seen her in this form before, but he knew the fire that burned within her almost as well as Reg did herself. She blew another breath of fire at the ceiling, and the building materials started to burn. Any fireproofing that had been used was no match for Reg's breath.

Chevy started to run, his arms closing around his head to protect it, running ducked low, closer to the ground, where the air was clearer and not yet superheated.

"Reg," Davyn warned. "Other people. And… your limits. Think about what you've learned."

If she let her fire get out of control, she could be consumed herself or, at the very least, become dehydrated with the effort.

But that was in her human form, not in this new shape.

She wasn't sure she cared about anyone else in the building. They had chosen to be there. At least some of them had imprisoned her, and the rest had probably at least known what was going on. They were not all innocent. And if a few innocents were consumed by fire, what was that to saving herself and Davyn?

The sirens had to protect themselves as a species. No sacrifice was too great if it would keep them alive.

And Davyn was her mentor—someone who understood fire.

In this form, Reg had mastery of all of the elements she wished to. The fire was hers and always would be. Water was hers as a siren. Her territory. Her home. What she gathered strength from. If she hunted on the water, no one could quote the human-siren compact signed hundreds of years earlier at her. She was entitled to pursue whatever she liked on the water.

And the air?

As the ceiling burned away above her, Reg gathered her strength and jumped and flapped her wings, and burst through what was left of the roof.

She was out.

She was free.

She was flying.

CHAPTER FIFTY-THREE

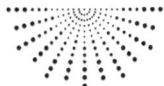

*I*n this form, she had no problem reaching out her mind to touch Ember's. She wasn't using her pale human telepathy or even her stronger siren consciousness that could spread out to connect all of the sirens in the world. Her mind met with Ember's one-on-one, dragon-to-dragon.

Ember soared up into the air, heading straight for her. She could feel the wind beneath his wings almost as clearly as the wind beneath her own. She rose high into the misty clouds and then dove back down to hover just above the building. Everything looked different from this perspective, and it took her a minute to orient herself.

Her guess that they might be imprisoned in a storage room at the grocery store had been correct. The building looked like a child's toy. Something unreal. She had difficulty comprehending that there could be people in there, people who she cared about or those she had no grudges against. Fire was pure. It would consume all of the impurities and sanctify it. There would be no more cabal of any kind. Stupid, weak humans who thought they could take over the world.

They couldn't even defeat the cats.

Reg glided in a circle around the grocery store, watching the people escape to safety. Davyn helped to clear everyone out, making sure that no one was trapped in the fire. Alarms were sounding and sprinklers spraying water and foam to douse the flames. By the time the volunteer fire brigade arrived, the fire would be out.

Ember sailed in from the north, letting out a long, delighted dragon cry when he saw her.

She was once again larger than he. A big, beautiful shape that he had never seen before, and he wondered at first why she had withheld it from him. She had always been his mother figure, and now here she was in brilliant mother form.

They flew around each other in the sky above the burning grocery store, swooping in and out in what felt like a square dance, where the dancers spun around each other and switched places and swung this way and that in tandem. She had never felt so free, except maybe in dreams.

"Reg! Ember!"

Reg focused in on the man on the ground below them. He looked so small and far away, but she knew it was Davyn. He couldn't be mad at her for what she had done. She had saved them both from having their powers stripped from them. It was inconceivable that anyone could ever take this away from her. She was more *Reg* than she had ever been before.

She and Ember both dive-bombed Davyn, falling out of the sky like missiles intent on destroying their target. At the last moment, they stopped above him and hung in the air as if on strings, floating on the air currents with hardly a movement.

"Reg!" Davyn laughed and shook his head. "You're as bad as he is!"

Reg snorted fire.

"Come down."

Reg reluctantly dipped her feet down to the ground and sat on the concrete in front of him. Ember did the same, making a noise that was an exasperated sigh. Just when they were having a good time, it was time to come in. The humans were always intent on wrecking his fun.

"The fire engines and police are going to be here," Davyn said. "I don't know what they're going to find inside. I want to get whatever the cabal has left inside before the non-practitioners can get their hands on them. Understand?"

Reg cocked her head at the building. The fire was almost all gone and everything was dripping wet. But Davyn was right. The firefighters and police would come anyway and would insist on going over every inch of the building to see where the fire had started and how it had spread. Any secret books or artifacts of the cabal would be exposed and confiscated.

"I can't go back in there," Davyn said. "They aren't going to let any humans back into the building. But you can go back in through the roof."

Reg lifted into the air and looked down at it. Ember followed her lead.

CHAPTER FIFTY-FOUR

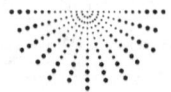

*R*eg and Ember flew down through the hole that Reg had made in the roof, charred and gaping wide, and dropped down to floor level to navigate the space inside. The room was too small for them to both fit in at once, so Ember hovered outside while Reg made her way through the room. Opening doors was tricky with dragon claws, so she gave up on trying to use doorknobs and just smashed her way through. There hadn't been a cage made that could hold a dragon for long.

The air was heavily perfumed with smoke from the fire but, sniffing carefully, Reg could find Chevy's scent and followed it through the back rooms of the grocery store, identifying the places he had been.

There was no bubbling cauldron, no pentagram inscribed on the floor. No black candles or animal sacrifices. It looked like just what it was, the employee area and storage spaces of a community grocery store. She nosed through the kitchen, stopping to eat a few charred donuts while she was there, and found another break room that included a vending machine, water cooler, and skinny employee lockers.

She ripped the door off the locker that smelled like Chevy and thrust her nose into it, snorting and snuffling around. He had a gym bag stored there, redolent with the smells of other people. Reg scooped it out and snuffled around for anything else she should take with her. She didn't know where Chevy himself had gone. He must have escaped the fire, since she hadn't found his charred body inside. That was too bad. She would have to hunt him down later. He couldn't be allowed to continue to prey on innocent victims, stealing their powers. She would put an immediate stop to that.

Ember was in the hallway outside, peering in. The rooms were much too small to be comfortable for dragons to move around each other. Reg broke open the vending machine and tossed Ember a few treats she knew he would like. He snapped them out of the air and swallowed them down. Reg had a couple of bites herself and went on.

Throughout the back portion of the building and the places Chevy had frequented, the only thing of significance she had found was the bag in his locker. She would have assumed he was working alone if she hadn't known he had at least one other partner in the cabal. Whoever else he was working with, they did not appear to work with him at the grocery store. That was good. Reg could continue shopping there and not be worried about further attacks.

When she was human again. And when the grocery store was rebuilt.

Rather than returning to the room they had come in through, Reg flew straight up and punched another hole through the roof. It was good to have two vent holes when there was a fire. It would air the building out faster.

She and Ember flew over the building, circling and looking down at the people on the ground. Reg could see Davyn, but not Chevy. The police and fire engines arrived, even though there wasn't much left for them to do. Few people seemed to see the dragons gliding overhead. Only those who believed that such a thing could exist would see them. Those who didn't believe would simply not see them. Their brains would shut the image out or replace it with birds wheeling overhead or something else that made sense in their reality. There was plenty else that was interesting to watch and distract them from any reality that they were not ready to accept.

Reg spotted a car she knew coming down the highway toward town, going a little bit faster than recommended, taking the curves recklessly. She floated down toward it and tracked it as it approached the town and then pulled into the grocery store's parking lot. The police were trying to manage the people and traffic, but hadn't completely cordoned the area off. Reg saw the white-haired man get out of the car and look around for his partner.

Ember dove down at Julian, making him jump away, startled. Then he laughed. "You get me every time, don't you, Ember?"

He was remarkably comfortable around Ember now. Funny to remember how floored he had been when he had first seen the hatchling not that long ago. Reg dived toward him on the other side, and this time, Julian's eyes went wide.

"Another one? How could there be...?"

Davyn had seen them and broke away from the crowd milling around the grocery store, taking pictures of the devastation. He greeted Julian with a quick squeeze around the shoulders and took in his astonishment at seeing a second dragon.

"This is Reg," Davyn explained.

Julian looked at her with his mouth hanging open. Davyn gestured to the gym bag dangling from Reg's claw. "Is that everything you took from the building?"

Reg appreciated that he had not just grabbed it without warning. Making a sudden movement toward a dragon was not wise, and she didn't know if she would have been able to school herself and avoid reflexively ripping his arm off.

She dropped the bag on the pavement in front of his feet. With his skinny human fingers, Davyn easily manipulated the zipper and opened the bag to see what was in it. Right on top was the poppet of Reg with long red braids and one of Davyn, with a face and black beard hastily scribbled on with black marker. Davyn moved them carefully to the side without comment.

There were a number of other poppets in the bag as well. Reg sniffed, recognizing Marta's scent among them. And Damon's. But where were they? Were they all at the cat sanctuary? And if so, where was it?

There were other pouches and jars of herbs and other ingredients in the bag, various raw materials for making the poppets; fabric, needle, thread, and markers. Some googly eyes purchased from Amazon. Reg pushed her snout into the bag and sniffed around, investigating more closely. The poppets were not just stuffed with cotton wool; there were other ingredients inside as well. Magical elements, poppets with pieces of their owners incorporated into them, whatever incantations and enchantments Chevy had put on them… it was hard to believe that so little was required to create a spell that would allow Chevy to steal powers from people just like Corvin. If there was anything more evil than a warlock with Corvin's curse, it was someone who chose to do what Corvin was compelled to.

She pulled her nose back out and sneezed. Davyn chuckled.

"All done?"

Reg nodded. Ember pushed forward and wanted a look at the bag too. Davyn stood patiently and allowed him to examine it.

He was a good dragon dad.

Eventually, Ember pulled his nose out and also sneezed.

"Did you see where Chevy went?" Davyn asked.

Reg shook her head. She flapped her wings and rose a few feet in the air. She tried to send Davyn a picture of them getting an aerial view so that they would better be able to find Chevy and scout out the area. She wasn't sure whether Davyn's mind would be able to receive this vision. Normally, she was the only one who could receive and interpret Ember's visions.

She didn't know whether he received the vision or understood the point of her lifting off but, looking at her with narrowed eyes, he asked, "You want to fly and get a better view?"

Reg nodded and lifted higher.

"Let's get in," Davyn told Julian. "We'll do our best to follow on the ground."

The two men climbed into the car and the two dragons flew

higher. Reg tried not to get too high or to go too fast, to give the humans a chance to follow them.

CHAPTER FIFTY-FIVE

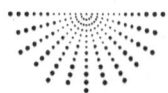

*S*he and Ember flew side by side, looking for any sign of Chevy. But Reg couldn't see or smell him. He had probably had a car in the parking lot and had driven away as quickly as he could from the burning building. The vehicle and its stinky exhaust would help to cover his scent and keep her from following his trail.

After circling a couple of times to find him, Reg gave up on the search. He would show up again sooner or later. And now that she knew who the leader—or at least one of the members—of the cabal was, she would be able to find him again, and she and the cats would put a stop to his exploits.

She doubted that Chevy was as important as he made himself out to be. He was more likely to be the most junior member of the cabal than the leader. But she didn't care, as long as by following him, she could bring down the group that had been trying to steal her gifts and those of her friends.

Reg turned her mind to her companion and pictured Starlight, Horace, and the other cats wandering among the trees, with some ancient buildings to shelter in, the same picture he had shared with her previously.

Ember blinked large eyes at her and looked around at the

scenery below them. Reg searched for some sign of the sanctuary. It was well-hidden. She looked at Ember, waiting for him to take her there. Of course, there was no guarantee that the sanctuary Starlight had been going to *was* local. Horace could travel through space. He could have taken them all to Egypt, a country Merneith had ruled anciently and knew well.

Ember changed direction, taking the lead.

Reg relished the freedom of flight, the sound of their wings flapping or the air skimming over their surfaces as they glided. After a few minutes, it was clear that Ember was searching for the place in his memory. Things had changed since his ancestor had been there. The trees were older and the town closer to the sanctuary than when it had just been a village. There had been no highways the last time a dragon had visited the sanctuary.

Eventually, Ember started his descent. Reg followed him. She scanned the highway below for Davyn's car, wondering whether he had been able to follow his airborne guides. She could see it poking along on the highway. Sooner or later, they would make it to the sanctuary. If they lost the dragons in their descent, Reg would go out looking for them and bring them to it.

Reg followed Ember to the ground, and they approached the sanctuary on foot, slinking quietly toward it. The air smelled green and earthy, so delicious Reg could almost eat it. She had never been so enthralled with the outdoors before. She liked her creature comforts. Or the water. But as a dragon, her senses brought her so much more information about her surroundings, she was enthralled.

She could smell and hear the cats before she could see them. And the humans were even smellier and noisier than the cats. Reg took the lead, since Starlight was her cat and Marta and Damon were her friends. They would be faster to recognize her than Ember. She entered a large clearing in the trees and looked around. It was remarkably similar to what Ember had pictured. Unchanged by the generations of cats and humans that had passed by during the interim.

One of the humans in the clearing let out a yell upon spotting the two approaching dragons. The humans moved quickly away, retreating to the other side of the clearing, some of them running away into the trees. They were a strange assortment of creatures, dressed in nightgowns, shorts, and worn old t-shirts, as if they were having a pajama party. Because they had all been taken at night, Reg realized. They had each been asleep when Horace had come for them. That was how he had been able to enter their homes. Through their dreams.

Only this time, he was no longer a draugr controlled by the Witch Doctor with an instinct to lie on their chests to smother them, but inhabited by Merneith, who was apparently more friendly toward humans, willing to help the cats save the victims of the cabal from a fate Reg considered worse than death.

Reg stopped advancing on the humans and sat on her haunches, trying to look non-threatening. Ember stopped beside her and looked curiously at all of the people who chose to inhabit a cat sanctuary. A few cats crept into the clearing, jumping down from trees, climbing down from the ruins or out from behind rocks and gullies where they had been watching from. Reg recognized the largest of the black cats as Horace. But she didn't rush forward to meet him. Horace-Merneith should still be able to touch her mind and recognize her, but she would wait for that recognition rather than advancing toward him.

CHAPTER FIFTY-SIX

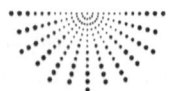

A woman broke away from the group huddling together on the other side of the clearing. This one braver than most. She was wearing a nightgown, but Reg quickly recognized Marta by her smell even before she could see her clearly.

"Ember?" Marta asked, "Is that you?"

Of course she would recognize Ember before Reg. She had seen him a couple of times since he had hatched, though he'd probably been much smaller when she had seen him last. But how many young dragons were there around Black Sands? The dragon population had doubled with Reg's transformation.

Ember took a step toward Marta and, following Reg's example, did not move too quickly toward the human, but allowed her to come to him.

The cats were taking up defensive positions, apparently not very happy with the invasion by the two unfamiliar dragons. Cats and dragons might not be enemies, but they were not exactly friends, either. Reg didn't know whether cats had generational memories like dragons, but some, like Starlight, had lived lives that stretched far back to ancient times.

"Ember?" Marta repeated, moving slowly toward Ember with

her hand held out. "I'm sorry, I don't have anything to give you. If I had crackers or some change, I would give you that. But they took us in our pajamas, and I don't exactly keep snacks and change in my nightgown." Marta gestured down at her filmy white dress, looking uncomfortable and embarrassed.

Ember sniffed the air as Marta approached him. Eventually, Marta was within an arm's reach and stopped, her hand held out in offering, not trying to touch Ember. Ember bent his head forward and touched his nose to it. Marta scratched the finely scaled skin around his nose and then reached up to scratch his ears as well.

"What are you doing here?" she mused. "Does Reg know you're here? Did she send you?"

Ember turned his head and looked at Reg.

"And who is this?" Marta asked, observing Reg but not reaching out to touch her or offer her hand as she did to Ember. Wisely not assuming that every dragon was so approachable.

Reg tried to send Marta pictures of herself and to describe the transformation to her, but Marta was not psychically gifted and did not receive them. Ember nudged Marta toward Reg.

Reg heard a yowl she recognized, and she turned to see her tuxedo cat stalking into the clearing, looking like he was ready to take a piece out of the dragons.

Reg sent her thoughts to him, reaching out and touching his mind, trying to soothe him before he got too far. He stopped and stared at her.

It's me, Reg told him, trying to communicate clearly with him. They'd always had a good psychic connection. His eyes riveted on her and he cocked his head, paying close attention.

Reg couldn't tell him all that had happened to her since she had been taken from the house. It was too complicated. Instead, she tried to communicate that she was there to help and that the cabal was still out there, the withered paw in hand.

Starlight hissed, making Reg laugh. She puffed out smoke and a bit of flame. Marta took a step back, looking alarmed.

Starlight started to pick his way across the field toward Reg.

The other cats watched. Marta didn't try to stop Starlight or tell him it was dangerous. At least she was smart enough to know that the cat had a better handle on what was going on than the humans, with their meager sense of smell and psychic abilities.

Starlight stopped in front of Reg and stood on his hind legs, looking at her. Reg wasn't sure whether she should try to pet him or not. He might object to being touched by a huge lizard. She held out her clawed forepaw, palm down, curled inward, knuckles toward Starlight.

Rather than rubbing against her or nipping at her fingers, both of which were equally likely, Starlight jumped onto her arm and scaled it to her shoulder. He sat there, looking down at everyone else.

She assumed he could communicate telepathically with at least some of the other cats, but none seemed inclined to come forward and meet and greet the large dragon sitting at the end of the field. The humans watched in stunned silence. It was strange to see a group of people without phones raised to take pictures of such an unusual sight, but Reg realized they had been taken in their sleep, and none of them had phones with them. She could only imagine how difficult a time the ones who had been there for more than a day or two were having. Reg didn't think she could manage to go a day without her phone. What would she do? What would she watch?

Marta stared at Starlight and Reg. She looked like she had an inkling of what was happening, but wasn't quite ready to talk to the dragon stranger and risk sounding like a fool.

Reg cocked her head as she heard a car turn off the highway onto the worn path leading from the thoroughfare to the sanctuary. It wasn't an actual road, not even graveled, but there was a worn spot in the grasses and other plants that had been traveled over the years. Had it all been trampled by cats? Or were there people who knew about the sanctuary and came out there regularly? Maybe not all of the people who were there now had been brought by Horace while they had been sleeping. Someone might come out with cat food or veterinary services for the animals who lived there.

Reg kept watching, her head turned to the side so her eye was toward the highway. In a moment, the car came into view, going slowly over the bumpy ground, and she saw that it was Davyn and Julian. They had managed to follow her and take the proper turnoff, even though it wasn't marked.

CHAPTER FIFTY-SEVEN

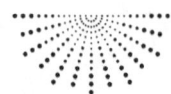

*D*avyn reached them first, with Julian trailing behind, his eyes big, looking at everything. For someone who worked for the magical endangered creatures division, he always seemed very surprised and excited to actually run into any endangered creatures in real life. And Reg seemed to be his favorite endangered creature, always providing him access to something else he hadn't seen before. Now, that something was her, yet again.

"Marta," Davyn called out to Detective Jessup when he saw her. "I'm glad to see you here! Everything is okay? You're unharmed?"

"Yes." Marta looked as if she thought it was some sort of trick. "I'm fine." She raised her brows. "You don't seem too surprised to see Ember's new companion. That must mean that you've already met?"

Davyn put the gym bag down at his feet between himself and Reg, smiling. "You've met her before too. Multiple times, I might add."

Marta looked at Reg again, sideways, as if she might be something different from when they looked the last time.

"Is it...?"

"This is Reg," Davyn confirmed.

"And... how did that happen? Did they put a spell on her?" Marta looked a little anxious. "Is that what they were planning to do to all of us? Turn us into dra—into other things?"

"No. What the cabal was doing had nothing to do with dragons."

"The cabal?"

"You hadn't figured out the details? The Cabal of the Withered Paw. I assumed that since you brought Reg the Withered Paw..."

Marta frowned, shaking her head. "I don't know what you're talking about."

Davyn shook his head, frowning at her. "You were raised in a magical home. Don't tell me you've never heard of the Cabal of the Withered Paw."

"Well... I mean, away at camp and stuff like that. Scary fireside stories. But... what does that have to do with anything? I mean, we're not here to tell each other ghost stories."

"The Cabal of the Withered Paw is real. Or if the stories themselves were not real, then the idea has been resurrected for real by a group in Black Sands who is determined to steal the powers of practitioners."

"The attacks? The attacks at the harbor were by the Cabal of the Withered Paw? That's crazy. They don't exist. They don't... really, do they?"

"You had the paw in your hand. You don't believe that it existed?"

"I... thought that was just a lucky rabbit's foot. I didn't think it was an actual relic of any importance."

"Whether that is what it was initially or it has just been pressed into service as one really doesn't matter. They believe it works to repel cats and keep them from interfering with the cabal's operations."

"The cats." Marta looked around at the cats sitting around the circumference of the clearing. She should certainly have figured out at least part of the story when she ended up stuck in the sanctuary with the victims of the attacks and a horde of cats.

A horde? That wasn't right. Reg turned it over in her mind,

trying to remember and make sense. A chowder? A crowd? It was going to drive her crazy all day.

"The cats brought you and the others here to protect you from the cabal," Davyn pointed out.

"The cats did?" Marta shook her head. "I'm sorry for sounding like such a dunce. But we just… sleepwalked here. We woke up and had no idea how we got here. Or why we had been abandoned at a cat sanctuary."

"I don't know for sure how it works," Davyn confessed. "I only got the barest inkling of it. I… wasn't in the best shape at the time and he didn't take the time to describe it in detail. Reg could explain it to you better, but until she returns to her usual form…" He looked at her expectantly. "You *are* going to return to your usual form, aren't you?"

Reg supposed that she would at some point, but she wasn't in any great hurry to do so.

"How could cats bring us here?" Marta mused. "I suppose it makes as much sense as anything. Since no one ever saw a vehicle coming or going when new people appeared."

Starlight jumped down from Reg's shoulder to investigate the gym bag. If he thought it was going to stink like used sneakers, he would be disappointed. Reg watched him root around in it for a minute. He pulled out the Reg poppet and threw it up in the air. He caught it between his paws and bit it, playing with it like it was a catnip mouse.

Reg snorted and moved closer to rescue the poppet. She didn't like the idea of her likeness being roughed up by a cat. She had already been pretty sore as a human and didn't need more aches and pains when she returned to her regular form.

Starlight tossed the poppet in the air again and, this time, Reg snatched it herself, and held it away from him in her claw. Starlight returned to the bag and pulled out another poppet. Other cats were curiously creeping closer.

Starlight pulled Davyn's poppet out and tossed it in the air. He grabbed at it, but missed it. Starlight snatched it again and darted away, arching his back playfully to encourage Davyn to chase after him.

"Starlight! Come back here!"

Davyn wasn't a cat person. He had no idea what Starlight wanted from him. But Ember recognized his body language and went chasing after the small cat. It was a good thing that Ember was young and agile. He and Starlight raced this way and that around the clearing, and a less dexterous dragon might have just flattened Starlight. Eventually, Ember managed to snatch the poppet away from Starlight and flew back to Davyn to award it to him.

The other cats who had been creeping up on the bag swarmed it, yowling and snapping at each other as they each tried to grab a poppet to play with. Hundreds of cats were now watching from around the edge of the clearing, and Reg was glad they didn't all try to join in. Even just those cats who had come over caused chaos, chasing each other around the field and playing with the poppets as if they were the best toys ever. Maybe one of the herbs in the stuffing was catnip.

As the cats played, Reg saw that they were taking the poppets back to the small group of people standing at the end of the field, still unsure about getting any closer to Reg and Ember, even though Marta had shown them that there was no danger.

The cats were making their way around the group of people, matching the poppets with their owners. Pretty soon, the fun and games of wrestling with poppets and tossing them around was over, and the people were each holding their own effigies, looking at them with consternation.

CHAPTER FIFTY-EIGHT

*W*hat are they?" Marta asked, taking the one offered to her by a short-haired white cat.

"It's a poppet," Davyn explained. He indicated the crudely stitched face on the doll. "It's you."

Julian leaned closer for a better look, impinging on Marta's space, and she gave him a small shove backward. "Get your own."

Julian looked in the bag to see if there were any left, but all that remained were the raw materials. His face showed disappointment.

"Poppets are powerful magical objects," he pointed out pompously to cover for his hurt feelings. He looked around at the cats. "They aren't toys. Something to be played with. Someone needs to tell these people that they have to keep their poppets safe until they can be properly unmade. It can be very dangerous."

Davyn nodded. He looked at Marta. "Maybe you could get everyone to assemble here and explain it to them. Since you're the authority, they'll be more likely to listen to you."

Marta shook her head. "If they were not practitioners, that might be true, but the magical community here has little respect for the police—especially those like me who have no gifts to speak of. You have far more influence as the leader of the coven. Past leader, I mean."

Davyn looked like he wanted to argue the point, but he nodded uncomfortably and accepted Marta's statement.

Reg heard the crunch of car tires leaving the highway and rolling onto the pathway that Davyn had followed to get there. Who else was coming? She wasn't sure they wanted anyone else to join their party. She turned her head and watched for the vehicle. She handed Davyn her poppet and crouched, waiting for the first glimpse of the approaching vehicle.

"What is it?" Davyn asked, unable to hear the approaching vehicle yet.

Reg looked around the clearing. She could be wrong. She didn't know anything about who might legitimately come to the cat sanctuary. But it didn't exactly look like the cats were waiting for anyone else to arrive. She withdrew into the trees, moving slowly so that she wouldn't attract any attention if the car's occupants could see the clearing before she expected them to. Ember followed closely behind her, the two of them fully in sync.

They disguised themselves in the trees the best they could, certainly well enough to keep themselves out of the dim sight of a human. The car pulled into view and Reg watched, her stomach in a knot of excited anticipation, as the driver of the car got out.

It was Chevy.

He looked both triumphant and furious as he looked around at the people and cats in the clearing. Since he had not known the location of the cat sanctuary a couple of hours earlier, Reg assumed that he had followed Davyn there, though maybe he had taken a couple of turns off the highway that led to farmhouses before finding the one that led to the sanctuary.

He was pleased at finding the cat sanctuary, but not so much at seeing that they had stolen his poppets from his locker and everyone was now holding their own images. Reg could feel the power of each person being magnified by holding their poppet.

Chevy had intended to drain the powers of each of them with his spell but, when they held their own effigies, it reversed the effect. Chevy looked around at everyone, shaking with anger. He tried to grab Davyn's and Reg's poppets out of Davyn's hand, but Davyn didn't let him get close.

"No, you don't," he told Chevy firmly, as if he were a three-year-old with his hand in the cookie jar.

"They are mine! I'm grateful to you for saving them from the fire at the store, but they are my property, not yours. I'll thank you to give them back." He looked around at the crowd. "All of them. They were not yours to give away."

"They are not yours," Davyn countered. "They are made in someone else's likeness using personal items or parts of their body. Under magical law, they belong to the person whose likeness they are."

Chevy sputtered angrily. "There is no such law! These are my things! You broke into my locker to get them. You had no right. And you have no right to take them away or to keep them from me!"

"I thought you just thanked me for taking them from the store."

"I was being polite. You should have left them alone. They would have been fine there. The sprinklers stopped the fire. They would have been safe until I could retrieve them again." Chevy made a dive at the poppets, and Davyn stepped back and held them high. He was taller and dangled them out of reach. Even though Chevy jumped several times to try to get them, there was nothing he could do about it. Davyn would win at the game of keep-away, unless Chevy had a power he had not yet revealed.

"I'm afraid Mr. Smithy is right," Marta said. "Effigies made in the likeness of a real person belong to that person. They have the right to control what happens to them and how their poppet is used."

Chevy scowled at her and shook his head. "Who are you? No one asked you."

He could be forgiven, Reg supposed, for not knowing who she was. Marta was in a nightgown, not the usual uniform of the Black Sands police department.

"I am Police Detective Marta Jessup," Marta said, drawing herself up and speaking in her no-nonsense cop voice. "And you are in a world of trouble."

He glanced at her and decided she was not a physical threat. Unable to get the poppets from Davyn, he decided to try to take back the others. He lunged at the pajama-party group holding their dolls and tried to snatch them all away, grabbing them from one person and then the next.

Several of the cats thought to protect the people who had been brought to the sanctuary, yowling angrily and advancing on him. Chevy pulled out the abhorrent cat's paw. He held it before him like a vampire hunter holding a crucifix on a bad TV movie, and all the cats who saw it fell back, staying well away from him.

Reg gathered her muscles to throw herself back into the clearing and take care of the threat. She was not going to let him get all of the poppets back and follow through on his evil plan after she had gone to so much trouble to break out of her prison and to steal them in the first place. She could dispatch the skinny young man in a bite or two. Then no one would have to worry about him and his plans again.

But the sleepwalkers had not been defeated. The first few had been surprised by Chevy's attack and had not managed to protect their poppets, but the others saw what was going on and were more prepared. They clutched the dolls to them, and maybe they could feel the way the poppets magnified their energy, because they started to stand tall and strong, their auras glowing brighter. They looked at each other and spoke out and encouraged one another.

Chevy turned to face them again, the cat's paw in his hand. His face paled and his eyes darted around, looking from one to the other for some weak point he could attack. Even the people whose poppets he had already taken stood there looking solid and strong, buoyed up by those around them. The magic being magnified by the poppets spread to touch all of them, becoming united, a group magic that was even stronger.

Chevy could feel it too, and he clutched the poppets he had

managed to take to his chest, desperate to keep them and use them as he had originally planned. Marta marched across the field toward him, looking very official despite her flimsy nightgown. She put her hand on his arm.

"You are under arrest," she told him sternly. "This is theft. I told you the poppets do not belong to you."

CHAPTER FIFTY-NINE

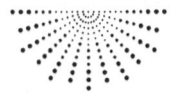

*M*arta didn't have any handcuffs, but Chevy didn't pull away from her and try to make a run for it. Reg could sense the little bit of magic that Marta had, magnified by her poppet, which held Chevy in place.

"Here," Julian offered, approaching the two of them. He pulled a couple of plastic zip ties out of his pocket. "I always keep a few on me, just in case." He smiled proudly. "You never know when you're going to witness a violation."

Marta didn't protest. She just took one of them from him and bound Chevy's wrists with it. She took the poppets from his hands and relieved him of the cat's paw.

"They're mine," Chevy protested, "I made them. You can't say that they belong to anyone else."

"That's not the only thing he did," Davyn told Marta. "He's the one behind the assaults as well. And he kidnapped Reg and me."

"He kidnapped you?"

"Yes. Disabled us with a curse and held us at the grocery store against our wills. The fire started when Reg... err... transformed and broke us out."

Marta gave Chevy's arm a little shake. "Fine, we'll add two

counts of kidnapping to the thefts, and an unspecified number of assaults, since I'm not sure how many were you and how many were your companion. Who are you working with, by the way?"

Chevy closed his mouth, tilting his head back and trying to look virtuous. "You'll never make me talk about the other members of the cabal," he told her haughtily.

"Then I guess you can go away for all of them."

He didn't look quite as pleased at this response.

Everything seemed to have calmed and quieted and, as far as Reg could tell, no one else was coming to join the party. She and Ember stepped out of the trees, returning to the clearing to join Davyn and Marta.

"You!" Chevy snarled at her. He looked at Ember and seemed momentarily disconcerted by the fact that he was facing two dragons rather than just one, but he focused on Reg and continued his tirade. "This is all your fault. You burned down my grocery store! You should arrest her for arson!" he told Marta.

Marta looked at Reg and raised her brows. "I can't arrest a dragon," she pointed out. "And I certainly can't charge a dragon with arson. There are magical compacts, you know. You can't prohibit a species from doing what comes to it naturally. We try to set reasonable limits, but not allowing a dragon to blow fire is beyond our purview."

"She's not a dragon. She just... she just looks like one!"

"Oh?" Marta asked politely.

"She's a person. A human. She was when she was in that room at the grocery store, and then she did something. She turned into... into this thing..."

"What room in the grocery store?"

He looked at her and didn't answer.

"Were you holding Reg and Davyn captive, as Mr. Smithy claims?"

Chevy shook his head, but couldn't find the words that would get him out of the situation he had gotten himself into.

Maybe there were none. As a dragon, Reg cared very little about words.

Actions were far more important.

She bent down and carefully picked up the cat's paw.

"That is mine!" Chevy protested. "You can't take it away from me!"

Marta looked to see what Reg had picked up, and shrugged. "I don't see any personal property."

"You can see it," Chevy spluttered, "It is right there! You can't let her take my paw! You're a law enforcement officer. You have to make sure she doesn't do anything to break the law."

"You have a permit to own an ancient, cursed artifact?"

His mouth opened and closed like a fish.

Of course he didn't. Who did? Reg didn't know much about such permits, but she had been told they were almost impossible to get. It took a ton of paperwork, character witnesses, a home study, gold, and years of waiting to obtain a permit issued legitimately. And when the artifact passed from one generation to the next, they had to go through the whole process again. Just because the father was approved to hold such a thing didn't mean the son was qualified.

"I don't see any personal property," Marta repeated. "Now walk."

She turned him to walk him toward her car and then faced her next roadblock.

No car.

She looked at Davyn's car and Chevy's. But she didn't have a police car. And getting one would prove tricky.

Even if she could get another police officer to come out there to pick her up, if they could find anyone with a working cell phone, they would have to explain what they were all doing out there. Why Marta was in her nightgown instead of in uniform and had no car and no phone? The location of the cat sanctuary was supposed to be a secret, though maybe if all of the cats hid, they wouldn't give it away. Reg and Ember could also hide, but the whole thing would be a mess to explain.

"You want me to drive you back into town?" Davyn suggested.

"We could do that, but then what about his car?"

"I could drive it," Julian suggested.

Chevy looked ready to have another meltdown. "No one is driving my car!" he insisted. "You don't have the right!"

Marta rolled her eyes. "Just leave it here. Maybe I'll have it towed."

That idea apparently did not comfort Chevy any more than the alternative. He choked, face turning red, unable to get the words out. If the guy didn't watch it, he was going to stroke out right there.

"Come on," Marta said unsympathetically, giving Chevy a tug. "We'll ride in back. Your car will stay here. If you have someone to pick it up, they can talk to me about it and we'll make arrangements."

If Reg were right, this would involve moving it to the highway so that the person picking it up would not know the sanctuary's location. Chevy could brag all that he liked that he knew where it was, but it wasn't exactly easy to give directions to the place.

Davyn and Julian followed Marta to the car. Davyn looked back over his shoulder at Reg and Ember. "I'll see you back at the house? You can get there on your own."

Reg flapped her wings in acknowledgment, and they opened their doors. Davyn looked past Reg at the people waiting in the clearing, clutching their poppets to them. "What about everybody else?"

Reg walked over to the car and bumped Davyn, encouraging him to get into the car. He got the idea and climbed in, but was still frowning.

"Do you want us to send someone back for them, then?"

Reg shook her head.

Davyn stood there for a minute longer, trying to understand the plan, but his mind was not open enough for Reg to share it with him, and she wasn't ready to resume her human form yet. If she did, she wasn't sure she would be able to get back into dragon form again, and she still had things to do, including flying back to Davyn's house when she was finished.

Davyn nodded. "Okay. Well, if you need me, you know how to find me. Or Ember can."

Reg waited for him to leave. She could see Chevy starting up another rant in the back seat of the car. It was probably good that Marta didn't have a nightstick or taser on her.

CHAPTER SIXTY

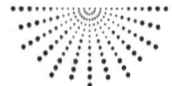

*T*hey were finally alone.

With the rest of the sleepwalkers.

Reg looked at the group, ridiculous in their pajamas. After all that they had been through, she wished they were wearing something more dignified. But what did a dragon care what anyone looked like? And the sleepwalkers had been with each other for long enough to overcome their embarrassment and didn't care how they were dressed.

She got closer, watching their faces for signs of fear. But they all seemed pretty calm about having two dragons in their midst. Maybe after Chevy, a couple of largish lizards didn't seem too bad. Reg studied their faces and reached out with her senses, looking for the one with the most promising psychic gifts.

She narrowed her attention to a man in baseball pajamas. Just like the blue and white striped ones little kids wore, except made for an adult. He reminded her a little of Harrison with his slightly inappropriate clothing and long legs. She narrowed her focus on the man, reaching out to touch his mind.

"I can hear you," the man said out loud, giving a nod.

Reg didn't use human words to communicate with him, but sent him pictures, explaining her plan. Jonathan—that was the baseball player's name—paid close attention, his earnest expression adorable. Then he turned back to the others.

"We're supposed to… go to sleep," he told them.

"Go to sleep?" one of the women repeated in a strident, complaining tone. "We want to go home! Someone needs to call for help. Won't that woman police officer send help?"

"We came here in our sleep," Jonathan told her, "And if we go to sleep now, we will be taken back home."

"I can't sleep," a balding man objected. "After everything that has happened? I'm way too wound up. I won't be able to sleep for hours!"

Jonathan sat down on the warm grass and stared up at the darkening sky. "It isn't like there's anything else to do. Do you think you'll get home and go to sleep there if they have to send an emergency evacuation bus out to get us? And then question us for hours about how we got out here in the first place and everything we've seen here? And get checked out by doctors, and then to arrange to have someone pick each of us up, because a bus isn't going to go to every individual's house. You'll be lucky to get any sleep tonight."

There were murmurs and further complaints from the rest of the sleepwalkers, but no one else raised their voices. They kept the complaints quiet, and must have thought that Jonathan was right about what would happen if they waited for a conventional rescue.

Jonathan stretched out on his back, hands clasped behind his head, and closed his eyes like he was going to sleep on a hammock.

Not everyone was ready to give it a try. But there was no point in standing around. Most at least sat down, gathered in little groups here and there across the field, and talked quietly about their experience or what they were going back to. Reg stretched her dragon body out long and soaked up the last few rays of the sun. Ember lay down beside her. Reg put down her head and watched over the humans as they talked and prepared for sleep.

Starlight came over to her and rubbed against her. Reg put her head down to him and they bumped jaws and foreheads, exchanging scent markers and memories. After a few minutes, Starlight curled up against Reg and waited.

Stars began to appear in the sky and, at first, Reg wasn't even aware that anything was happening. She noticed that Jonathan was gone and thought he must have gone into the trees to relieve himself, but she knew he hadn't walked past her. The humans lay down and quieted and their numbers became fewer as they slept and dreamed, and Horace took them home.

* * *

The field was empty. Reg stirred, waking Starlight and Ember.

Starlight rose to his feet and quivered from tip to tail as he stretched each muscle in turn. Reg stretched her body, marveling at her strength and flexibility. She had seen how agile Ember was, but had assumed that was just because he was a youngling. She pictured adult dragons as slow and ponderous, unable to move around very fast because of the vast bulk they carried. But she didn't feel heavy at all. She felt like a bird, light and quick.

Reg picked up the cat's paw, which she had kept hidden under her large, clawed forepaw when she had lain down. Starlight hissed at the sight, but he did not fall back or act afraid of it as the cats had when Chevy had wielded it. Holding on to it, Reg took flight.

In the dim light of the moon—by which she could see perfectly —Reg soared over the cat sanctuary, examining its layout, the ruins of old buildings and a few new ones to provide the comforts to those who needed them, and the many dark shapes and shiny eyes roaming around the property.

Eventually, she settled on a place. She landed near one of the ruins on the far side of the property, as far from the highway and human infiltration as possible. Ember landed silently beside her. Starlight and some of the other cats who had been watching her took a few minutes to assemble a short distance away.

Reg used one of her sharp claws to dig a hole. It didn't have to be large or deep, and her claw did the job very nicely. Then Reg gently laid the withered paw in the hole. She nudged the pile of dirt she had made so that a bit of it trickled into the hole.

Starlight approached. He pawed at the pile of dirt to sprinkle a little more onto the ancient relic. Then he moved to the side and each of the other cats who had come, the leaders among them, she assumed, came and scraped a little more dirt into the hole until they had all participated and the hole had been filled in. Reg packed the earth down.

Now the owner of the paw could be at rest.

* * *

Reg waited until Horace had returned for Starlight, and the two of them had disappeared. Then she and Ember took to the air and pointed their snouts toward Davyn's house.

They flew in silence, a few pictures shared between them, but mostly thinking their own thoughts. Reg enjoyed the feeling of her wings flapping and the air streaming over her face and body. It was like swimming, except through the air instead of the water. In all of her dreams, it had never been so wonderful.

She saw the lights of Davyn's house glowing below them. He had lit a fire in the big fireplace. Julian was probably cooking, but it was a welcome to the dragons. They glided around the property a few times before landing.

Ember was more experienced with doors than Reg was as a dragon. He gave the lever handle of the screen door a little flick and let them both in. Reg let the door flap shut behind her.

"Well, hello," Davyn greeted, looking up from his book to watch them enter. Reg went up to the fire to bask in the welcome warmth. Ember stayed for a minute, then squeezed down the staircase to his basement lair.

Davyn looked Reg over. "Are you ready to transform back?"

Reg's shoulders didn't work the same way as a dragon, and shrugging was impossible. She raised the palms of her forepaws up instead.

I suppose.

Of course, that was assuming she knew how to take back her usual form. Reg wasn't quite sure how it worked. And Davyn would not be able to tell her. Even with all that he had learned about dragons lately, she was sure he had not come across anything in the literature that told him how to transform into or away from one as a siren.

She reached out to the siren sisters, listening for their song and words as she stared into the fire. Their chorus was soothing and pleasant. All the anger she had felt when she had transformed into her dragon form had gone and she was at peace. It had been very nice to spend the afternoon and evening as a dragon, but she was ready to return to her own form and relax with Davyn.

"Welcome back," Davyn said.

She turned and looked at him, and then looked down at herself. The same Reg as she had been before. Pink and soft and weak.

Human.

"What a day," Reg sighed. She ran her hands over her arms, examining herself curiously. Her body had never been so familiar and so foreign.

"Come tell me about it," Davyn suggested, patting the couch beside him. Reg looked at it and wondered about Julian. Had he gone back home? Or was he still there, too, waiting for Davyn to go to bed?

"He went to sleep a few hours ago," Davyn told Reg, interpreting her glance toward the upstairs rooms. "I wanted to wait up for you two."

"You're probably tired."

Davyn shook his head. "After all of that fire that you fed me? I could go for three days without sleeping. Tell me what happened after I left."

Reg sat down next to him on the couch and did.

EPILOGUE

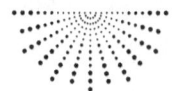

$\mathcal{R}$eg hung up the phone after talking to Etienne. It would be nice to go on a little vacation. She sat in the car staring at the store for several minutes before working up the energy to break through her inertia to unbuckle her seatbelt, open her door, and get out of the car.

Reg was hesitant to walk in through the doors. But the store looked completely different from before the fire. It had been an old, small-town grocery store before. A bit too small. A bit too old. Maybe not quite up to code, but there was nowhere else for the members of the community to go unless they wanted to go all the way across town to the "new" (at least ten years old) grocery store, or all the way to the city if they needed something that wasn't stocked in town.

Now it was a behemoth. Well, maybe not as bad as the big box stores, but still too big and too modern for this small town.

"Go on in," a voice encouraged.

Reg turned around and saw a woman clerk, still dressed in the same color of smock as the clerks had worn in the old building. Her face was vaguely familiar. Her name tag said Val.

Reg looked around, thinking that Val was probably talking to someone else, but Val smiled and nodded, motioning her to go in.

"We have all kinds of fun activities planned today," Val told her. "Go on in and have a look around."

Reg took a long look at Val, then went in through the doors that whisked open in front of her.

Inside, an old-style swing band played. The aisles stretched impossibly far in every direction. It would take an hour just to walk through the store to find what she was looking for.

Reg walked by a small pyramid of Tia Mia's Handcrafted Smokey Salsa. She stopped and looked at it carefully, then looked around.

No one was watching her, but she remembered Chevy's words.

People you wouldn't even consider. People you overlook all the time. You don't even see them around you.

Maybe she would go into the city to shop.

Did you enjoy this book? Reviews and recommendations are vital to making a book successful.

Please leave a review at your favorite book store or review site and share it with your friends.

Don't miss the following bonus material:
Sign up for mailing list to get a free ebook
Read a sneak preview chapter
Other books by P.D. Workman
Learn more about the author

DON'T MISS A THING! GET THE LATEST NEWS AND A FREE EBOOK

Your First Taste

PREVIEW OF TAINTED TRUFFLE TREACHERY

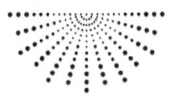

PREVIEW CHAPTER 1

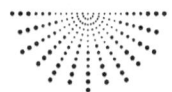

*R*eg was happy to be home. Going to the Everglades for a few days to visit Etienne and his new wife, Ilka, had been a nice diversion and helped her to get her mind off of recent events in Black Sands. Still, it was always nice to get home again. She was happy to have a home to go to after so many years of being shuttled from one place to another every few months. She had been in Black Sands for over a year. A lot had happened during that time, and it was home now. The little guest cottage she had rented from Sarah on her first day in Black Sands had become her sanctuary and home base. She ate and slept there, ran her psychic business holding readings and seances there, and of course, there was Starlight.

She put down the cat carrier and let out the black and white tuxedo cat with a white splash on his forehead. Starlight took his time oozing out of the carrier, arching his back, and then elongating all his muscles, vibrating with the joy of the stretch. Reg reached down and scratched his ears and then along his back, hoping it would help to work out any fatigue or soreness from their trip. She wished someone would come and give *her* a back rub and massage. It wasn't like she'd been traveling all day, but the three-legged trip—first on donkey, then airboat, and then car—had seemed very long.

Of course, Corvin would be happy to get a call from her to massage her sore body, but he wouldn't stop there. She would feel good for a while, but he would strip her of her powers, which she knew from sad experience was not something she could tolerate. She would go crazy with the silence in her own head. She was too used to the other voices there, always vying for her attention, and didn't know how normal people lived with the silence.

She let out a noisy sigh at the thought of Corvin. She had expected the phone to ring as soon as she got in the door, Corvin asking if she was home and when he could see her. Having shared magic, memories, and thoughts with her before, he had an uncanny sense of where she was and what she was doing. She could never quite keep him out of her head.

He had told her he had some news she would be interested in. Something that he couldn't tell her over the phone—though that was probably just a ruse. He wanted a chance to see her face to face, just as he always did, so that he might get the opportunity to seduce her and take away her gifts.

But his words echoed in her mind. "I have a job for you. Something you're going to want to do."

A job? What would Corvin need her to do for him? He was very powerful and grew stronger all the time. She had to be careful of him, to always be aware that today he might be stronger than yesterday and that what had worked before would not necessarily work again.

She would find out tomorrow. She had managed to put him off for a day, which was probably why he hadn't phoned the minute she walked in the door. Then she and the handsome warlock would sit across from each other at the restaurant of their choosing, and he would tell her about... whatever it was he wanted her to look into. Some little thing that he had made up to get her interest. A lost ring. A haunting. A friend who wanted a psychic to do readings at her birthday party.

It wasn't going to be anything earth-shattering. She was sure of that.

* * *

Starlight marched directly to his bowl. It was, of course, empty. They had been away from the house for several days and she had not left food out for him.

He put his ears back in a grumpy cat scowl and narrowed his mismatched blue and green eyes at her.

"I'm sorry, Your Majesty," Reg told him, rolling her eyes. "I'm sorry that food doesn't instantly appear in your dish the second we walk in the door. I think you can wait a few minutes while I put down my bags and splash some water on my face."

Starlight gave a short yowl, which indicated he would not be happy to wait for Reg to take care of her own physical needs while he waited.

"At least you could curl up and go to sleep in your carrier on the way home," Reg pointed out. And, of course, the carrier was lined with a soft blanket for his comfort. "You're not the one who had to sit on a donkey. And those hard boat chairs."

He did not seem sympathetic. Reg grabbed the plastic box of dry kibble and trickled a little into Starlight's bowl. He stared at her, waiting for the good stuff.

"That will hold you for now," Reg assured him, and walked by him to put her suitcase in her bedroom and take care of other matters.

When she returned to the kitchen, he was still sitting in front of his food dish, looking offended that she had only offered him dry kibble.

"You're spoiled, you know that?" Reg asked as she opened the door to the fridge and started rummaging through the plastic bowls to find some tuna or stew that he would enjoy. "First, you insist on coming with me to the Everglades—and I told you it was a swamp, so you can't complain if you got your paws a little wet—when you could have been nice and comfortable at home with

Sarah looking after you. You're the one who decided to go galli-vanting around with the panther while I was visiting with Etienne and Ilka. I don't know what you guys got into, but if you have an upset stomach or ticks, that's your own fault, not mine. You're the one who insisted."

Starlight just stared at his bowl, unmoving.

Reg got the distinct feeling that he was trying to train her to serve him properly, and he could do without the constant babble. She looked at him and raised an eyebrow.

"Really?"

He just looked at her, long-suffering, waiting for her to finally get around to putting something edible into his food dish.

Reg picked it up and added a couple of generous spoonfuls of tuna casserole, then put it on the floor in front of him. Starlight pushed her hand out of the way as he lunged forward to attack the tuna, poor starved cat that he was. His rumbling purr filled the room, and Reg couldn't feel too annoyed at him. The purr was soothing and assured her that she had done what she was supposed to.

A positive reinforcement for performing the expected behavior, she supposed. All part of her training.

Humans took a long time to train.

PREVIEW CHAPTER 2

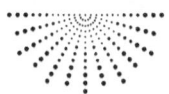

*E*tienne and Ilka had been diligent in providing Reg with everything she needed while visiting them in their remote Everglades cabin. But all of the comforts of someone else's home couldn't replicate the feeling of falling into her own bed at the end of her workday, pulling up her sheets, and going to sleep. The bed was the right height and softness, not a hulking great thing she felt like a child climbing into. She couldn't deny that her bed in the cabin had been comfortable, but it had not been *right*.

She slept well. She did not have any nightmares. She actually woke up in the morning feeling well-rested and refreshed. Exactly how she should feel after a holiday.

She could hear someone moving around the house and knew without seeing that it was Sarah. Firstly, because Sarah was the only one who had a key and could get past the protective wards that she and Reg had set to ensure that Corvin couldn't walk into the cottage. Or anyone else who intended her harm. Also because Starlight had left the bedroom at the first stirrings of sound and there was no indication that he had attacked the intruder. Starlight was very territorial, and if someone who was a threat entered the cottage, he wouldn't hesitate to shred their lower limbs. He wasn't yowling for his breakfast, either, so Sarah had fed him.

For a while, she just luxuriated in the lazy morning warmth of her bed. What could be better? When she got up, she would have a good cup of coffee, check her planner schedule to see if Sarah had written in any new appointments for her, and just relax while she started the day at a nice, slow pace.

Sarah hung around longer than Reg expected, but she didn't poke her head in to tell Reg it was time to get up. Reg heard her leave the cottage and decided it was time. She just didn't want to have to deal with company before she saw Corvin. And if Sarah sensed that she was planning to visit Corvin... the old witch would not be happy with her, that was for sure.

When Reg got out to the kitchen and front room, Starlight was sitting on the back of the couch, watching birds out the window. He turned his head to look at Reg and made a small, satisfied noise of greeting. Sarah's feeding Starlight before Reg got up eliminated the need for the dance around a howling, rubbing cat doing his best to trip her up and insisting that he needed to be taken care of before she'd even had one shot of caffeine. It was the perfect morning.

The new coffee maker was already queued up and ready to go. All Reg had to do was push one button, and the dark, fragrant coffee started to fill her mug. Reg breathed in the high-octane fumes, ready to enjoy her liquid breakfast.

And then the phone rang.

Of course.

And it was Corvin.

Of course.

Reg looked at his name and picture on the screen of her phone and didn't answer it immediately. She waited for her coffee cup to be filled, then picked it up and carried it over to the couch, where she sat with her feet curled up under her, within petting distance of Starlight. By this time, her phone had stopped ringing, but before Reg could tap the screen to call Corvin back, it was ringing again. Reg swiped to accept the call and left it on the coffee table in speaker mode.

She took a sip of the scalding hot coffee before saying anything.

"Reg, are you there?" Corvin asked, sounding confused and irritated.

"Yeah. Just got to get some coffee in me."

She expected to hear his usual low, sexy chuckle and for him to make some comment about how late she had slept in. But he didn't. Reg took another sip of coffee, then reached out her senses toward him, curious about the lack of banter.

He was serious. Maybe not angry, but close to it. Not in any mood for Reg to be lighthearted or teasing. Definitely not the usual state of affairs.

"What's going on?" she asked him.

"We'll discuss that when we get together. Which I am hoping is before too long."

"Well… I *just* got up."

"Maybe we could meet for a donut. Or whatever other sugary confection grabs your fancy. Or one of those dreadful coffee-choco-late-caramel-cinnamon-whatever drinks you like so much at The Witches' Brew."

"I thought we could do a late lunch or early dinner. I'm not really ready to start into anything I have to think about this morning."

"It won't be morning much longer."

"Which is why I suggested lunch instead of breakfast."

Corvin gave an exasperated sigh. "When is the earliest you could drag yourself out of your lazy morning routine to meet me?"

"I'm not lazy. I was up late."

He knew that she was normally up into the small hours of the morning dealing with seances or other readings. That was why she slept so late in the morning, not because she was lazy. Reg's foster moms had always criticized her for being lazy, but Reg couldn't help the fact that her brain was built to stay up late and not fully engage until late morning or early afternoon.

Corvin didn't have to know that she hadn't actually had any readings the night before and had gone to bed early, considering her usual schedule. She *was* being lazy. But that was the only way to start the morning after a vacation. The only right way.

"When, Reg?" he asked impatiently.

"Late lunch or early dinner," she repeated evenly.

"So... one o'clock?"

"One thirty," Reg negotiated, without even looking at the clock to see what time it was. She did not want to go with his first suggestion. She needed to show him that she had a mind of her own.

Though it wasn't like he didn't already know that she had her own ideas about things. She hadn't exactly cooperated with him in the past. Except on a few occasions, which she usually regretted.

"One thirty, then," Corvin said sternly. "Where do you want to meet? The usual?"

"The Crystal Bowl," Reg confirmed. It had been a while since they had been to his private club, and she didn't want him to think that the club was "the usual." She didn't have any intention of going back *there*.

"Good," Corvin agreed, not arguing with her that he would prefer the club's privacy, as he often did.

His behavior was certainly different from usual. Did he have something really serious on his mind? He'd tried to emphasize that in his previous call, but Reg was too suspicious to believe everything he said. Not even most of it.

"Don't be late," Corvin growled.

Then he disconnected. Reg looked at her phone for a minute, then sipped some more coffee, still piping hot.

What was eating Corvin?

* * *

Tainted Truffle Treachery, Book #20 of the *Reg Rawlins, Psychic Investigator series* by P.D. Workman can be purchased at pdworkman.com

* * *

ABOUT THE AUTHOR

P.D. Workman is a USA Today Bestselling author, winner of several awards from Library Services for Youth in Custody and the InD'tale Magazine's Crowned Heart award, and has published over 100 mystery/suspense/thriller and young adult books, including stand alones and these series: Auntie Clem's Bakery cozy mysteries, Reg Rawlins Psychic Investigator paranormal mysteries, Zachary Goldman Mysteries (PI), Kenzie Kirsch Medical Thrillers, Parks Pat Mysteries (police procedural), and YA series: Tamara's Teardrops, Between the Cracks, and Breaking the Pattern.

Workman loves writing about the underdog, who the reader may love or hate. She has been praised for her realistic details, deep characterization, and sensitive handling of the serious social issues that appear in all of her stories, from light cozy mysteries through to darker, grittier young adult and mystery/suspense books.

> P. D. Workman, does not shy from probing the deep psychological scars of childhood trauma, mental illness, and addiction. Also characteristic of this author, these extremely sensitive issues are explored with extensive empathy, described with incredible clarity, and portrayed with profound insight.
>
> — —KIM, GOODREADS REVIEWER

Some of Workman's titles have been translated into Spanish, French, Portuguese, German, and Italian.

Workman began writing at an early age and is a prolific reader as well as writer. She is also passionate about teaching and learning, expresses her creativity through art and cooking, and loves exploring the Calgary parks and green spaces where the Parks Pat Mysteries are set. She was a legal assistant for many years and has done extensive charitable work.

Workman was born and raised in Alberta, Canada, and is married with one adult son.

* * *

Please visit P.D. Workman at pdworkman.com to see what else she is working on, to join her mailing list, and to link to her social networks.

* * *

If you enjoyed this book, please take the time to recommend it to other purchasers with a review or star rating and share it with your friends!

tiktok.com/@pdworkmanauthor

facebook.com/pdworkmanauthor

x.com/pdworkmanauthor

instagram.com/pdworkmanauthor

amazon.com/author/pdworkman

bookbub.com/authors/p-d-workman

goodreads.com/pdworkman

linkedin.com/in/pdworkman

pinterest.com/pdworkmanauthor

youtube.com/pdworkman

Find P.D. Workman's books at

PDWORKMAN.COM

Scan the QR code below